SELFISH: A PSYCHOLOGICAL THRILLER

BOOK 3 OF WHEN BAD THINGS HAPPEN

SHARON A. MITCHELL

"*I* never want to see the inside of a courtroom again. Ever!"

"Well, hello to you, too, Elizabeth."

"I'm sorry, Anna. Your door was open, so I just walked in and started at you. That's not like me."

"A lot that's happened to you lately isn't like you."

"Or the me I ever wanted to be. Growing up, I was a goody-goody, always the rule-follower, never making waves. And yeah, look what that got me." She grimaced. "But not everything that happened was bad. I met you." She walked around Anna's desk to give the woman a hug. "Who'd have thought that being kidnapped and my husband trying to kill me, would bring me friends I never knew I needed. For you, I might consider stepping foot inside this courthouse." She thought for a second. "Unless you're about to move your office to a better location?"

"Being a court-appointed social worker pretty much means that I hang out here."

. . .

"How'd the pre-sentencing go?"

"Dr. Mayberry won't be seeing daylight for a long time. Judge Bursey was not pleased with her. She not only took us all for a ride, she made him look foolish for having approved of her." She twisted her hands together. "But at least she didn't get Timothy."

"How is your little man?"

Elizabeth brightened. "He's great! He seems less traumatized by all that happened than I am. Maybe it's the resiliency of youth, or maybe," she regarded Anna from the corner of her eye, "it's your Dr. Murphy working his magic."

Anna blushed. "He's not my anything."

"That's not the sense I get from him."

"We're friends."

"No, Murph and I have become friends. He does not look at me in the same way he looks at you."

"Knock, knock," came a deeper voice from the doorway. Both women jumped as he continued. "Anna, you should close your door if you don't want people walking in on you."

"Hey, Murph," said Elizabeth. "We were just talking about you."

He raised an eyebrow; his steady gaze rested on Anna's blush. "Hopefully nothing bad."

Anna's hair partially hid her face, but she was smiling. Arnold Murphy pushed off from the doorjamb and strode to Anna to give her a kiss on the cheek, then did the same to Elizabeth, but this one was briefer, as he asked, "Are you joining us for lunch?"

"Lunch?" Elizabeth looked from Murph to Anna. Behind Murph's back, Anna nodded her head vigorously. Her eyes said, "Please" even before her lips did.

Grinning, Elizabeth pretended to consider. "Thanks, but I'd better get home. It was rough sitting in that courtroom all day and I need to get in a workout before I pick up Timothy."

"If you're sure..." said Murph.

"We'd love to have you come with us..." said Anna at the same time.

"If I didn't have a healthy ego, Elizabeth, I'd swear that she'd rather have lunch with you than with me," said Murph. His twinkle told Elizabeth that he'd picked up on Anna's nervousness. "She's a hard one to pin down, although I think I'm growing on her."

"Hellooo, I'm right here," interrupted Anna.

"And I'm not," said Elizabeth, "or I won't be in a minute." She gathered her purse and phone. "See you later and have a nice lunch date."

"It's not a..." started Anna.

"We will," said Murph.

HE WAITED while Anna finished up the email she'd been working on, then set her phone to take messages.

"Shall we?" He held out his elbow to Anna.

She'd have to be rude to not take his arm. But in some ways, even though the contact flustered her, it was easier than looking him in the eye. They had to walk right through the reception area where the secretary sat and past the other social workers. Anna was positive that Murph knew this and had her on his arm on purpose.

"Did Elizabeth tell you about the pre-sentencing hearing this morning?"

"Just a bit," answered Anna. "She didn't think Hanna would get out for a long time."

"Probably true. But I don't know. Elizabeth might have put her own spin on things." Murph picked up his menu. "This was an attempted abduction. Timothy's mother willingly handed the child to Hanna, and Hanna had a judge's approval for the plan. But it was her intention to keep the boy. And the prosecution argued that she meant the boy harm by pushing him out on the lake in a boat by himself. I don't know how much time she'll actually get."

"She tried to steal Timothy!"

"You and I know that. I testified to her worsening mental health."

Before Anna could interrupt, he added, "Yes, I know. It wasn't my fault, and she showed her 'together' side to me, but I'm a psychiatrist. I should have seen through her. I was growing concerned but had no idea she was that far gone."

"She's clever," said Anna. "And she knew just what to say to you."

"Yes, she is clever. That's what worries me. She will know how to play the system. Whatever her sentence, I'm positive she'll be released early. She'll know all the right things to say and do."

"At least Timothy's safe."

"Yes, and so will other children be safe from her. She'll not be allowed to practice child psychology ever again."

"I can't bear anyone harming a child."

Murph wrapped his hands around hers. "Now, let's talk about something more pleasant."

Anna relaxed.

"When are you going to agree to move in with me?"

ONE YEAR AGO IN TIJUANA, MEXICO

Turning into a side street, Evaline leaned her back against the cracking concrete wall. Taking a deep breath, she listened carefully, then stuck as little of her face as she could around the corner, checking that no one followed.

No, no one.

Bending her knees, she let her back slide down the wall, scraping away some flaking paint as she did so. Sitting on the sidewalk, she brought her knees up to her stomach. They didn't come as close as they once had; the bulge of her stomach held them off. She rubbed a hand over her belly.

How had this happened? Well, she knew how. She even

knew when. What she didn't know was how she had let herself get into this predicament.

She thought Cal loved her. Yeah, he loved to get into her was about it. It had only been a couple of times, but that was enough to cause this.

She hid it for a while. The puking was only for a few hours each morning, and since she was the only one up at that time, it was not hard to hide her nausea. Not that anyone would notice if she was pale. She could continue at her job. The money certainly was not great, but enough to help her family, plus give her a bit to spend.

Then her mother noticed her bulge. They were alone, just the two of them that afternoon. Her madre had pulled up Evaline's shirt and then shrieked. A torrent of words came out, but all Evaline heard was shame and sin.

When her padre came home from the cantina that night, there was more hollering. Then a beating. Then nothing. Exactly nothing more for Evaline. They'd kicked her out for shaming the family. That was it. No clothes, no money, no place to stay.

The first few places Evaline tried to find to sleep didn't work for long. Dogs found her and were suspicious that she was a rival for the food they scrounged by the dumpsters. She spent much of that first night walking, keeping to the shadows, leery of strangers who might come across her in the night.

CHAPTER 2

There. Anna thought she spied her again.

Although not rare, it wasn't that common to see children in the courthouse. Sadly, sometimes their family circumstances brought them here. But to see a child wandering the halls alone was not the norm.

Although not positive, Anna thought she had noticed this young girl earlier in the day, not just once but possibly several times. She was always alone, always walking and watching, but never seeming attached to any of the staff or clients who had reason to be in the building. Now, it was nearing the end of office hours and the building would shut down soon.

Grabbing an empty coffee cup, Anna set out on a path to intersect the girl. She looked to be around twelve or so, a pre-teen or early adolescent, anyway. The child looked more nervous than she had earlier in the day.

"Hey there, hi," she said. "I'm about to get some hot chocolate. Want some?"

The girl didn't reply, but her eyes said what her words didn't. She looked longingly at Anna's cup, making Anna wonder when the child's last meal had been.

"Our break room's just up here. Come on and I'll get you some." She didn't turn her head, hoping that the girl would follow her. She did.

"I'm Anna," she offered.

The girl didn't speak.

Not usually one for small talk, Anna chatted away about nothing, wanting to put the child at ease.

As the TASSIMO machine churned out the first cup of hot chocolate, Anna passed the mug to the girl. The child's hands trembled slightly as she took the mug. Low blood sugar from not eating? Either that, or she was extremely shy.

The girl downed half her drink before Anna's brewed. Immediately, Anna started a third cup coming. Once ready, she swapped it out for the empty mug the child clutched. "One's never enough for me," she said.

The child sipped this one more slowly as Anna rummaged in the cupboards for some cookies, anything to fill the hole in this little girl's stomach.

She gestured toward the table and pulled out a chair for herself. Elbows on the table, Anna tried to portray as much nonchalance as possible. She heard another chair scraping on the floor tiles as the child sat down.

"My name's Anna." She held out her hand.

The child set her cup carefully on the table and took her hand in a quick, tepid, shake.

"What's your name?"

No response.

To fill the silence, Anna made some inane comments about the cookies they were consuming, how she preferred the brand with more chocolate chips in them, or at least the oatmeal/raisin kind.

"Are your parents with you?"

Nothing

"Did you get lost?"

No response.

"Is someone coming for you? Are you supposed to meet them?"

The girl shuffled, then pushed back her chair.

Worried that she was about to bolt, Anna feigned an enormous yawn. "Goodness, this has been a long day, hasn't it? I'm beat. Some days are like that, you know." From the corner of her eye, she watched the girl's shoulders relax, just slightly.

"Tomlins will be happy to see me. He's my cat, you know. Do you have a cat?"

The girl shook her head.

"Want to see a picture of him?"

Anna wasn't sure, but the child might have inched a little closer. Pulling out her wallet, Anna showed her pictures of her beloved cat, a twenty-pound tabby who loved his kibble and treats. It showed.

Yes, she hadn't imagined it. The girl leaned closer. Anna handed her the case that held the photos, pointing out various features as the girl shuffled through the pictures. At one photo of the cat sprawled on his back, luxuriating in the sun, the girl gave a half-smile. Almost.

. . .

PUTTING her arm under the table, Anna gave a surreptitious glance at her watch. The offices closed in half an hour, as did the main desk at Child Protective Services.

"The cleaners will be here any minute to start work on this room. Why don't we take our hot chocolates back to my office? We can finish them there in peace." Again, she rose, hoping that the child would follow. The sound of the chair legs scraping on the floor told her she was.

Keeping up her chatter, they made their way back to Anna's office. Passing through the reception area, Anna made eye contact with the receptionist, trying to convey without words that something was going on. Betty nodded she got it. There was a real plus to working closely together with a team. As she turned the corner to her office, Anna saw Betty heading into the door of their supervisor's room. Good to have a team behind her.

Anna pointed to the couch, telling the girl that it was much more comfortable than the hard wooden chair by her desk. Plus, it was far from the door in case the girl wanted to run. Once the child sat, Anna said she'd be with her in just a couple of minutes; she had a few messages she needed to return, then she could relax with her hot chocolate. First, though, she pulled from her bottom left drawer, a package of crackers. "Want some?"

She picked up her phone. "Hi, Betty. Could you get CPS on the line, please? Tell them to hold and make sure that someone's around. Thanks." Anna logged in to her computer. She turned her chair, so that she was sideways to both the girl on the couch and her desk. She angled her computer monitor so that she could still work, yet the girl could not see the screen. She pulled up her email program and sent a message to Betty saying that she'd noticed this young girl several times since that morning. She was always wandering the hallways alone and didn't seem connected to anyone. So far, the child had not responded to questions, or said a word. Anna wondered if she was a runaway or abandoned? Had someone reported a child as missing? Had there been any family court hearings involving a twelve-year-old girl?

Anna knew Betty would take the message to their supervisor. Surely this girl belonged to someone who must be frantic with worry about what had become of her.

As Anna sipped her now-cooling hot chocolate, she watched the girl. She devoured a dozen crackers in short order, but the two cups of hot chocolate plus the cookies and crackers seemed to have taken off some of the desperate edge. Still, the child did not seem disposed to conversation. She listened, though.

So Anna prattled. She was not skilled at small talk at the best of times, and no one would call her gabby, but her chatter seemed to calm the child. Maybe if she relaxed some, she'd be willing to give up her name, her story, and where she was from. Surely someone was frantic about her disappearance by now.

Or maybe she was hiding here, just as frantic to not

be found. In that case, Child Protective Services was definitely needed.

ABOUT FIFTEEN MINUTES later there was a quiet knock on the door. Betty poked her head in and said, "Anna, CPS is here. It's Jillian."

Thank goodness. Jillian was great. "Come on in. Hey, Jillian. How are you?"

"Great, thanks." She turned towards the child on the couch. "And who's this?"

"I'm not sure of her name, but we met in the hallway here and have shared some hot chocolate." She grimaced. "And some stale crackers."

"At this time of day, I'm on board with any kind of snack." She put her hand toward the box on the couch. "May I?" she asked the girl. Without waiting for an answer, she planted herself on the couch and reached for the box. "Ah, Ritz. And not the low sodium kind, either. Excellent choice." She grinned at the girl as if the child had made the best decision in buying this type.

There was a half-smile, but not much more in response.

Trying a more direct approach, Jillian said, "So, where are you off to when these offices close for the day?"

The child blanched. Maybe she hadn't thought that far ahead.

"Are you here with someone?" She popped more crackers into her mouth and chewed for a few moments. "Anna, do you have a pen and pad of paper we can use, please?"

With these implements on the couch between them, Jillian suggested the girl might be more comfortable writing answers than saying them.

The child made no move to reach for the pen.

"Is someone coming to pick you up?"

No response, no eye contact.

"Can you tell us where you live?"

Nothing.

"Anna, would you please tell Betty to get things moving?" They had a plan in wait.

There was movement in the hallway as staff packed up and shut their doors for the night, ready to head home.

"Bonnie. May I call you Bonnie/" Jillian said to the girl. "I've always liked the name Bonnie and you really seem like a Bonnie lass."

The child's eyes remained glued to the hands in her lap that she twisted and untwisted into knots.

"Bonnie, you can't stay here. You know that, don't you?" Her warm eyes urged the child to trust her, to talk to her. "Don't worry. We'll find a safe place for you to spend the night." She waited. Nothing. "Is that what you want?"

A gentle tap on the door and two women entered.

"Bonnie, these are my colleagues, Hillary and Pam. They run a receiving home. It's a safe place for you to spend the night. They'll take care of you."

The child raised her wide eyes to Anna's. A film of tears covered them.

Anna went to her and squeezed her hands. "It'll be all right. You'll be safe with these women; they'll take care of you. They've had lots of experience with kids."

The child's eyes never left hers.

"And I'll come see you tomorrow." Now, where did that come from?

CHAPTER 3

"*A*re you ready to go?" Murph was at the door, a picnic basket slung over his arm. "I thought you might want to check that I've packed the things you like."

Anna stood frozen in the doorway. Hastily, she tried to plaster on a smile of anticipation, but Murph knew how to read her.

"You don't want to go?" He tried to keep his tone neutral, but he'd been looking forward to this all week.

"Sure. Of course, I want to go."

He heard the 'but' in her voice. "But?" When she hesitated, he said, "Come on, Anna, just tell me."

She sighed. "I'm so sorry, but I forgot." At Murph's raised eyebrows, she hurried on. "When I got up this morning, all I could think about was that child, Bonnie. I keep wondering where she came from, what her story is, and why she won't speak. I'm not usually intimidating to children, but maybe it was just me and she'd told everyone who she is by now."

"Wondering about this child means that you and I should not go on our picnic?"

Looking even more uncomfortable, Anna explained, "I sort of promised Bonnie that I'd see her today." Raising her eyes to meet Murph's, she said, "Not sort of. I told her I'd see her." She hurried on. "At the time, I forgot all about our picnic. Sorry."

Murph brushed past her and entered the kitchen. "Do you think you can make room in your fridge for this?" He set the picnic basket on the counter and began emptying it, placing items into the fridge. He straightened. "If we leave now, we can go see this child, then have a picnic, just a little later than planned."

ANNA'S JOB required her to assess children in various environments, including their home and their foster placements. For emergency placements, she placed kids into designated receiving homes, a temporary safe place until she could arrange a regular foster home. Anna'd been to this home several times.

While waiting for their knock to be answered, Anna and Murph surveyed the yard. It needed tending to, but these parents devoted more of their time to the charges in their care. With new children landing in their home with alarming frequency, the yard got neglected, but not the children.

Janice opened her door and her arms to Anna, engulfing her in a big hug. "What brings you here, my dear?" Although her smile for Anna was warm, there was wariness in her eyes as she regarded Murph.

"Hi, Janice. I'm here to see Bonnie. I'm the one who found her, and I promised her I'd come see her today." She noticed Janice's eyes looking over her shoulder. Turning, she wrapped a hand around Murph's arm. "Janice, I'd like you to meet my friend, Dr. Arnold Murphy. He's a psychiatrist who does work at the courthouse."

Janice relaxed somewhat as she shook Murph's hand. Over her shoulder, she called, "Kevin!"

Her husband appeared in the hallway with a diaper over one shoulder, a baby in one arm, and a bottle in his hand. Seeing a strange man in his doorway, he turned, putting his body between the baby and this unknown person. This would not be the first time that an irate father had tried to take back his child, despite what the courts decreed.

He bent down to give Anna a peck on the cheek and nodded when introduced to Murph.

"She's here to see Bonnie," she says.

"Good. The child could use a friend. She's not warmed up to us."

Anna and Murph exchanged a look. There went Anna's hope that Bonnie was only silent with her.

"Has she spoken to you?" asked Murph. "We've been talking about the reasons she is not talking."

"Not a word," Kevin said. He nodded toward the rabble coming from the interior of the house. "Although with seven others, it would be hard to get a word in edgewise. There's always the chance that even if she said something, we'd not hear it amid all the babble that's going on around here all the time."

"We tried to spend some time with her last night, after we got the younger ones to bed," said Janice. "Thought she might like some of our attention all to herself. Apparently not. We invited her to watch some television with us. She looked nervous, like we'd make her even if she didn't want to. She perched on the edge of a cushion, staring at the screen, but not looking at either of us once."

"Before bed, I always make us some warm milk. She accepted hers and drank with us, but fast enough that I'm sure the poor lass scalded her tongue." Kevin pointed to the dregs in three coffee cups sitting on the coffee table. "Finally, I took pity on her, and told her she was welcome to stay and watch the next show with us, or free to go to bed. The girl looked scared out of her skin at being in the same room with us."

"That's right. It was like she was trying to escape," said Janice. "Bonnie seemed to relax more around the kids. She even helped with the little ones, as if she was used to babies and toddlers. She pitched in without asking, smiling at the children, but not saying a word. They seemed to take to her. I guess wee ones don't notice or care if you're a non-talker."

Murph had to ask. "Did she seem afraid of men?"

Kevin knew what he was getting at. "Not especially, at least not as much as many other unfortunate kids who have passed through these doors. She was leery, but not terrified."

.   .   .

THERE WERE sounds of a scuffle in the other room, then a sharp cry. As the adults moved toward the noise, the crying quieted and they could hear soft, comforting sounds. As they entered the doorway, Bonnie stood with her back to them, swaying side to side. A toddler's dripping nose pressed into her neck and crooning noises came from Bonnie as they comforted the child.

The adults exchanged glances. While not really words, those were definitely sounds coming from Bonnie, the first that any of them had heard.

ANNA CALLED the girl's name. Bonnie turned, startled to see four adults staring at her. She went silent but continued to rock the little boy in her arms.

Janice stepped forward to take Jeremy from her. "There, there, little man. It looks like Bonnie has fixed you right up. Did you have a fall?" She beamed at Bonnie and mouthed, "Thank you."

Anna stepped forward. "Hi, Bonnie. I told you I'd come to see you today. How are you?"

Bonnie stood immobile.

Janice put a hand on the girl's shoulder. "Why don't you take Anna and her friend into the living room and visit with them?"

Obediently, Bonnie started down the hall to the room with the empty mugs.

Murph trailed behind. To Kevin he asked, "What do you make of her?"

Kevin shrugged. "This is a new one on me and we've

had hundreds of kids stay with us. Some are silent because they're angry, some because they're scared, but by the next day, they've at least said something, even if it's only to blow up when one of the other kids does something to them." He gestured around. "As you can see, we pretty much live on top of each other here."

"Yes, it looks crowded, but comfortable. And safe. That's something many of these kids likely haven't experienced before."

"That's why we're not warm when an unknown man suddenly shows up on our doorstep."

Murph nodded. "Fair enough."

"But if you're a friend of Anna's, you must be all right."

"Yeah, I am," grinned Murph.

"What's the story with Anna and Bonnie? Sometimes we don't get many details when kids are dropped off here."

"Apparently, Anna noticed her in the hallways of the courthouse a few times in the morning, then several times again that afternoon. She assumed the girl was waiting for someone, but she was still there long after all the court sessions ended. When she tried to talk to her, she got no response, but Bonnie followed her to her office. From there CPS was called, and she ended up here."

"Did she have some ID on her? How do we know her name's Bonnie?" He jostled the increasingly restless baby in his arms.

Murph grinned. "We don't. That's the social worker's

doing. She thought she had to call her something and said that she looked like a Bonnie. When the girl didn't object, the name stuck. Guess it's as good as any until we find out more about her. She had nothing with her, no purse, backpack, or even a jacket."

"HMM. Well, she's safe here for now."

An odor filled the air, an odor that could not be mistaken for anything other than what it was. The infant smiled up at Kevin. "Guess that's my cue. Looks like a diaper change is needed. Again." He left the room.

MURPH LINGERED in the hallway outside the living room, giving Anna and Bonnie some time to bond. He smiled to himself as he listened to Anna's one-sided conversation. At the best of times, no one could call Anna chatty, but here she was, doing her best to hold up both of their sides of the conversation, without putting pressure on Bonnie.

Murph entered with a smile, his arms open, making himself as unintimidating as he could. He took a seat where he could see both Anna and Bonnie, without intruding on their visit.

Anna turned to him in relief. It was hard work talking to someone without the normal back-and-forth interchange. Bonnie's facial expression showed little, although Murph thought her eyes followed Anna's every movement with interest.

Anna stood, smiling brightly at Bonnie, explaining that they had to get going. She promised to come to see her again. Murph thought that something in the child's eyes faded as she learned her friend was leaving.

CHAPTER 4

"Well, that was awkward," complained Anna.

"She seemed to react to you positively," was Murph's opinion.

"Do you think?" She shook her head. "It's so hard to tell."

"You have nothing to go on but her body language."

"Hopefully, the police will have some luck finding out who she is."

As they drove through the sunny streets, Anna rubbed her eyes. She asked Murph if he minded if she pulled down her sun visor.

"Now why would I mind if you put the visor on your side of the car up or down?"

Anna shrugged and lowered it to block some sunshine. She massaged her forehead.

"Headache?"

"A bit. I didn't sleep well last night."

"Do you want to take it easy today? We can do our picnic some other day."

"No," protested Anna. "It's fine. You've gone to a lot of work for this picnic."

Murph tried to keep his voice even. "Anna, if you don't want to go, just say so."

"It's fine. It'll be fun."

"Your words and your body language don't match."

They drove the rest of the way in silence, not the comfortable silence that Anna enjoyed. This reeked of tension, and Anna longed to smooth things over.

SHUTTING off the ignition in front of Anna's house, Murph draped his wrists over the steering wheel and stared straight ahead. He sighed, then started. "Anna, you're a lovely woman."

Oh, no, thought Anna. This is the kiss-off. She braced for what was to come.

"I think I've made my feelings for you pretty clear and where I hoped things would go with us. But this isn't going to work, is it?" He shifted in his seat to look at his passenger.

Anna's fingers twisted around each other. Looking at her lap, in a voice barely above a whisper, she said, "I guess not. I'm sorry that it's not good for you."

"But it is. It is good for me, but it's not for you. And, I guess that it's not what I want for me, either."

"What do you want?"

"You, Anna, I want you."

She shot him a quick look from behind the curtain of her hair.

"But I want the real you, not the polite facade you show all too often."

Now Anna was confused. Since when was it bad to not be rude?

"By the real you, I mean the person you are inside, not just the polite stranger you present so well. I want you to trust me, to believe that I love you and want to be with you. That means all of you, warts and all."

"But...".

He held up his hand to stop her. "Just hear me out, please. I've kept this inside for too long and I don't want to do the same thing I'm accusing you of." Through the windscreen he watched a child riding a wobbly bicycle down the street. "Real people don't always agree. They don't always like the same things. Sure, it's okay to be accommodating sometimes, but not all the time. You need to feel free to tell me the truth, that you have a headache and want to lie down, or you just don't feel like going on a picnic today. That's okay. People in a relationship can be honest about things like that, knowing that the other person will understand, and that there will be another time. They plan for a future together and don't act like polite strangers." He drummed his hands on the steering column. "That's what I want with you."

A small voice said, "Me, too."

Murph turned his head to look at her. "Really? Can you trust me? Trust that I'm here, even if we disagree or want to do different things?"

Anna nodded.

He reached out a finger and gently turned her chin toward him. He winced at the sheen of tears in her eyes. "I've asked you to move in with me. Or to let me move in with you. I love you, but I know you need time. I'll wait. I can be a patient man when it's something important. But I need to know that I'm not waiting in vain."

"You're not."

"Then why do you keep me at arm's length? Why do I feel that I've not yet peeled away the layers to find the true Anna?"

"You might not like what you see."

"Now, that's exactly what I'm talking about. I know I will. I'd like you to trust me by showing your real self, knowing that I'll love all the parts of you."

"There's stuff you don't know."

"No kidding!" He softened it with a smile.

"There are some things I don't think I could ever talk about." She peered at Murph, this good man who was coming to mean so much to her. "Things that I don't even want to think about."

Murph raised an eyebrow. "Is that the best way to cope with them?"

"It is for me." For once Anna's voice was firm.

Murph grinned. "I like that!" He squeezed her hand. "Maybe not those exact words, but the spirit behind them. I asked, and you told me in your oh-so-polite way to butt out. I may not like that you don't want to share your secrets, but I do like that you feel okay to stand your ground."

He opened his car door and came around to her side. "Come on. Let's go inside. There are some picnic fixings waiting to be consumed."

As they sat on the stools in front of the kitchen island, they started first on the chocolate-covered strawberries. The main course could wait.

Murph turned to face Anna, popping a cheese cube into her mouth. "Did you ever read anything by Ayn Rand? I think she wrote in the '60s or '70s. One of her books is *The Virtue of Selfishness*."

"I think I might have read something of hers back in college. Didn't she have a sort of cult following?"

"I think so, but it was a bit before my time." He took a sip from his glass. "She defined selfishness as concern with one's own interests." He topped up each of their wineglasses. "One of your admirable traits," Murph told her, "is how you put others first. That's a lovely part of you, your kindness and how giving you are. But that's only good sometimes. It's okay to plant your feet and state what you want and need for yourself."

"Okay." She stood, feet apart, hands on her hips. "I'm claiming that last strawberry."

Murph laughed and threw his arms around Anna. "You are quite the woman." He backed her up toward the counter.

"Oh, no you don't. You're sneaking up on my strawberry." She pounced on the fruit, gobbling it in one bite.

TWELVE YEARS AGO, IN ENSENADA, MEXICO

"But I don't even know him. Why do I have to marry him?"

"Hush, Anna."

"I don't want to!"

"You have no choice."

"Why? Why are you doing this to me?"

"It's a matter of honor. You must do it for your family."

PRESENT DAY

This was the time of day Anna relished. Each evening, before bed, Murph called her. It didn't matter if they'd seen each other earlier in the day, or even for supper, he still called. It was their time to talk, to wind down.

Somehow, it was easier on the phone for Anna. She could let her guard down and speak freely, without Murph's attractiveness impeding her thoughts.

Murph was a good listener; well, of course he was. That's what he did for a living. He wouldn't be much of a psychiatrist if he did not listen well and encourage others to speak their mind. Now was time to tell him the full story about Bonnie, or at least as much as Anna knew.

"There was this little girl. I saw her hanging around in the hallways of the courthouse in the morning. Then when I came back from our lunch, I saw her again–

several times. At first, I assumed she was waiting for her parents who were attending a trial, but then it was getting close to closing time and all the court sessions had finished by three o'clock."

"Did you ever see her talking to anyone?"

"Never, but I could have missed it. It seemed odd that she was still around, so I tried to talk to her. She wouldn't say a word. She accepted some hot chocolate though and ate the cookies as if she'd not eaten all day. I got her to my office, and she snacked a bit more but still wouldn't speak. I called Protective Services and Jillian arranged a home for her for the night."

"Odd that you couldn't get anything out of her."

"Usually, kids warm up to me. This time though, she acted like she trusted me, at least enough to follow me to my office, but she didn't utter a sound."

"Do you think she can talk? How did she seem cognitively?"

"Hard to tell without talking to her, but she seemed to follow everything I said and to be aware of her surroundings. She didn't strike me as a child with a cognitive disability, but who knows?"

"Do you think she is deaf? Unable to speak? Did she appear to be watching your lips to get what you were saying?"

"No, not that I noticed. She responded even when she was looking down at her lap."

"Maybe she was told by someone not to speak and she's frightened."

"That crossed my mind, too."

"Or maybe she has selective mutism."

"What's that?"

"It's a form of anxiety disorder. The person can physically speak, but anxiety gets in the way, preventing them from talking in certain situations. They may converse freely with some people in some circumstances, but freeze at other times, unable to get any words out."

"I wonder what might have happened to a child to make her selectively mute?"

CHAPTER 5

"Ms. Sanchez, may I see you in my chambers when I've dismissed court."

"Certainly, Judge Bursey."

"WHAT DO you think of our mystery little girl, Anna?"

Seated in front of the his desk, Anna shook her head. "I don't know, Judge."

"Anna. We've worked together long enough. There's no one here but you and me. It's Frank, remember?"

"Right, Frank. I've been to see her at the home she's in. Several times. She'll smile and look pleased to see me, but I'm not getting anything out of her. The foster parents say that she doesn't speak to them, either. When they ask her a direct question and wait for an answer, she looks uncomfortable. And twice had tears."

"How is she getting along there?"

"She helps with the little ones. They never told her to, she just automatically involves herself with the toddlers.

The kids seem to respond to her, too. Janice and Kevin think that they've heard her making some sounds when she's soothing a crying baby, but no real words."

"Apart from the small children, is she interacting with anyone else there? Getting close to them?"

Anna shrugged. "They say that whenever she can, Bonnie slips away to her room. She reads a book, or doodles, but often just sits."

"Is she ill?"

"Janice says that she eats all right and they don't see any signs of anything amiss physically."

"How many kids are in that home right now?"

"Eight, is what Kevin told me, although it's hard to take a count because they never seem to hold still for more than a minute at a time."

Frank rested his chin on one fist. "Does this child strike you as the kind to flourish in such a busy household?"

Anna shook her head. "Not really. She seems quiet, like one who would relish some peace and alone time. It's hard to have private time in a small house with ten people."

"That's what I wanted to talk to you about."

"Have the police located her family?"

He shook his head. "No. Nothing. There's been no missing children reported that even remotely fit her age and appearance."

"How could a young girl just suddenly appear in our building?"

"Good question. It looks like she's our responsibility

for now." He picked up some papers. "I'm signing the temporary custody order now. She's a ward of the State, at least until we find out who she is and why no one has come looking for her."

Anna nodded.

"That brings me to what I wanted to talk to you about." He rocked back in his chair. "I think we can agree that the present home is not the best place for Bonnie."

Anna nodded again. "Janice's and Kevin's place is only supposed to be for emergencies until CPS can find a more permanent placement."

"Permanent placement. We both know that in the foster care world, 'permanent' can mean anything from a month to several years."

Where is he going with this, wondered Anna.

"At one time you were a foster parent, yourself."

"Yes, that was some time ago."

"Would you consider fostering Bonnie?"

SALLY TRIED NOT to take a step back. That would mean showing fear, and Archie thrived on that, especially when he was in this mood. But, oh, his breath. That stale tobacco smell, laced with cheap whisky and a mug or two or three of beer.

"Where is she?" He grabbed her shoulders and squeezed.

"Who?"

"You know who I'm talking about." He shook her. "Where is that brat?"

"I don't know." At least that was the truth. He could spot when she lied, but this time she was being forthright. Sally honestly had no idea where her daughter was. She just knew that she wasn't here in this house any longer.

"She disappears, just when she was getting interesting." Archie's leer gave her the creeps. It was different when that look was directed at her own body.

In the other room, a small child let loose a wail. Almost immediately, the brother struck up a duet, each competing to be the loudest.

He shoved the woman toward the living room. "Go see to your brats and shut them up."

ELIZABETH COULDN'T SLEEP. It was one of those nights when thoughts just wouldn't stop running around in her head. The psychologist Murph recommended assured her it would get better, but not fast, and that she'd still have torments about what she and her son had been through lingering for a very long time.

As she thought over all that had happened to them, she smiled at the thought of Murph. At first, she'd hated him; she felt he was in cahoots with Dr. Mayberry, the nutsy psychologist who tried to steal Timothy. Dr. Murphy was Mayberry's psychiatrist. Most people in their professions had one, someone like a mentor, someone to check in with when the strain of their jobs wore into their psyche. Most psychologists and psychiatrists learned to find a balance, to practice self-care, and to not lose themselves in listening to other people's problems day in and day out. Turns out that Murph was as taken in by Dr. Mayberry as was Elizabeth.

Now, she trusted him and called him a friend.

That said a lot for Elizabeth as she did not give her trust easily. Not after what her ex-husband had done to them. Not after what Dr. Mayberry had done. Elizabeth had been urged - no, not urged, but ordered by the court otoget professional help for Timothy after the kidnapping. This, when all Elizabeth wanted to do was wrap her arms around her son and hold him snug and safe with her alone at home.

But, 'twas not to be. She'd complied and was let down yet again, by those she trusted.

No, that was not entirely true. Through all this she'd become close friends with Keira and Cynthia, then Anna. She included in her circle of close friends Jake and Murph and, of course, Brendan. Who ever thought that she would consider letting another man into her life?

GROWING UP IN HER FAMILY, she was taught to shove away unpleasant things and not discuss them. In retrospect, Elizabeth was not sure that was the best way to handle the punches life threw at you. But she had a decision to make, and the time was coming soon.

School. Should she let Timothy go to school? That

would mean letting him out of her sight for half a day, five days a week. Sure, she could bear to be away from him when she knew he was with someone like Keira or Cynthia, people who knew and loved him. But school?

Who were these people? One pre-kindergarten teacher might have two dozen little people in her charge. How much attention would she pay to Timothy? How much care would she take with him?

It's not paranoia if someone really was after you, thought Elizabeth. Most kids, heck, most adults sailed through life with nothing too traumatic happening to them. But before Timothy's fifth birthday he'd been kidnapped not just once, but taken a second time. What were the odds? Most kids also sailed through pre-K and kindergarten with nothing amiss, but Timothy wasn't most kids.

Apart from those situations, he had more of a medical history than most people did by retirement age. On the upside, his seizures were under much better control now. Rather than occurring multiple times a day, they were down to maybe one a month, and the ones he had were not as serious as they used to be. His pediatric neurologist, Dr. Muller, was pleased with Timothy's progress and even talked about the possibility of slightly reducing his medications this fall. Elizabeth was leery about rocking the boat now that things were settling down, but on the other hand, she didn't want her kid on meds if it was possible to quit them. Sadly, Dr. Muller said that the only way to know was to try it. Sheesh.

Then there was Timothy's speech. He used to say

some words, and she and Jackson had thought that his vocabulary was growing. Then, in his third year, they noticed he spoke less and less. This coincided with the onset of his seizures, so they assumed the two were related.

Maybe, Dr. Muller had said. Maybe. They'd wait and see how he was once he was medically more stable.

She turned over. Enough. Nothing was getting solved tonight.

But one niggling thought remained. Dr. Muller wondered if there might be something else going on with Timothy.

CHAPTER 6

*A*nna didn't hear a colleague saying hello as they passed each other in the hallway. Walking back to her office, her vision narrowed to just the tile flooring in front of her.

Foster a child? It had been years since she'd done that. It was a way to earn a bit of money while she put herself through school. But more than that, it was a way of giving back. She was free now to live her own life, yet so many children did not have this opportunity. She understood what it was like to have circumstances work against you. Maybe she could give some of these kids a fresh start, or at least a glimpse of what life could be like. Oh, how she would have appreciated that growing up.

She had taken small children into her home back then. Toddlers and preschoolers who were in daycare during the day while she took classes, then they went to bed at a reasonable hour, giving her time to catch up on housework and homework.

Bonnie was twelve, or so they estimated. The nurse practitioner who examined her had found no evidence of sexual assault, thank goodness. Judging by her bone size and development, Bonnie was an adolescent.

Although she cooperated with the physical exam, she only complied when Anna promised to remain in the room with her. That had to mean something, didn't it?

How could she bond with a child who would not speak to her? Yes, Janice and Kevin felt Bonnie perked up whenever Anna came around. They swore Bonnie remembered the date and time that Anna said she'd return and stayed by the window watching for her. Those were plusses.

So far, they'd not enrolled the child in school, not wanting her to go through the stress of joining one school class only to be moved to a different school within a few weeks. If she lived with Anna, she would have to begin school.

Would a school even take a child who would not or could not speak? She'd have to ask Murph about that. He'd know.

MURPH. He filled her thoughts as she drove home. What would this mean to him if she agreed to foster Bonnie?

Used to acting on her own, it was new to Anna to have to take someone else's wishes and needs into account. Sure, she was good at that, a master, even when in polite company. But her life behind her closed door was her own. Or had been.

Was she seriously considering letting Murph in? Or letting him in further?

He'd been talking for some time now about the possibility of them living together. Could she do that?

She'd been clear, actually more than a little forceful, in stating that she had no interest in marriage. Not that Murph had asked, she remembered red-facedly, but his demeanor had changed from eager to rather sad on hearing that she would not want to marry him. Ever honest, he'd said that he hoped that's where they were heading, but he was fine with just living together, if those were her terms.

Living together would mean increased intimacy. Not that she didn't find Murph attractive–she most definitely did. But she had scars, both external and internal. Baring herself to him would mean that he'd seen her physical scars. Would he accept she couldn't talk about them? Could he just leave it alone, or would he probe her mental scars as well?

Then there was Bonnie. If Anna agreed to foster this child, that might be a reason to put anything further with Murph on hold. Is that what she wanted?

Where would she put Bonnie? Her rental unit was a small two-bedroom half of a duplex, a perfect size for one person. The second bedroom was her office, with only room for one filing cabinet, a futon, a desk pushed into one corner and a small bookshelf. Many walk-in closets were bigger than that room.

Bonnie needed a place to call her own, a place where she felt she belonged.

Now she was into the details of how to rearrange

her place to accommodate a young girl. What was she thinking? Was she actually considering bringing this child into her home? She knew nothing about her; to be fair, Bonnie knew nothing about Anna, either. Bonnie had secrets; so did Anna. Anna wasn't usually much for gabbing; neither was Bonnie, obviously. She smiled. Maybe they could get along and form a family of sorts.

A family was a dream Anna had given up on ages ago. It could never happen. Perhaps an unconventional family was in her cards.

Back to Murph. Argh. There were too many thoughts running around in her head.

She could use Bonnie as an excuse for putting off any decision about moving her relationship with Murph closer. He'd understand that she and Bonnie needed time to get used to each other, to settle in.

Did that mean that she'd see less of Murph? She hoped not.

～

HER CELL PHONE RANG. These thoughts whirling around in her head had filled the evening.

"Hi, Murph," she said into the phone without checking the caller ID. This was the time of night that he always called. His voice echoed; he was in his car on speaker phone, coming back from a meeting.

They chatted for a while, but something in their usual give-and-take was missing. Sensing something, Murph asked, "Is everything all right?"

When she hesitated, he interrupted. "Just hold that

thought. I'm not that far from your place and I'll be there in ten minutes." He hung up.

Anna surveyed her living room. It was a mess. She'd tried rearranging her furniture so that she could move the desk in there to give Bonnie more room in the spare bedroom. It hadn't worked. She'd bought and positioned the furniture specifically for this room, choosing each piece with care, ensuring that it fit. Now, it just looked crowded.

SHE HAD the couch half pushed toward another wall, when there was a knock at the door. Murph entered and raised his eyebrows at the mess in her usually well-ordered room. "Moving somewhere? Going for a fresh look?" he asked.

"Have a seat. Want some tea or coffee or wine?"

"The latter, please." He perched himself in the middle of the couch, even though it jutted into the center of the room. He hooked one foot around the coffee table's leg and pulled it toward himself. He stood to take the wine goblets from Anna's hands and placed them on the table. "Now, what's going on?"

"It's Judge Bursey. He started it."

"What's Frank done this time? He's not upset Elizabeth again, has he?"

Anna shook her head. "Nothing to do with Elizabeth or Timothy this time. It's about me." She hesitated. "And Bonnie."

"Have they found her family?"

"No. That's all still a mystery."

Murph handed her a glass of wine.

Taking a deep breath, Anna started in. "Bonnie can't stay with Janice and Kevin much longer. They're not set up to be foster parents; they just provide emergency respite. Bonnie is now a ward of the State, and so needs a foster home of her own." She swirled the merlot in her glass. "The judge asked if I'd be Bonnie's foster parent."

Murph went still, his expression neutral.

Anna sometimes wished that he wasn't so good at his job, at masking his thoughts when he wanted to. She had trouble guessing what was going on in his mind right now.

He regarded the disarray in the living room. "So, you were rearranging your place to accommodate another person?"

"I was thinking about it."

"And I take it that that person you were thinking of bringing in wasn't me?" He could tell from the startled expression on her face that that had not occurred to her. He sighed and leaned back. Now was a good time to take a few sips of wine. It would give him time to think. "I'm not giving up on you, you know," he reminded her. "I'm not giving up on us." He moved his wine glass back and forth between them.

"I know." Without meeting his eyes, she added, "Neither am I."

"Taking a child into your home is a big decision."
Anna nodded.

"Have you decided?"

"No, I'm still thinking about it."

"Where does that leave me?"

Anna looked at him pleadingly. "Please. Nothing has to change between us."

"It doesn't work that way. Things are changing. I'm changing, growing closer to you, wanting more of you."

"But Bonnie..."

Murph set his wine glass on the table, then set Anna's alongside its mate. He rested the side of his knee on the couch and turned to Anna, taking her hands in his. "I'm not a child and I'm not jealous of the time you want to devote to a child. I like kids, too. But it doesn't have to be Bonnie, or me. You can have us both. She can have us both." He looked around the small room. "I've seen your home office. Do you really think that you have enough room here for you and Bonnie to co-habit without treading on one another?"

"No. I was trying to think of a way that it would work out, but this place is pretty small. It was fine for just me, but now...".

"I have a solution." He held up a hand. "Now before you think I'm railroading you into anything, it's just a suggestion, just an offer. It's one that would please me very much."

Anna waited. It was unlike Murph to seem nervous.

"Why don't you and Bonnie move in with me?"

Silence.

He hurried on. "I have a three-bedroom place, plus a big office; we could share it, or you could take one bedroom for your own office." He hesitated. "Or your own bedroom. We could play this any way you want."

⁓

SLEEP PROVED ELUSIVE THAT NIGHT. There were far too many problems floating around in her mind to allow for a peaceful rest.

Problems. Was that the way to look at things? She had two big decisions to make, both life-altering. But were either of them truly problems?

Contemplating living with a wonderful man should not be a problem. It would thrill many women to have such an invitation from a man like Murph. And he truly was quite wonderful. The only time she'd really seen him out-of-sorts was when he was annoyed with her for giving in too often, for not stating what she wanted. Like that was an undesirable trait in a man.

She should know. She'd experienced her share of undesirable characteristics in men. Murph never treated her like a commodity.

If she had only herself to consider, if only her life was an open book with no past to haunt her, then yes, she'd adore living with Dr. Arnold Murphy.

Could she take a chance? It had been a decade since she'd escaped her past. There'd been no sign that anyone knew where she was or cared. Could she trust it would stay that way? Was it fair to Murph to involve him on the slight chance her past would come to call? What were the odds?

THEN THERE WAS BONNIE. An innocent child. What had happened in her world that she had turned up in a courthouse alone? No frantic family crying to the police about their lost little girl. Not even a school alarmed that a student had not shown up for weeks. It's as if she belonged nowhere.

That was not right for any child, especially one like Bonnie. Something about the girl tugged at Anna's heart. Maybe she recognized her younger self in Bonnie, way back when Anna was unsure about the world, but hoping for her parents' continued protection. She'd often felt that she straddled two worlds with their constant traipsing from southern California to Mexico and back. The only time she had felt safe and wanted was when she was with her abuela in San Felipe, Mexico. A few times, when Abuela was ill, Anna's parents left her to look after her grandmother. Those were happy months.

With Abuela, there were no threats. Anna did not need to worry about making herself small or staying out of everyone's way. Abuela wanted her and liked her company. It was nice to feel loved and valued.

Had Bonnie ever felt that in her life?

CHAPTER 7

*A*nna woke up not refreshed but determined. Her churning mind weighed up the odds and decided. She picked up her phone. "Murph, I've been thinking."

"Me, too. I'm sorry if I've been pushing too hard. I'm patient. I can wait for you to catch up to me." He paused. "You will catch up to me at some point, won't you?"

"Yep." A grin entered her voice. "I'm there already."

There was a longer pause.

Oh, no, Anna thought. He's reconsidered. I took too long to decide, and he's changed his mind.

"What are you drinking?"

That was weird. "Ah, coffee."

"The good stuff?" Before she could answer, he bit in. "Never mind. Hold that thought. I'll be over in twenty minutes with some coffee to celebrate."

The line went dead. Anna couldn't hold in her grin. Guess he didn't change his mind. She raced to the

49

shower. Celebration coffees required better attire than ancient sweatpants and hair that was past its best-before date.

ANNA SHUT off her hair dryer and heard her phone chirp. She had several text messages from Murph.

The first one said, "B there in 5."

The next one said. "There was no answer, so I used my key and let myself in."

Then, "Just heard the shower go off. Wanted you to know that I'm here."

Finally, "There's a cruller here with your name on it, but there might be a bite out of it if you don't hurry."

That made her move. "Don't you dare! That's my cruller."

Murph stood in the hallway, the cruller in question in one hand, making its way toward his mouth.

Anna snatched it from his hand, tore the thing in two, stuffed the smaller piece into Murph's mouth, then savored smaller bites of her own half.

Reaching behind him, he picked up a large cup from the coffee table. "Here, my dear. Your favorite latte."

Anna moaned her pleasure and plunked herself onto the couch. Then she noticed. "Hey! You put the furniture back in its place."

"You could hardly operate with the couch sticking into the middle of the room."

The silence stretched.

"So, you've been thinking?" Murph broached the topic.

"Yes." She took a deep breath. "I'd love to live with you."

Murph gave an un-Murph-like whoop. "Yes!" He hugged her, rocking them from side to side.

"Hey, watch the latte." She quickly downed more to prevent it from slopping over the edge in case Murph did more of this rocking stuff.

"Where and when?" Murph wanted to know.

"I'm not sure. I didn't get that far yet."

He tried to hide his disappointment. Tomlins, Anna's tabby cat jumped onto his lap.

"That's what I wanted to talk to you about." She set her cup down and turned to face him. "All night I thought about us–you and me, and about Bonnie. There's something about her that gets to me.

"I didn't always have the greatest childhood, but sometimes I felt secure and wanted. I keep wondering if Bonnie has even felt that. I kind of doubt it, since in all these weeks no one has come looking for her."

"You're likely right."

"I thought I could give her some of that, at least a safe, secure place to live, even just for a while." This was the harder part. "I wondered if you would want to work with me to help her feel secure and wanted?" There. It was out. This was a big ask.

"Okay."

What? No discussion? It couldn't be that easy.

"I like kids. I was sad that we had none of our own, but my wife died too young. We were both just getting started in our careers and thought there was lots of time to think about a family down the road. There's been no one else that I've wanted to make a family with. Until you, that is."

Anna could not contain her grin.

"It might not be that easy," Murph continued. "While I'm willing and you're willing, Bonnie looks old enough to have some say in this. She's met me, but just twice. You're the one she's bonded with." He looked pained. "Maybe she would like to be with you, but not if you and I are together."

Anna wrapped her arms around him. "Any child would be privileged to have you in her life and in her corner. I know she'll learn to love you."

"Still, she's likely felt that nothing in her life is under her control lately. I think we should ask her what she thinks, rather than just tell her that this is our plan."

"There are logistics," said Anna. "I'm already on the approved foster care list, but you'll have to apply. There'll be a background check, and a home study."

"The background check's already done. I had to be cleared before the courts could have me confer on child custody cases. But I'll get on with the rest of the application today. Will you help me?"

They checked online and submitted the initial application. A couple of calls later, a home study appointment was booked. It thrilled Child Protective Services personnel to have a psychiatrist they'd worked with before applying to foster one of their harder-to-place older children.

~

"CERTAINLY," said Janice. "It'll do her good to get out of here for a while. She's been cooped up too long with no one but us and the little ones to talk to." It pleased Janice to receive Anna's call and request to take Bonnie out for a drive with her and Murph.

"Talk to. Is she speaking?" Anna asked.

"Sadly, no, at least not that Kevin or I have heard."

ANNA AND MURPH picked up Bonnie for their afternoon together. They went to an amusement park first, a small one, across from an art gallery. The three of them shared a seat in the rickety open train carriage that trundled around the edges of the park. Bonnie's face glowed. They weren't sure if she'd ever been on such a ride. Next, Anna and Bonnie took a seat on the Ferris wheel. As Ferris wheels went, it was pretty tame, but watching Bonnie's expression as she surveyed the city from the apex made it all worthwhile. Murph remained on the ground, his eyes fixed on the ladies who he hoped would soon live with him in his house.

Afterward, they crossed the street to tour the art gallery. While viewing fine art might not be high on a twelve-year-old's list of fun activities, they thought she might like the conservatory on the side of the building. It was a huge glass-walled building with skylights that seemed to touch the clouds. Opening the atrium doors ushered in another world. The lush plant growth, freshly turned soil, the scents of roses and other flowering species, plus the bubbling water in the fountains filled their senses as they strolled the paths, each turn in the walkway bringing them fresh sights from the world of nature.

The plan was to make themselves a late lunch at Murph's house, to let Bonnie see the grounds of his acreage and meet his dog. As they passed a Kentucky Fried Chicken, Bonnie turned in her seat, her eyes not leaving that big bucket high in the sky. Anna and Murph looked at each other, then at the child in the back seat. Murph turned on his signal light, made a loop around the block, then pulled into the parking lot. It looked like they were having to-go fried chicken for lunch.

Morgan, Murph's ancient Corgi, and her sidekick, the much younger German Shepherd, Sandy, glued themselves to Bonnie's side. Although they knew they had to stay back from the table when people were eating, they were all too willing to lick Bonnie's fingers clean when she left the table.

After Anna and Murph gave her a tour of the house, Murph led Bonnie and her new canine buddies outside. He showed Bonnie how to use the Chuckit–a contraption that launched the tennis balls the dogs so loved to retrieve. The first time Sandy brought back the ball, Bonnie bent to pick it up, then hastily dropped it, wiping the dog drool off her hand. Murph laughed. Bonnie stiffened and looked at him from the corner of her eye.

"Gross, isn't it?" he asked. Then he showed her how to use the Chuckit to pick up the ball, slobber and all. He handed it to her to throw.

Soon, Bonnie and the dogs were engrossed in their

game. Murph returned to the house to help Anna clean up the remnants of their lunch.

"Do you think she'd like one of the rooms upstairs for herself?"

"What kid wouldn't love to live here?" asked Anna.

"What about you? Would you love to, as well?"

She smiled. "Yes, I think I would."

They stood at the picture window, watching the young girl and the dogs play. Bonnie's grin matched that of the dogs.

Anna leaned forward. "There. Did it look like her lips moved? Did she say something?"

"Hard to tell. If it is selective mutism, maybe she'll feel safer with the animals than with people. It may be easier for her to speak to them. Pet therapy can work wonders for some people. These aren't trained therapy dogs, but they're splendid companions."

Anna leaned back against Murph as he wrapped his arms around her and leaned his chin on her head. She moved away as Bonnie turned in their direction, but Murph held her still. "If we're going to make this work with the three of us, she has to know that we're together."

Anna relaxed as Bonnie gave a smile in their direction, then turned back to throw the ball in a high arc. She laughed as Morgan tripped then righted herself as she raced to get the ball.

CHAPTER 8

*H*er knock wasn't loud. Somehow, despite working with him for years, there was just something about a judge's chambers that was intimidating. It wasn't just with Judge Bursey, but with all the magistrates in the building. Maybe it was the austereness of the furnishings. Not that Anna regarded a judge as godlike; no, she had seen them err, most recently at her friend, Elizabeth's expense. She heard his muffled voice directing her to enter. Couldn't he say, "come in" like a normal person?

"Hi." She closed the door behind her.

Judge Frank Bursey motioned her forward. He rose and headed for his credenza. Holding up the pot, he asked, "Care for some coffee?"

Something to do with her hands would be good. Part of this conversation would be easy, part not. She was a private woman and didn't enjoy needing to share personal information.

"Thanks." When settled, she took a deep breath. "I've

given it a lot of thought and yes, I'd like to be a foster parent to Bonnie."

Judge Bursey's eyes crinkled at the corners. "Good, good. Bonnie's a lucky child." He waited. "I'm sensing a but…".

"Well, yes, it's not that simple."

At his frown, she hastened to add. "No, nothing with Child Protective Services. I already talked to them and they're working on the paperwork."

"They'd better." He hated when bureaucracy impeded what was best for a child.

"The part that's not simple is personal."

"I'm sure that you and Murph will work it out."

Anna's eyes widened. "Murph?"

"Anna, Anna. This is a small building. Did you think I didn't know about you and Dr. Murphy?"

She blushed.

He smiled at her discomfort. "You cannot keep a budding romance quiet in this courthouse." He sipped his coffee. "Good taste, by the way - on both your part and on his."

"Ah, thanks." Goodness, this was uncomfortable. "There's more, though. Um, Murph and I were thinking of moving in together."

"Even better. Then Bonnie gets the benefit of both a social worker and a psychiatrist on her team."

"You'd just asked me to foster Bonnie; we had not talked about adding Murphy into the equation."

"No. While I didn't say so in as many words, I knew things were heading in that direction. It was only a matter of time. Murph will be good for her."

He motioned toward Anna with his mug. "As will you."

"Glad you feel that way. We'll try. We have to wait now for Murph to get approved as a foster parent. He's started the process, but things take time to work their way through the system."

"Not a problem. Murph already talked to me and I'm one of his references."

"He did?"

"He seems to go after what he wants."

"I'll do what I can to push things through quickly. CPS will cooperate. They have other children who need a spot in that temporary home and it's difficult to find foster placements for older children like this."

"How does Bonnie feel about this?"

ANNA AND MURPH agreed to meet with Janice and Kevin when the youngest kids were napping. Hopefully. Their nap times were not an exact science.

They came armed with pictures. Murph had taken photographs of Bonnie playing with his dogs, of them sharing greasy chicken at the kitchen table together, then of two bedrooms. He wanted Bonnie to have her choice of rooms. So much had been done to her young life recently; he wanted her to have at least some semblance of control. The major choice, though, was if she wanted to come to live with them.

If she hated the idea, then the next move was unclear. She couldn't stay where she was, there was no trace of a family frantically searching for her and the options for adolescents in foster care were bleak.

THERE WAS no simple way to broach the possibility of more change to Bonnie, so they got right to it. Responding to Janice's call, Bonnie slipped into a kitchen chair, joining them at the table. She smiled shyly at Anna, including Murph in her gaze.

Janice started. "Bonnie, honey, we've loved having you here with us and the kids think you're wonderful." She squeezed Bonnie's folded hands. "But you know that this is not your forever home, just temporary. Until we find your family, you'll live in a foster home."

With each of her words, the muscles in Bonnie's small body got tighter and tighter. Her head lowered, her hair hiding her face. Bonnie's shoulders shrank in on themselves.

Anna's turn. "I used to be a foster parent," she told Bonnie. "I haven't done it for a few years, but am thinking of starting again."

No response.

With a look at Murph for courage, Anna continued. "Would you consider being my foster child, sort of easing me back into things?"

That caught Bonnie's attention. She peeked at Anna from beneath her bangs.

"I'd like it if you wanted me to be your foster mom. How would you feel about moving in with me?"

"With us," added Murph. "It would be you, Anna, and me, living together in my house. Would you like that?"

A smile broke through the veil of hair. Bonnie raised her eyes to meet Murph's.

He pushed the pictures across the table toward her. Laying them out one at a time, he explained that he'd been showing them to Kevin and Janice. Patiently, he explained again to them how Bonnie had entertained the dogs so well and how much they loved her. Finally, he placed pictures of the two bedrooms in front of Bonnie. "Anna and I talked about lot about you coming to live with us, but we couldn't decide which bedroom you might prefer."

Bonnie's eyes widened.

"We thought we'd leave these pictures with you so you could decide."

Bonnie's smile lit the room as she pushed back her chair.

"Where are you going?" asked Janice.

There was no answer.

They could hear rummaging from upstairs and in just a few minutes, Bonnie returned with a plastic grocery bag brimming with clothing.

Anna was the first one who got it and shook her head. "Oh, my dear. We should have explained better."

Bonnie's face fell and her posture returned to that of a small child trying to make herself invisible.

"We want you," explained Murph. "But we can't take you home with us just yet."

Bonnie didn't trust what she was hearing.

Anna wondered how many times this child had been let down in her life, how many promises not kept, how many people pretending they wanted her, but not following through. "Soon," she said. "Maybe a week, although I can't promise. We have to get the paperwork from Child Protective Services and plan."

Janice put her arm around Bonnie's shoulders. "In the meantime, you'll stay here with us until it's time for you to move."

Bonnie sagged against her.

"We're going to need your help," added Murph. "We'll have to decorate your room, so think about what you'd like."

Anna nodded. "Then, we have to pack up my stuff to move to Murph's. Do you think you could help me with some of that work?"

Bonnie nodded, her smile breaking through.

"Oh, and there's one other thing," added Murph. He watched Bonnie tense, waiting for the other shoe to drop. No, things had not always turned out well in her world. "It's about Morgan and Sandy." He stretched out one arm and massaged his bicep. "They're waiting in the car, wanting a trip to the park. They expect a lot of ball-throwing, but my arm's on the stiff side. Do you think you'd be willing to come with us and use the Chuckit with them?"

She might not have uttered a word, but her grin spoke volumes.

THE PLACE WAS IN DISARRAY. While not a neat freak, Anna usually kept her place reasonably tidy. Today, not so much.

She'd spent the week sorting her belongings. In boxes in the hallway were things she'd likely never use again - clothes she'd bought on sale that looked great on the hanger, but not so good on her. One box contained kitchen gadgets, the kind that looked great on infomercials, but once home didn't seem nearly so handy after all. She'd carefully sorted through her kitchen cupboards. How many glasses and cups did she really need? The previous weekend she'd investigated every cupboard and drawer in Murph's kitchen, determining what he lacked and what she should bring, how much duplication there was and which of her things she'd prefer to take precedence and space over Murph's.

He assured her he was attached to none of it. Still, she carefully stacked on the table things she thought could go to make room for her belongings. This was a test of their diplomacy, but it had worked. Murph genuinely seemed not to care about his stuff mostly, but pointed out the objects he felt strongly about retaining. After helping her box up those items, he hauled them to Goodwill and to the women's shelter.

Making the same determinations about her own things was harder, but mostly done.

The tearing sound of packing tape ripping from its dispenser came from the next room. Bonnie entered, proudly carrying another box she'd just reinforced. She was spending the day helping Anna prepare for their move. They sat on the floor, wrapping newspaper around glass stemware, Bonnie handling it like she'd never touched such fragile items. Gently, Bonnie lay the first wine glass on a bed of scrunched-up newsprint covering the bottom of the box.

They'd have more help later in the afternoon when Elizabeth and Keira came over to assist. For now, they were content with each other's company, getting tasks completed and enjoying the oldies station blaring on the radio. Anna wasn't sure and didn't want to make a big deal out of it, but she thought she caught the sound of humming coming from Bonnie just before the child rose to her feet, leaving the room to tape up another box.

~

ONE YEAR AGO IN TIJUANA, MEXICO

Evaline tried returning to her job. She knew she looked rough, as if she had spent the night sleeping on the street. Funny that she'd look that way, because that's exactly what had happened. Stopping at the washroom of an OXXO service station, she cleaned herself up just a little. There was only so much the finger-combing of her hair could do and there was no way to remove the dirt patches from her clothes. They would frown at that in the taqueria.

But her filthy clothes were the least of her problems when she entered the taqueria, where she had worked for almost two years. Her boss spotted her immediately and shooed her out. He said that they did not want her kind there.

Her mother had been round first thing in the morning and told the boss about her shame. Now Evaline was severed from her family, her home, and the only source of income she had. There was no discussing this; her boss was adamant. She was to leave and never return.

Head down, she let her hair hang in her face to hide her tears. She was so wrapped up in her grief that it took several seconds for her to realize that someone was calling her name. Turning, she saw it was Madeline, her boss's wife. She also worked at the taqueria and had always been kind to Evaline. Madeline motioned for her to come into the back alley. Glancing around to make sure that no one was watching, Madeline handed her a small bag. Inside were some pesos and several steaming fish fajitas.

"No more," Madeline told her. "Do not come here again. Lo siento."

When Evaline looked up to express her gratitude, all she saw was Madeline's back.

EVALINE HEADED FOR A PARK. She avoided Parque Morelos; it was too near her home and someone she knew might see her. But she found a bench to sit on in a quieter area and bolted down the first fajita. After the first hurried bites, her queasy stomach reminded her to slow down. She really didn't want to barf right here where anyone could see her, nor did she want to waste any bit of this warm food. Who knew when she'd get more?

Carefully, she folded the last fajita, so its filling wouldn't spill out. She glanced around. No, no one seemed to pay her any attention. She reached into her shirt, between her breasts, and pulled out the carefully folded pesos. Sheltering them from sight using her hands and the plastic bag, she counted them out. Then counted them again. This was her past week's salary. It wasn't much, but it was more than she'd had as of last night. She was grateful to Madeline for this.

But it was not much, she knew. She would need to find a way to replenish this money now that she had no job.

Would it be enough to get her off the street for the night?

CHAPTER 9

*I*n a house across town, a pot of spaghetti
boiled over, but no one was there to notice.
The splashes sizzled on the stove top, some puddling,
some evaporating, some sticking. The brown scorch
marks grew, as did the smell of scorched starch.

Two children hid in a back bedroom - one silent and
terrified, the other wailing. The older brother tried to
shush his baby brother, but he was a little past
toddlerhood himself and not up to providing comfort.

"I expect food on the table when I step through this
door." He gave his sister-in-law a shake. "Do you
hear me?"

Trying not to whimper, she nodded, glancing behind
her to be sure that the boys were out of sight. As bad as
this was for her when Archie was in this mood, she
didn't want the babies on the receiving end.

Over the last year, Archie had started in on her
daughter, and it was getting worse. Thank god she was
out of harm's way now. At least, that's what Sally

insisted on telling herself. Surely her daughter had ended up in a better place than this.

Archie's nose moved away from Sally's face and sniffed the air. "What's that?"

Oh God, oh God, thought Sally. No, not again. She'd been cooking when Archie came through the door in one of his moods. Had she forgotten to turn off the burner when she left the room?

Her nose told her she had. Ducking under his arm, she tore into the kitchen. Now that all the water had evaporated, the pasta that wasn't burned to the bottom of the pan was a pasty, gelatinous mass. The stench of burning starch filled the air. Tendrils of smoke rose from the cooktop. Much longer and she'd have had a real mess on her hands. Not that this one wasn't bad enough.

Reaching for the kitchen towel, she used it to grab the broken pot handle. She tossed the pot into the sink where it hissed when its bottom contacted the wetness and old food scrapings accumulated in the sink's bottom. She turned on the faucet to add water to the pan. Steam rose, along with it the scorched aroma. Great.

"THIS is how you cook my supper?" She was sure that everyone up and down the block could hear his roar. "I. Work. All. Week. Hard. To provide for you, my brother and your brats, and all I ask is that you have meals ready on time." He took a step backward from the stink. "Now what is a starving man supposed to eat?"

"I have meatballs in the oven. They should be ready by now. And I can make more pasta." At least she thought she could. Maybe enough for just Archie. She'd thrown almost the entire box into that pot, trying to make enough filling food for the four of them. The grocery money Archie gave her did not go far enough. Nothing did.

"Forget it. I don't deserve to be treated like this. I'm out of here. You'll be lucky if I come back."

The front door slammed, then there was silence. Blessed silence. She pondered his last statement and wondered if it was true.

WITH HER BACK to the hallway, the music filling her ears, and plans running through her mind, Anna didn't hear the front door open. It was always locked, anyway, as were all of her doors and windows. Always.

She didn't see the man standing in the entrance to the living room with his hands on his hips, his feet planted far apart. "What's my wife up to?" he asked. "Are you moving in or out?"

Anna stiffened, the whites of her eyes showing. NO! No, no, no. It could not be. Slowly, she inched her body around. The Austrian crystal goblet fell to the carpet, not shattering, but rolling safely under the couch. This could not be. No.

It had been over a decade, but she'd recognize this man even if it had been a century. He haunted her dreams, or rather her nightmares.

She was sure that he'd lost interest in her since she was deficient and could not do what he wanted. She had no sign that he was even looking for her. Only in the last few years had she relaxed, finally thinking she was free of him and the burden that had been thrust up on her.

"What's mi esposa been up to?"

Anna's mouth opened, but no words escaped.

"Aren't you inviting me in?"

Again, Anna couldn't reply.

"But then I suppose that mi casa es su casa and all that, so my wife's home is my home." He lounged in her recliner. "Not bad, not bad," he said as he looked around. "A little messy for my taste, but you could fix that, couldn't you?"

Stretching toward the coffee table, he picked up the television remote. "Turn that racket off," he ordered. "Let's see what's on. You're not much into big screens, I see."

When Anna remained frozen to the floor, he lowered his brows, narrowing his eyes. "I said turn off that noise."

She still couldn't move.

With an expletive, he took two steps, wrenched the cord from the wall, then strode to the front door. Opening it, he chucked the offending radio onto the concrete walkway where it bounced and cracked apart.

Pleased with himself, he returned to the lounger and flicked through the channels with a complaint. "No Netflix?"

Anna's wits were returning from the far land of her memories, images flooding her mind that she never wanted to live through again.

"What? No offer of food or drink? That's no way to treat a long-lost marino. What's with you since you moved up here? Have you forgotten how to treat a husband?"

Slowly, Anna got to her feet. She used the coffee table for support, her legs suddenly feeling forty years older than they were. "Get out," she said. Then louder, "Get out of my house, now." There was steel in her quiet voice.

He laughed and pulled the lever to extend the recliner's footrest. "I don't think I will. I like it here." He gave her a look that she remembered oh so well. "Now get me some food. I've come a long way, and you put me to a lot of trouble trying to find you." His look cut through her. "You'll pay for that, you know."

Footsteps sounded on the hardwood flooring in the hall. Bonnie entered, bearing another box, this one so large that it obscured her head. She peeked around the right side of her burden to see where the coffee table was, then set the box on top of it. As she stood back, she noticed the man in the room. Instantly, she tightened. Her eyes darted around the room, then to the hallway from which she had entered, her gaze searching for the best hiding place.

Alejandro sat up straighter, looking between Bonnie and Anna and back again. The look in his eyes did not bode well for anyone. He lowered the footrest and planted his boots on the floor.

As his glare penetrated Anna, she put an arm around Bonnie, pulling the child behind her.

"You've been holding out on me," accused Alejandro.

Anna shook her head.

"You had a kid."

Again, Anna shook her head. She could see how he might think that Bonnie was hers, since they both had thick, straight, dark brown hair. "She is not my child. She's the daughter of someone else, just here helping me today." Please, she pleaded in her mind to Bonnie. Don't think that I'm denying you or that you'll be my foster daughter. I just don't want this man anywhere near you.

"You never could tell a lie to save yourself." Alejandro laughed. "I always knew when you were hiding something." He eyed what he could see of Bonnie, only partially covered by Anna's body. "This is a pretty big something."

Anna watched as he did some figuring in his head, knowing that he was adding up the years, guessing at Bonnie's age.

"You're sure she's not mine?"

"No! Definitely not, of course not." Anna took a small step backward so that she could feel Bonnie's trembling body against her own. "She's not my daughter or yours."

"Then tell me, kid, who's your daddy?"

Bonnie's enormous eyes looked at him from the side of Anna's head.

Alejandro slapped his palms on the arms of the recliner. "I asked you a question. Who is your father?"

"Alejandro, she doesn't talk. She can't tell you."

"Right. A big kid like that doesn't talk. You expect me to buy that she's some kind of deaf mute or something?" He got to his feet. "You know better than to mess with me." He cracked his knuckles. "Or has it been so long that you've forgotten your lessons?"

EIGHTEEN YEARS AGO IN ENSENADA, MEXICO

"Who is this priest?" The abuela didn't like this.

"He's someone Alejandro knows," replied her daughter-in-law.

"I've lived here all my life and I've never heard of him. There aren't that many priests in these mountains."

"I don't know. It doesn't matter. Alejandro took care of everything for the wedding."

"Why does our girl look so sad?"

"She's not sad. What girl could be sad on her wedding day? She's nervous. It's a big day for her." A big day for all of us, she thought.

"I don't like it," insisted the abuela. "Something's not right."

CHAPTER 10

*H*is advance halted as the doorbell chimed. They heard the door open, then a woman's voice yelled, "Hey, Anna. It's just us."

Then another female voice said, "Your door was open. That's not like you. And what's with the radio on the ground outside?"

Elizabeth and Keira dropped their purses in the entryway and headed into the living room.

"What do you want us to do first?" Keira's voice trailed off as she saw the back of a large man in the middle of the room, a man with clenched fists and stiffness in his stance. "Hey," she yelled. "What are you doing in here?"

Elizabeth skirted around the couch to take a stand beside Anna. Her arm brushed her friend's in solidarity.

Keira pulled her phone out of her back pocket. Pushing the home button, she said, "Hey, Siri, call Jake."

A voice echoed, "Calling Jake."

The dark-haired man turned to face the woman who had spoken. "Who's Jake?"

"My boyfriend." Thinking quickly, Keira added, "He's coming to help us carry boxes."

While Keira had the guy's attention on her, Elizabeth pulled her phone from her pocket and punched the buttons to speed dial Brendan. She made sure the volume was all the way up, put the phone on speaker, then slipped it into her side pocket.

"Anna, who is this?" Keira asked, glaring at the man. She wanted to keep his attention focused on her as Elizabeth edged toward the fireplace where the poker hung.

Taking one step back into the hallway, Keira reached for the heavy vase that adorned the side table. "Anna, what are you going to do with this? If you're not planning to take it, do you think I might have it? I've always loved this thing." She hefted it in her hands, getting a feel for its weight and balance. While not an ideal weapon, it was better than nothing and certainly better than the roll of packing tape sitting on the floor.

While his attention was on Keira, Anna pushed Bonnie and herself several steps backward. She motioned to the wing chair to Bonnie, hoping that the girl got the message to scrunch down behind it. She wanted Bonnie out of the range of fire if things got bad. And from her experience with Alejandro, things could very well go bad.

She straightened as she felt Bonnie slip away from her. From the side of her eye, she saw that Elizabeth now held the metal poker behind one leg. Not that either of them had any practice using such a thing for a weapon, but it might help.

Anna told herself that she was no longer a frightened, helpless twenty-year-old, powerless against this man and at his mercy. She was not alone. She had friends. She had a life. She had skills she'd fought damned hard for.

Alejandro laughed, not a humorous laugh, but one full of evil intent. How often had Anna heard that before? She knew what could come next. "Who are these chicas caliente?" His smile turned into a leer. "Aren't you going to introduce them to your husband?"

Keira and Elizabeth exchanged looks. Still clasping the heavy vase, Keira positioned herself on the other side of Anna. "Guess not. Looks like she doesn't want us to make your acquaintance." She looked him up and down. "I can see why."

Anna gasped. Red flag to a bull, Keira, her mind screamed. Don't antagonize him.

Alejandro's laugh burst from him. "Ah, Anna. I like this one. She has spunk. You never had much of that, did you?" His gaze swept Keira from head to foot, then back up again, lingering in certain places. "Wonder what she's like in the sack?"

As Keira opened her mouth to retort and Elizabeth brought the poker to her side, there was a click from the doorway.

"Stop! Hold it right there. Don't anyone move," ordered Brendan James from the doorway where he stood with arms extended, both hands on the gun pointed at the floor near the man's feet. A quick glance told him that Elizabeth, Anna, and Keira were all right. Frightened for sure, but not hurt.

He advanced into the room, watching intently as the man shuffled his feet to face him. Brendan edged toward the woman, intending to place himself between this guy and them.

"Who are you?" he asked.

The guy smiled. He had the nerve to smile. He nodded toward Anna. "Aren't you going to introduce us, little wifey?"

Wife? Brendan didn't dare take his eyes off the fellow long enough to look to Anna for confirmation. "Down," he ordered. With his revolver, he motioned to the floor. "Get down on your stomach."

The guy's smile creeped out Brendan. He'd seen that look before on punks, and it never boded well.

Anna spoke up. "Just go, Alejandro, leave. You're not wanted. You have no business being here."

"A man doesn't have the right to see his wife?"

"Please," Anna asked. "Go. We don't want any trouble."

"Elizabeth, call 911," Brendan told her.

"No need," a voice said from the hallway. "Backup's here." Jake, Brendan's partner, entered the room, his weapon held at his side. "Are you hurt?" he asked the women.

They shook their heads.

"What's your name?" he asked the guy.

"Alejandro Sanchez."

Jake and Brendan exchanged looks. Anna flushed.

"Sanchez, like Anna?"

"Doesn't a wife usually take her husband's name?"

"Anna, what gives?" asked Elizabeth.

Keira didn't let her answer. "I don't care who he says he is. Do you want him here, Anna?"

Anna shook her head.

"Then he can't be here." It was clear to Keira.

"Are you married to this guy?" Brendan wasn't clear on what was going on.

"No." Anna was definite. "I was, once, a long time ago. But not anymore."

Alejandro brought a hand to his chest. "Oh, you wound me, la mujer."

Anna explained, "I've not seen him or heard from him in over ten years."

Brendan summed things up. "It doesn't sound like she wants a reunion with you. Leave or face trespassing charges."

"He was threatening her, too," added Elizabeth.

Brendan motioned toward the door with his gun. "Leave now, or we arrest you."

Showing that he had some sense of discretion, Alejandro moved to the doorway. He stopped and nodded his head at the women. "Nice meeting your friends, Anna." He narrowed his eyes at her. "This isn't over."

∿

"Hey, can anyone help with the door?" Murph's voice from the entranceway broke the spell. Like statues coming out from under a spell, everyone moved at once, unfreezing themselves and loosening the tension created by Alejandro's exit. "Who was that guy I saw leaving?"

Jake opened the door and took half of the pizza boxes from Murph's arms, setting them on the hall table. Then Jake's long strides took him back to the living room where he wrapped his arms around his girlfriend, Keira. Brendan had already done the same with Elizabeth. Only Anna stood there, a solitary figure.

Murph soon fixed that. As he folded her gently in his embrace, he whispered in her ear, "What's going on here? Why's everyone acting so strange?" Then he spied Bonnie, crouched behind a chair, watching them all with wide eyes. "Come here," he said to her. When she walked closer, he included her in the hug he shared with Anna. Bonnie's arms remained at her side, but she rested her head against Murph's chest.

Keira and Elizabeth shared a glance. Keira grabbed Jake's arm, tugging him after her. "Come on. Let's see to these boxes."

Jake looked puzzled, but allowed her to lead him into the other room. Elizabeth and Brendan followed. Elizabeth turned. "Bonnie, please show us where things are?" The child went with her.

"Okay, what's going on?"

"It's a long story," began Anna.

"I've got time. Why is everyone acting so weird?"

"We had a visitor. That guy you saw leaving? I used to know him. I haven't seen him in years and years, thought I'd never see him again. I thought I was free of him and that he had no use for me anymore."

Murph frowned. "Who is he?"

"My husband."

Murph froze. Of all the words that could come out of Anna's mouth, those were not the ones he'd expected. He rubbed his hand across the top of his head and half turned away. "You're married?"

Anna shook her head. "No. Once I was. I had to."

"You had to? You mean you were pregnant?"

"No, nothing like that. At least not then," she added.

"Why in god's name would you have to marry him or anyone?"

"It was a family thing, an honor thing."

Without saying a word, his face said, "What?"

"I can't talk about it. It's not my story to tell. Please trust me. It was an honor thing I had to do for my family. I filled my obligation, then got out."

"So you're not married?"

She shook her head.

"To him or to anyone else."

"No."

"I still don't get it. He just dropped by to see how you were doing?"

A noise from the hallway distracted them. Turning, they saw four adults filling the small space.

"Sorry, man," said Brendan. "We're not just being nosy. We're worried."

"Why was everyone so tense when I got here?" asked Murph.

"This didn't appear to be a friendly visit," Jake explained. "When I got here, Keira was toting that enormous vase in her arms and Elizabeth had the fireplace poked clenched in her fists."

Murph held Anna by the shoulders. "Is this man dangerous?"

There was no swift denial from Anna.

"That settles it." Murph was definite. "You are not to be in this house alone. We're speeding up your move-in date."

Jake and Brendan relaxed.

"We'll help," said Elizabeth.

The other three echoed their agreement.

"But we need a break now." Elizabeth was definite. "Since Murph already picked up the pizzas, and we were planning on coming to my place to eat, I say we head there now."

"Cynthia has probably had enough of our sons anyway," said Keira.

"We'll make the rounds first and make sure that everything's locked up tight." Jake headed off in one direction, Brendan taking the opposite route.

CHAPTER 11

*W*hile the men arranged the pizza boxes on the dining room table, Anna got out the plates and cutlery. Elizabeth had gotten used to others making themselves at home in her house. At first this casualness had felt uncomfortable and against her upbringing, but now she appreciated the informality of sharing chores and her space with people who had become important to her. She'd learned that neither she nor her house had to be perfect. They liked her anyway.

Keira and Elizabeth went next door to her neighbor Cynthia's house to retrieve their sons. Cynthia's Amy loved playing with the boys and Cynthia was happy to babysit during playdates.

Interrupting the kids' game was not easy, but the mention of pizza did the trick. Amy led the way as the kids scrambled to put on their shoes and run next door.

"We were planning to invite you and Amy anyway," Elizabeth assured Cynthia.

"Thanks. As if my daughter left you any choice."

Backing up what Elizabeth just said, the women and children entered Elizabeth's house to find the table set with eleven place settings. Bonnie placed a folded paper napkin on each plate.

SUPPER WAS RELAXED, if somewhat messy, the pizza accompanied by the Caesar salad Elizabeth had made earlier, home-made garlicky bread sticks supplied by Keira, and wine, beer and sparkling juice brought by Jake.

As the youngest three became restless, Elizabeth turned to Bonnie. "Would you mind helping? Would you take the kids into the other room and put on a movie for them?"

Bonnie nodded. She'd been here several times before and knew how to run the equipment. The three children loved her. They didn't seem to notice that she didn't speak; somehow, communication between the four of them was easy. Of course, it probably helped that Daniel spoke only a few words. Although Timothy's speech was coming, it was by no means fluent and easy for him. Amy, on the other hand, made up for any speech lack in the other three put together. They could hear her chattering in the other room.

~

WITH UNSPOKEN ASSENT, they all agreed to ignore the elephant in the room and not talk about the visit at Anna's house this afternoon. But, soon....

Filling a lull in the conversation, Cynthia told the group that Amy was driving her crazy with her continuing questions about school supplies. Yes, they already had everything on the list, but Amy constantly took them out of her backpack, sorting them, worrying that she didn't have enough different colored pencils and crayons, or enough glue to last the year.

"Have you thought about school for Timothy?" she asked Elizabeth.

"No." Elizabeth shook her head. "I feel like I'm still catching my breath after all that's happened to us."

Keira gave her a skeptical look. "Riiight."

Jake and Brendan smirked, Brendan squeezing Elizabeth's hand. "We know you're nervous," he said.

"True."

"Understandable," assured Cynthia. "But he has to start sometime, doesn't he?"

"But he's been sick so much," protested Elizabeth.

"The seizures aren't happening nearly as often now." Brendan was around often enough to keep tabs on such things.

"The local school knows what to do if he has one there." Jake used to be a community police officer, regularly dropping by the school Amy and Daniel attended.

"Still…," worried Elizabeth.

"No one was leerier about letting their kid start school than me last year," Keira said. "I stormed in there with a list of demands on how they must watch Daniel and accommodate him." She thought a moment. "They listened politely to me, took some of my ideas, but mostly did the things they do best. They even helped me with some strategies, especially around communication."

That interested Elizabeth.

Keira continued. "They didn't seem flapped by a kid who doesn't talk. They didn't force him to speak, (as if they could anyway), but focused on giving him ways to communicate."

"Didn't you have some trouble with them?"

"Other than that they lost him once, no."

"*Lost* him? How do you lose a kid?"

Jake took this one. "He wandered off at recess and no one noticed at first."

"They were supposed to always have an eye on him, but he got away on them." Then she added, "He has on me a few times, as well."

"Did they keep someone guarding him after that?"

"Not really. Instead, they worked on strategies for Daniel to stop himself, taught him boundaries and kept a closer watch on him. Some of their ideas helped us at home as well."

"That worries me, too. Timothy can get so engrossed in something that I could see him forgetting where he was, or wandering away to look at something."

"Sounds like he could use some of the strategies they implemented with Daniel. They helped," said Jake.

"I'll go with you," offered Keira. "It's great that we're in the same neighborhood and the kids will all go to the same school. Let's just go once, the two of us alone, so I can introduce you to some staff and you can check things out."

"Maybe." Elizabeth knew that the time was coming soon, but she wasn't quite ready yet.

"Amy's going into grade two now; she'll watch out for the boys." She added, "And, she might just tell them what to do."

The adults laughed. Yep, they could definitely see Amy ordering the boys around. Somehow, Daniel and Timothy took it well and followed her directions.

THROUGHOUT THE DISCUSSION, Anna and Murph were quiet. School had crossed their minds also, but they didn't know how to approach it.

"What about Bonnie?" Keira asked.

"We're not sure," said Murph. "There are concerns. We have no idea what grade she's in or even if she's been to school."

"We know that she can read because we've seen her with a book."

"We don't know if she can write because she puts up a face like a blank wall when we offer her a paper and pen or even a keyboard."

"Plus, how can a school handle a child who doesn't talk?" Anna asked.

There was silence.

It was unlike Anna to put her foot in her mouth. "Sorry. I didn't mean that the way it came out."

Elizabeth looked skeptically at her.

Anna tried back pedaling. "I mean, I know that Daniel doesn't really speak, and Timothy is just starting to use some words, but they're still so young, just five.

Look how they get along with Amy. Little kids are accepting and find ways. But what about a twelve-year-old who doesn't speak?"

"Yeah, about that," said Keira. "What's up with that?"

"We don't know," Murph explained. "Some kids who are deaf don't speak because it's difficult to produce sounds when you've never heard them. But Bonnie's hearing seems to be okay. I haven't peered down her throat, but she eats all right, and doesn't seem to have breathing problems, so I'd assume that there is no oral motor structural reason she can't speak. Sometimes people will become aphasic after some trauma to the head, but they often try to talk, but can't. I don't see evidence of Bonnie trying."

"So what's going on then?"

"Another possibility is selective mutism. This can happen when a child becomes increasingly anxious, afraid to speak in certain situations. Those situations can increase until the child only feels safe talking with a few people and under specific conditions."

"Or," Anna added, "maybe someone has warned her not to speak."

"ONCE YOU MOVE IN TOGETHER, the two of you will need to be at work all day, right?" asked Cynthia.

Murph and Anna nodded.

"Bonnie's too young to be left alone all day, every day."

True.

"Most parents handle this by having their kids in school during the work week, or put them in day care. Bonnie's old for day care, don't you think?"

This was just one of the many logistics they still had to work through.

"We talked about hiring someone to come in to be with her during the day, at least until she can go to school," said Murph.

"But who would we get? It's not like we can go to a temp agency and put in a request, or hire a nanny for an almost teen."

They all pondered this predicament.

"I'm a teacher," announced Cynthia.

No one spoke.

"It's what I trained for and what I did before we had Amy. I'd planned to stay at home until she reached school-age, but after Tim died, I just wanted to be at home with her."

Understandable.

"Now that Amy's in school full time, I'm at loose ends most days." She looked at Elizabeth. "I love it when I can babysit Timothy for you and enjoy it when he and Daniel come over. But I could do more." She turned to Anna. "If you're not opposed to homeschooling and would trust me, I could teach Bonnie at my house until you decide to place her in a school."

"Seriously?" To Murph, this seemed too good to be true.

Cynthia nodded. "I'd enjoy it. I used to teach middle years, grades six to eight. It wouldn't take me long to get a handle on what Bonnie knows or doesn't know. If she has some weak areas, we could work on them together to help her get caught up to her peers before she enters a classroom."

"We're worried that if she has selective mutism, then the added pressure of a new school, new teacher, and classmates could increase Bonnie's anxiety and make her recovery all that much slower."

Anna added, "But she already knows and likes you. She's relaxed around you." She turned to Murph. "This could really work." Turning to Cynthia, she asked, "May we get back to you later this week?"

CHAPTER 12

*A*cross town, two wee boys huddled together on yellowed bed sheets. The older, little more than a baby himself, tried to cuddle his little brother. He gave him the corner of a blanket to suck on. There was nothing else.

They had already been through all the cupboards in the kitchen. They took turns grabbing and gobbling fistfuls of dried cereal, the only thing they could find to eat. The younger toddler gathered the bits that spilled onto the floor. He wasn't much good at walking.

Sometimes there was soda in the fridge, but not today. Or milk. Daddy liked milk with his cereal. He would be mad when he found out that they had none.

Benjie slid off the bed and toddled back to the kitchen, Jordy following. Pulling over a chair, Jordy used it to climb onto the counter to get a glass. Carefully, he cradled it in his hands. Once he'd dropped one and it had smashed to pieces all over the place. Daddy had been so mad and spanked him. Hard. Then when daddy left for work, mommy spanked him some more and made him pick up all the little pieces of glass with his hands. It hurt when they got in his fingers and his bare feet. For a while it was hard to walk around, but then it got better. Mostly.

He saw a bottle on the counter. He was proud of himself; only recently had he learned to turn caps. Some he just could not get off, but some he could open. Setting the glass beside the sink, he used both hands to unscrew this one. It wasn't on tight and came off easily. Raising it to take a drink, he stopped. He knew that smell. Mommy called it Daddy's mean juice. His little brother might be thirsty, but Jordy didn't want Benjie to get mean. He cried and yelled enough as it was. And if he tried it himself and got mean, who would look after Benjie?

Water it would be then. Stretching out along the counter, Jordy held the glass carefully by its rim, then stretched out his other hand to turn on the tap. The one nearest him stuck. He could not turn it on. Sitting up and holding the glass between his thighs, he tried using both hands on the stubborn tap. Nothing.

Carefully, he crossed the sinkful of dirty dishes, trying not to put his weight on any of them. He'd get in trouble if he broke any. It was hard because they were greasy and slippery. They smelled bad, too.

This wasn't working.

He crawled back down to the chair, and then onto the floor. Pushing, he slid the chair to the other side of the sink and the other tap. Maybe this one would work.

Perched by the other tap, he realized that he'd

forgotten the glass on the other side. Carefully he placed one palm, then one knee on the haphazard stack of dirty dishes. Not much farther and he could reach the glass.

Crack! His knee fell down, his slight weight breaking a teacup. His jarring descent threw him off-balance, and his chin cracked against the edge of the sink. He rested there a moment, feeling his world spin. Using his hand to raise himself, his palm landed on a knife protruding from a pile of plates. Its blade sliced across the base of two fingers. It happened so quickly and so cleanly that he didn't feel any pain. What he saw was blood, lots of blood dripping all over the dirty dishes. Mommy would be mad. He stuck his hand into the murky water and shook it around. Pulling his wet hand out, it dripped blood on the counter, but his little brother's screams were louder now. He needed something to eat or drink.

Jordy reached for the glass he'd carefully left by the sink. His fingers were now slick with blood and grease, making it hard to grasp the glass properly. It slipped from his grip several times as he inched his way back across the sink full of dishes. Back by the tap he had not yet tried, he set the glass down. Using both hands, he grasped the tap on the left, turning with all his three-year-old might.

Water erupted from the tap into the dirty water, sending cascades of grease and old bits of food flying all over Jordy, the counters, the wall and the floor. Frantically he tried to decrease the flow, but his greasy hands kept slipping. The water spilled over the edge of the sink, at first in a trickle, then a torrent onto the floor.

Benjie, caught in the waterfall, stopped his crying. After some gasping breaths, he laughed.

A key turned in the front door's lock.

ELIZABETH GOT up to check on the kids. The only sounds came from the Disney channel playing on the television. From experience, Elizabeth knew not to rock the boat when the kids were quiet.

"Hey," she whispered.

Bonnie turned her head and smiled at Elizabeth. Each of her arms was around a sleeping little boy. On the floor, at Bonnie's feet was Amy, her head on a pillow taken from the couch, her body sprawled in slumber.

"Everything okay? Elizabeth asked.

Bonnie gave her a thumb's up.

"Can I bring you anything? Want me to move the boys off of you?"

Bonnie shook her head and smiled before turning back to watch the movie.

"KIDS ARE FINE," she announced to the adults. "Amazing that they get along so well."

"They're good kids." It was novel for Anna to feel included in a parenting role. It felt good, filled a void she'd had for a long time.

Understanding, Murph squeezed her hand. "Now,

on to tomorrow. After what happened this afternoon, we need to speed up your moving plans."

Nods all around.

"How much more would it take to get you packed up?"

"Maybe a few days. I have some vacation time saved up and could use some of it now to finish packing, then clean the place."

Keira asked, "If it would take you a few days, how long would it take with all of us helping?"

"If you're thinking of tomorrow, I can keep the kids again, if that would help," offered Cynthia. "I'd come myself, but with three little ones underfoot, I'm not sure how much we'd get done. I might be of more use keeping them out of the way."

"Seriously?" Elizabeth wanted to know. "You're up for it *again*?"

"It often feels easier to look after two or three kids at once, rather than just Amy alone. They entertain each other."

"I'm off tomorrow," said Brendan.

"Me, too," threw in Jake, "and my truck's available."

"That would make six of us. We can get a lot done."

"Do you need some of us to go to your place, Murph, to help you move things around to make room for Anna's stuff?"

"Nope, that's done. Anna did a good job of cleaning me out already."

Anna whacked his arm. "And, I've gotten rid of most of the stuff I don't plan to take with me. It's just the boxes in the hallway that need to go to the Salvation Army."

"Why don't we load those up tonight, then I can drop them off first thing in the morning, before helping with the packing," offered Jake. "Sound all right?"

ANNA AND MURPH helped extricate Bonnie from the little bodies that were using her as their pillows. Then they drove to Janice's and Kevin's house to deposit a reluctant Bonnie. They assured her this was to be one of her last nights there, before moving into Murph's home.

Jake carried Daniel out to Keira's car and expertly strapped the child into his car seat. He was getting good at this.

Elizabeth, Brendan, and Cynthia cleaned up after their supper. Although she took a significant ribbing from the others, Elizabeth could not bring herself to allow guests to eat off of paper plates in her house. It simply wasn't done; she could only ignore her mother's voice in her head so much. So, they loaded the dirty plates and cutlery into the dishwasher.

Brendan carried Amy home, with Cynthia leading the way to the child's bed. Amy never woke up. Kids. Amazing how boneless they became in slumber and could sleep through almost anything. Returning to Elizabeth's, he helped her settle the dead-to-the-world Timothy into his bed.

With things straightened away in the kitchen and Timothy asleep, they had a few moments to themselves.

"I can't tell you what it did to my blood pressure to

see that guy in the room with you. He had bad news written all over him." He put his arm around her shoulders. "Nice to see you prepared to defend yourself. Do you know how to wield a fireplace poker?"

"No idea. But it couldn't be any less effective than the vase Keira grabbed."

He laughed, but his face didn't register humor as he pulled her closer. Not wanting to gossip about their friend, he vowed to get Anna alone tomorrow to find out more about who this guy was and just how much of a threat he might pose to their friends.

CHAPTER 13

*A*fter Murph helped load the boxes into the covered truck and Jake left, Anna flitted about her house, touching some things, moving others from one box to another, taking things down, putting them somewhere, not being her usual, productive self.

Murph took her hands in his. "Enough." He led her to the recliner.

"Not there." Anna shuddered. She would never look at that chair in the same way again, picturing Alejandro's leering face peering from its depths.

Tossing throw pillows onto the floor, Murph sat on the rug with his back against the couch, pulling Anna down to nestle between his legs. He wrapped his arms around her as she leaned back, her head on his shoulder. "Want to tell me about it," he asked.

She shook her head.

Flummoxed, Murph called on all his professional training to know how to proceed. But it didn't work. This wasn't a client, this was Anna, this was their lives.

As much as his mind told him to distance himself to get perspective, it wasn't happening.

He tried. "We each had a history before we got together. I don't expect you to bare every corner of your soul to me and I probably won't to you." Although, I'm tempted to, he thought. "But if something about this man puts you in danger, or interferes with our lives together, I should know."

"There's nothing."

Murph turned his face to search Anna's eyes. "That didn't seem like nothing." He so wished that he had been present, rather than having to glean what he could from those who were there. If only there hadn't been that delay at the pizzeria.

"Are you married to him?"

"No."

"Does he have a claim on you?"

"No."

"Will he be back?"

She shook her head. "I have nothing he wants."

"Then why was he here?"

THE LITTLE BOYS FROZE. Even Benjie knew to grow silent at the sound of the key in the door. You never knew who would enter. Some didn't like little boys who made noise.

Benjie's face broke into a grin. He crawled over as fast as his hands and knees would take him. Sometimes that was still faster than getting to his feet, then walking.

The man in the doorway stooped to pick him up and hoist him high into the air. Father and son smiled at each other. "Da!" called Benjie.

"Dadd..., um, Unc," yelled Jordy. It was so confusing, this business of his name. For all of his young life, he'd thought of him as daddy. But lately, mommy hit him whenever he called Carl daddy. Mommy would correct him and say this was now Uncle Carl. Daddy was the other man, the one Jordy didn't like.

As this man approached, Jordy launched himself off of the counter, utterly confident that the man would catch him. Carl hugged his sons to himself. Oh, how he loved these little boys. It pained him that his wife was training the kids to call him uncle. How could she?

He had little say. He has little say in anything anymore. Since being laid off from his job, his status in the home had sunk to a new low. That was saying something, because he had felt that it couldn't sink any lower when he was still the primary bread-winner in the home.

Then his older brother lost his house. More like his latest girlfriend kicked him out of her place. So, he'd showed up at their doorstep. Sally always liked Archie. She became different around him, sort of like the girl she'd been when Carl and Sally first began dating, when she was a single mom with a baby girl, what seemed like so many years ago.

When she spied Archie's duffle bag and his pickup truck full of stuff, and heard that he was homeless, she insisted he stay with them. Just until he got on his feet, she said. Archie agreed; neither of them asked Carl.

"But we only have three bedrooms," Carl protested. "And this couch isn't long enough."

"Lily can move into the boy's room. She spends all her time with them anyway," was Sally's solution.

No one asked Lily, but knowing that kid, she'd do so without an argument. Carl loved his stepdaughter; she was a great kid. The little boys loved her also, but he wasn't sure about Sally. Surely she must. What mother wouldn't?

The sensation of wet on his back brought Carl back from his thoughts. Did one of the kids have an accident? No, wait, the wet was on his back, not his side. He set both boys on the edge of the counter, steadying each with a hand. He looked at his left shoulder and saw the red stain. That wasn't there when he walked in. His gaze fell on Jordy's pants. The child's hand rested in his lap with a spreading pool of red.

Carl scooped Benjie back onto the floor where he would get into less mischief. He grabbed Jordy's hand. "What happened, buddy?"

"Don't know."

Spreading the child's palm in his larger hand, Carl gently probed, seeking the source of the blood. There it was, a line near the base of his index finger, spreading toward the middle finger. "How'd you cut yourself, bud?"

Jordy glanced toward the sink.

Carl could see pools of pink congealing among the

grease and murky water. He sighed. When had Sally last done the dishes?

Holding Jordy on one hip, he took the child's injured hand in one of his, then turned on the tap to run cold water over the cut. He could see now that it was not that deep. Even so, it must have hurt, and he needed to clean it. "Hold on bud, I need to pour more water over this." Some fat from the leavings in the sink clung to one edge of the cut. Carl winced to think of what else might grow in Jordy's flesh if the child had stuck his hand into that filthy, old dishwater.

Turning, he carried the child to the bathroom, clasping him while he rummaged under the sink. Where was that first aid kid that he'd stashed there? You needed such things when you had kids in the house. You never knew what they'd get up to. When Lily was younger, he'd patched up countless skinned knees and scrapes for her. She'd never been a dare-devil kid, but even the careful ones had accidents.

There. There was the peroxide. "Okay, Jordy. I need you to be a big boy for me. This is going to hurt, but it will be over soon. I have to do this to get the cut clean."

Jordy nodded. It made Carl's heart swell, the faith this little boy had in him.

Pouring the peroxide all over the cut, Carl quickly brought the child's palm to his face and blew on the offending cut. Jordy tensed, but didn't cry out. He was a tough kid, a good kid. The kind a father was proud to call his own.

That's why it hurt so much that his wife was now wanting the kids to call Carl's brother, Archie, daddy.

She said that a dad was the man who brought home the bacon.

It was not Carl's fault that his company went bankrupt. With the senior Mr. Barkley at the helm, it had been well run. But after his sudden, fatal heart attack, his son took over. That son knew nothing about the business and seemed to care even less. It took two years, but its demise was inevitable, no matter how much loyal employees like Carl tried to keep things afloat. The son took out more money than the company brought in.

In the meantime, he'd not been able to find full-time employment. He filled his days with job searches, sending out resumes, and lining up for temp day jobs. They paid only minimum wages, but he had a family to support and needed to take anything he could get.

At least that was his thought until his brother knocked on their door. Now, Archie had his foot firmly in their house, their family. *He* had a full-time job. *His* salary paid their rent. *His* salary paid for the groceries, or at least he said it did. In reality, Carl's temp positions bought the groceries and paid the utilities. But these odd jobs he picked up weren't enough to cover the rent. Nor would they extend to the things that Sally felt were her due, like shopping and spa days and nights out with the girls. Although lately the nights out were more with Archie than with girlfriends.

Enough. Carl pulled his thoughts back from that abyss.

He gave his brave son a tight hug, then set him on the bathroom counter. Rummaging in the first aid kit, he found salve, then bandages that would keep the cut clean and secure while the skin knit. Hmm, he'd have to restock this kit soon. He thought Sally took care of that. Guess not.

Sally. Where was she? Why hadn't she come out when she heard all the ruckus? Was she not home? No, she wouldn't leave the kids home alone. "Where's your mom, buddy?"

CHAPTER 14

"*M*urph, he's not a problem for us," Anna assured him. "It's been almost a dozen years since I've seen him. It's over."

Then why did he show up today? Murph tried hard not to press Anna. His priority was to keep her safe. Tomorrow, he'd have her out of this place and her ex would not know how to find her again. Now it was Murph's job to keep her safe. Her and Bonnie, his family.

He rose and began moving boxes off of the couch.

"What are you doing?"

"Making my bed."

"You don't need to sleep here. A bed will more comfortable."

"No, I'm sleeping here tonight. If anyone comes through that door, I want to hear. Anyone after you will have to get through me."

MANY HANDS MAKE LIGHT WORK. A cliche, sure, but it
was true. With Anna, Keira and Elizabeth packing,
Murph, Brendan and Jake hauling, by mid-afternoon, all
of Anna's belongings were on their way to Murph's.

"Thank goodness your place is small." Keira blew a
strand of hair out of her face. "And you're not a slob."

"Keira!" Elizabeth rebuked.

"Well, she's not. I've helped other people move and
packing up their stuff didn't take nearly as long as
scouring the place afterward so that they could get their
damage deposit back. And it sometimes didn't work."

"I think you need a better class of friends," retorted
Elizabeth.

Just then Jake entered, toting a floor cleaner. "I
rented this thing. Is it any good?"

"Yes!" Keira read the directions, then put Jake to
work, beginning with the kitchen floor.

Anna worked on the bathroom; Elizabeth
vacuumed, while Keira swept any trash their packing
had left behind and ran a Swiffer duster over every
surface she could find. It was actually easier to clean a
nearly empty place, especially one kept in excellent
condition, anyway.

"There," she said. "I defy any landlord to rescind
your damage deposit. You could eat off of these floors."

SINCE THEY'D each brought their own vehicles, Jake
headed back to the rental store to return the cleaner,
while Keira followed Elizabeth to Murph's house. Well,
Murph and Anna's. She'd not yet been there.

Since Anna had labelled each box with a black felt marker, they were fairly confident that unpacking would go smoothly. *Fairly.* Keira recalled some of her own moves. They had not been smooth. But then, she'd had Daniel with her, and he required more attention than did the boxes. Child-free, she'd be way more efficient this time. Thank goodness for Cynthia.

"Wow!" Keira just sat and took in the views. What a place. She'd known that Murph lived on an acreage, but she'd not thought much about what that would look like. The five acres seemed to extend forever; when you are used to a fifty-by-one-hundred-foot lot, this was a paradise of open space.

Well, it wasn't all open space. There was a bluff area of trees, maybe more than she could see from the driveway. Meadows surrounded the place. She could see one huge, solitary tree in the meadow. Towering, it dominated the space. The sun was just thinking about setting and reflected through the leaves at the top of the majestic tree. She'd love to bring her computer out here and work on her latest coding project while sitting under its shade. Maybe she'd ask Murph about that.

MURPH WASN'T KIDDING when he'd said that Anna had cleaned him out to prepare for making room for her stuff. Anna opened the doors to the empty kitchen cupboards to show Elizabeth where to stow the things from the box labelled "dishes". She pointed to a couple of empty drawers and the boxes containing the items to go there.

Keira was at work in the bedroom, following Anna's directions as to which boxes needed to be hung up in the half-empty walk-in closet and which were to go in the dresser Brendan and Jake were hauling in.

Anna was an organized woman, with only one last-minute change. The recliner in her living room didn't end up being moved to Murph's house. After a detour, it was donated to Value Village.

IT WAS A TIRING DAY, but the three couples powered through, determined to get as much accomplished as possible before Elizabeth and Keira needed to collect their sons from Cynthia's house. They left at seven-thirty; they'd tested Cynthia's good will as far as they thought it should go. The boys would be nearly ready for bed.

Brendan and Jackson stayed a while longer, moving the remaining boxes into the rooms where they'd be unpacked and rearranging furniture according to Anna's directions, until the blend of her things and Murph's pleased her eye.

Then they left.

"THAT WAS A GOOD DAY, EH?" Murph sensed a tension in Anna. Moving was trying on anyone's spirits. But was that all it was? "I'm beat. Shall we hit the hay?"

"Hit the hay. That's fitting. I feel like I'm in a rural

area now. Looking out the window, I can't see any other houses."

"Does that bother you?" Murph tried to keep his voice light. He knew that not everyone adjusted well to living out of an urban area.

Anna turned to him. "It's just different. I love it. At least, I'm sure I'll get to love it here. It's all so new and different. Give me a little time to adjust, will you?"

He kissed her forehead. "You have all the time in the world, my dear." Putting his arm around her shoulder, he turned out lights as he went, steering them toward the bedroom.

Anna tensed.

"What?" he asked.

"I forgot. I'm out of my routine. Did you lock the doors?"

Understanding her need for security in a strange place and after yesterday's unexpected visitor, he changed their direction. "Let's go check." Together, they made the rounds and yes, each door locked, and each ground-floor window latched. Quietly, they opened Bonnie's door. She was dead to the world, her face relaxed in sleep.

ANNA DAWDLED in the ensuite bathroom. She knew her nerves were silly. She was not a teen; neither of them was. They'd both been married. But, still...

Finally, she could stall no longer. She shut off the bathroom light and crept to what was now her side of the bed. The bedside lights were off. She wasn't sure if Murph was asleep or awake.

As quietly as she could, she lowered herself to the bed, her silk pyjamas sliding easily on the sheets. She'd just pulled the covers over herself when Murph turned on his side toward her. "Are you okay?" he asked.

A slight pause, then she found her voice. "Of course. I'm fine."

"Are you nervous?"

"No. Well, maybe a little." It wasn't the thought of having sex with this man. She'd thought about this often, too much over the last half-year. Murph was an exceedingly attractive man; she could not fathom what he saw in her, but she'd take what he offered.

"Then what is it?" He rubbed his hand up and down her arm, loving the feel of the silk that was almost as smooth as her skin.

"I'm just tired, I think. It's been a big couple of days."

"That is has." He'd take her cue, let her take the lead in this. Even if it killed him. "Second thoughts?" he asked her.

She shook her head. About Murph? No.

He slid one arm beneath her shoulders and pulled her close.

It felt good, she thought as she relaxed into his touch.

His hand slid over the bare patch of skin where her pajama top rose, separating from the elastic of her bottoms. His fingers skimmed the skin just under her waistband and stilled. He was a physician, and his trained fingers hovered over the scarring he could feel there.

Anna froze.

He stilled his fingers and kissed the side of her head. His gentle fingertips explored just a bit further.

Anna tensed. Would he guess what he was feeling? She had hoped that in the dark, he wouldn't notice.

To a doctor, there were few things that would create such scarring in that particular place. Nothing but a caesarian, and an emergency one at that. Generally, the incisions for a planned C-section ran horizontal, not up and down.

"Anna, have you had a child?"

CHAPTER 15

*C*arl set the boys to play on the kitchen floor. They didn't have many toys, but wooden spoons and pot lids did the trick.

He couldn't find any paper towels. Using some toilet tissue, he wiped the blood droplets off the floor. Next, he surveyed the mess on the counter. Blood there, and on the taps. Regarding the disgusting mess in the sink, he wondered how long it had been since Sally did the dishes. Not that he believed it was the woman's job to clean up, but she was the only adult at home all day, so couldn't she do her part?

But where was she? How could it be that these little boys were on their own? Often he'd come home to find their older stepsister with them. Sally insisted the girl was old enough to babysit; Carl didn't mention that the child had been babysitting for the last three years. She was a good kid, though. They got on well together and she felt like his own.

Where had Sally sent the girl?

Grimacing at the smell and feel, he plunged his hands into the sink, pulling out slimy dishes one by one until he could reach the bottom and pull out the plug. The water didn't just drain out, of course it didn't. A multitude of disgusting things clogged the drain. Using a dirty fork, he scraped out as much of the gunk as he could, depositing it onto one of the plates. Finally, the water seeped through, sluggishly, but at least it was draining.

Checking that the boys were content, Carl went into the bathroom to retrieve a plunger. He didn't want to think about what that plunger had last touched, but hoped that it would work to clear the rest of the sink drain.

Finally, finally, water ran free down the drain. He poured dish soap all over the outside and inside of the plunger, hoping to kill any creepy crawly things, then stowed it back in the bathroom.

Next, he scoured both sinks. The scrapes and stains made the old sink look dirty, but he thought he got it as clean as he could. Filling the one sink with hot, soapy water, he began the grim task of washing this mass of dirty dishes.

How could Sally have let the kitchen get into such a state? Ah. The answer dawned on him. It had been Sally's daughter who kept up with the dishes. With her absent, Sally had not thought to take up the slack.

·   ·   ·

FOOTSTEPS SOUNDED ON THE PORCH, amid giggles and laughter. Carl braced himself for what he was about to face.

His older brother, Archie, and Sally burst through the front door, Sally clinging to his arm, neither of their steps too steady. Carl paused in his dishwashing to regard the pair. And a pair is exactly what they seemed like.

"Where's supper," Sally asked. "Aren't you planning on feeding my boys?" She made kissy noises toward her sons. Both children sat still and silent; neither went toward their mother or uncle.

"What, no kisses for your mommy?" Benjie struck a pot lid with his spoon. Jordy just stared.

Archie put his arm around Sally and drew her with him toward the living room. "Come on. We'll watch us some TV while my baby brother makes us some food."

Wiping his hands on a semi-clean towel, Carl followed them. "Sally, when I got here the boys were alone."

She waved her hand. "Oh, it wasn't for more than a few minutes. We knew you'd be home soon, didn't we, Arch?"

Archie settled himself deeper into the couch, his arm around his sister-in-law.

Carl tried again. "Sally, Jordy's not even four yet. They cannot be left alone."

"Well, you stay with them, then. I'm here all the time and need a break sometimes. Isn't that right, Archie?"

"I was working all day. And when I'm not working, I'm out looking for more work."

Archie raised one eyebrow as he flicked stations with the remote. "Bully for you."

ANNA AND MURPH spent the next day settling in. While their friends helped enormously the day before, there were still finishing touches to do, stuff to rearrange, things to get in order to begin their lives together. And yes, that's how it felt to Anna and Murph, that these were the first steps to their forever lives.

Almost. Bonnie would fill the remaining gap, at least for as long as she was to live with them.

Anna and Bonnie had been shopping, Bonnie choosing how she wanted her bedroom to look. Most of the things were in place, but Anna would leave the final bits for Bonnie to arrange herself. The fresh lilac paint on the walls blended with the ivory furnishings. The decorations reflected a girl midway between childhood and the teen years.

At first reluctant to select her preferences, Anna was not sure that Bonnie had ever had a say in what went into her room before. Not wanting to put undue pressure on Bonnie, at first Anna had stood back, waiting for Bonnie to make a choice. But, not wanting to see her foster daughter overwhelmed, Anna selected a few items and had Bonnie choose between them. This went on for several shopping trips, with Murph patiently schlepping the bags for them.

Now, things were almost ready. They were waiting on the final paper approval from Child Protective

Services, but were assured that that would come through within the next few days. Judge Bursey was on it; he would not let things stall past this weekend. Besides, CPS had pressure. They had other children to place with Janice and Kevin and needed Bonnie to move out. Callous, perhaps, but that was the way it was with the demand of children in need of protection.

FRIDAY AFTER WORK, Murph and Anna collected Bonnie. Her pitifully few belongings fit in one garbage bag. Never mind. There was more stuff awaiting her at their home, including a full wardrobe.

Supper was, of course, Bonnie's favorite of takeout fried chicken.

"Don't get used to this," Anna warned her. "We eat healthy around here."

Murph winked. "But the odd treat won't hurt us, will it?"

SATURDAY THEY HAD A FULL HOUSE. The party was to celebrate Anna and Bonnie's move. Although Anna and Murph cooked, their friends brought plenty of potluck fare, enough for even the pickiest of appetites. Keira even brought some avocado and hummus dip that Timothy adored, but everyone else hated. The guests arrived mid afternoon, anticipating that their fun wouldn't run late into the evening with Timothy, Daniel and Amy in attendance.

This was the first time Cynthia had seen Murph's

place. She wandered around taking in the stone fireplace that dominated one wall, the u-shaped kitchen with the center island and bar stools along the counter separating that area from the great room. To the side of the kitchen was a farm-house style table with seating for twelve. Backing onto that was the great room with its two seating areas - one circling the fireplace and the other pointed at the floor-to-ceiling windows looking out on the meadow.

Not as picky about such things as Elizabeth, Murph had a stack of paper plates set out on the counter. Anna drew the line at plastic eating utensils, so there were stainless steel knives, forks and spoons standing in metal tubes, ready for people to grab what they needed. An array of tacos, tamales, enchiladas, fried chicken, bread sticks, guacamole, and toasted pita squares stood on one side of the open counter. Along its other side were Caesar and fruit salads, along with platters of cut-up vegetables and cheeses.

"Help yourself, everyone!"

Amid the laughter and scramble for food, first one child's plate, then another hit the floor. The first to overturn was Amy's. In her rush to reach for another taco, she didn't quite balance her current load correctly and over it went.

Bonnie's eyes widened, and she froze. Her head swivelled to see how the adults would react. She took a step closer to Amy, as if to protect her. In her anxiousness, she didn't notice the protruding leg of a bar stool. Her foot snagged it, throwing her off-balance and her plate hit the floor.

"I'm sorry, I'm sorry. I didn't mean it."

The adults froze.

Bonnie, terrified of the trouble that she was in, continued in a smaller voice. "I'll clean it up right away."

Anna was the first to react. She drew Bonnie into her arms. "It's all right, sweetie. It was an accident." Her eyes met Murph's across the room, silently asking how they should react to Bonnie's words.

He gave an imperceptible shake of his head. Now wasn't the time. He smiled and nodded at Anna embracing the child, rocking her gently from side to side. She was doing the right thing.

Meanwhile, Elizabeth grabbed a handful of paper napkins and was making quick work of making the plate Anna had dropped disappear.

"Amy, give me a hand here, please," asked Cynthia.

"Did I ever make a mess, eh mommy?" Amy was in awe of the patterns the salsa and sour cream made together.

"You sure did. We'd better get this off of Anna's floor before it stains," her mom said.

At the word 'stain', Bonnie stiffened.

"Sh, it's all right." Anna stroked Bonnie's hair. "It won't stain. And even if it did, so what?"

Bonnie relaxed, but her face remained perplexed.

Then Elizabeth was in front of her with a new plate. "Here. You'd better start again." She smiled at the child and ruffled her hair.

"Unless you want to eat this!" Amy held out the mess she'd scraped from the floor onto her soiled plate. "Gross, eh?"

The rest of the group laughed.

Brendan produced a garbage can from under the sink. Cynthia guided her daughter towards the garbage can so that she could throw the dirty plate away before she dropped it on the floor a second time.

Standing near the fireplace, Keira and Jake watched the scene. As mother to a young boy, she was no stranger to spills. Jake had nieces and had observed his share of plates upended. Neither had witnessed a child's terrified reaction to such an accident, though.

"Well, at least it got her talking," whispered Keira.

"Makes you wonder what that poor kid's been through."

THE REST of the meal went smoothly, or as smoothly as one can go with four kids and seven adults filling their plates, shuffling seats and enjoying one another's company.

As the adults put away the uneaten food and readied the fire pit for later in the evening, the kids were getting restless. Bonnie came to stand in front on Anna and Murph. Her eyes pleaded for something. Her look went from her new foster parents, to the younger kids getting underfoot and the beckoning outdoors, then back again.

Murph took a guess. "Do you want to take the kids outside to play?"

Bonnie grinned. She opened her mouth. Anna thought she heard a small "please". Her eye caught Murph's. Yes, he'd noticed as well.

"Sure," he said. "But stay between the house and the

tree." He pointed out the window at the lone, spreading tree standing like a sentinel in the middle of the meadow. "That is, if their moms are okay with it."

Elizabeth, Cynthia and Keira had hardly spoken their approval before the kids dashed for the door. Like gazelles, they raced to the tree, circled around it, then tore back to the house.

Bonnie organized them in a game of tag. How she did that without talking was a mystery, but it seemed to work, and the kids fell in with the activity.

THE ADULTS DRAGGED chairs in a semi-circle facing the picture window where they could watch the kids. Some cradled a bottle of beer while others preferred stemmed glasses of chardonnay. Swirling her wine, Keira said what they were all thinking. "She spoke."

CHAPTER 16

*W*ith that many people helping, it didn't take long to put the house to rights after their dinner party. Men hoisted sleepy little people into their arms and deposited them gently into car seats. Keira, Jake and Daniel headed out. Brendan, Elizabeth and Timothy followed Cynthia and Amy's car home. When they arrived in their adjoining driveways, Brendan carried Amy in for Cynthia, before returning to Elizabeth's car to do the same with Timothy.

WITH BONNIE TUCKED in and asleep, Anna and Murph cuddled in bed talking over the day.

"The highlight was Bonnie!" Anna could not get over the fact that the child had finally spoken. They'd known the child for over a month, and this was the first word any of them had heard her utter. "Sad that it took feeling distressed for her to be able to speak."

"At least now we know for sure that she *can* talk. I

wasn't sure before. Did you see the look on her face when she dropped her food?"

"It terrified her. I wonder what she's experienced before and who's come down on her for making a mistake."

"I don't think the answer to those questions is anything good."

"I'm glad she's here with us now. Maybe we can show her a different way to live."

"I hope that the safer she feels here, the more likely she'll feel that it's okay to speak."

"Is that how selective mutism works?"

"It varies with the individual. Usually they come out of it the same way they slipped into it, a bit at a time. Initially, it might be certain situations or people who make them feel anxious. They begin to shut down in those circumstances, worried about saying or doing the wrong thing, or the ramifications of making a mistake."

"But this time it was a mistake that caused her to speak."

"Yeah, I wonder about that. You know, it's crossed my mind that she may keep silent out of fear. Maybe someone threatened her or warned her not to talk. Being a kid, she might have taken the warning more literally than it was intended."

"Then again, maybe not. From the look on her face this evening, I'd say that her young life has not been an easy one."

"She's here with us now and we'll do our best to make her feel secure and wanted."

. . .

THEY SNUGGLED FURTHER into the sheets. Anna's head was on Murph's shoulder, his one arm draped across her middle.

Murph debated letting it go, but they'd never finished their discussion the other night. This was not the way he wanted their relationship to go. Sure, they both had a past, but walls might only grow.

Cradling her head, he broached the subject again. "Anna, tell me about it."

She stilled.

"You had a child, didn't you? I recognize the scarring of a caesarian section. And my guess is that it didn't go well for you. Planned C-section incisions are usually across the abdomen, but yours goes up and down. That suggests that they had to do it in a hurry."

Still nothing.

"Was the baby in distress?"

"Yes," admitted Anna. "I was in labor for almost two days. The baby was breach. They kept trying to turn her, but it didn't work."

Murph winced. He knew, at least academically, the degree of discomfort those efforts would have caused this sweet woman, on top of her labor pains. "You must have been exhausted after all that time."

Anna nodded. "Near the end, I think I was only semi-conscious. I have no recollection of the decision to do the section. I woke up to a flatter belly and to pain."

"I'm sorry you had to go through that." The doctor in him couldn't resist. "But didn't they know ahead of time that the baby was in breach position? Things like that are monitored closely."

"I had a partera, a midwife. They only brought her in after my water broke and I was in labor. We were far from a town and it took her a while to get there. Then they had to get me to the clinic. It took time. By then I was pretty out of it."

"Where was this?"

"Near my grandmother's place. It's near Ensenada, Mexico."

"What were you doing there?"

"We went to stay with her often while I was growing up. Some of my best memories are of the time I spent with her."

Murph raised his eyebrow.

"Well, not this particular time. That one's mostly a blur of pain."

Murph wondered if it was just physical pain she referred to. "And the baby?"

Anna didn't speak.

Gently, he asked, "Did the baby not make it?"

A tear slid from the corner of Anna's eye. "She was alive. Or so they told me."

"Told you?"

"I never got to see her. They took her."

Murph went up on one elbow. "Who? Who would do such a thing?"

"My husband."

~

"So far, it's going well." Cynthia and Anna were on the phone discussing how their homeschooling plan for Bonnie was going.

"From my preliminary assessments, she's about where she should be with reading, if we assume that she's a grade six student. Mathematics is a bit more of a mixed bag. I'll need to work with her more, but I'm not getting the sense that she has dyscalculia, a learning disability in math. When I show her things, she catches on fast, then can practice them on her own. The gaps she displays make me wonder if she's been exposed to some of these concepts before. Or, if she has, she might not have much time to practice them."

"What do you mean?" Anna asked.

"I wonder just how regular her school attendance has been."

"Did she say anything to you about that?"

"No, not a word. She's pleasant and cooperative, but I haven't heard her say anything since that evening at your place when she dropped her plate."

"She doesn't seem sickly, like someone who would be home ill a lot. In the time that we've known her, she hasn't come down with anything."

"Yeah, even that weekend when Amy was sneezing all over everyone, Bonnie didn't catch it."

"Doesn't someone keep track of school attendance?"

"Each school does, but attendance doesn't get reported to some central agency, if that's what you're thinking. There are little teeth in the law to force parents to send their kids to school. Maybe she's from a transient family who moves a lot. Bonnie's previous school might just assume that they've moved again."

"Maybe. It's almost like no one cares."

MURPH, Anna, and Bonnie traipsed up the interior staircase. This was a space neither Bonnie nor Anna had seen before.

"What do you think?" Murph's arm swept toward the unfinished area that made up the second floor of the double garage. "It's called an attic garage, they told me when I bought the place. The previous owners did nothing with it, other than store some boxes. There's almost eight hundred square feet here, although that's just floor space. Since the walls slope to the whole way on two sides, that's not useable space. I clad those walls in drywall, and the floors were just plywood, but the space had possibilities. So? Are you game to help me transform this into something?"

Anna's grin was slow in coming. "Me? What do I know about building?"

"Probably about as much as me and Bonnie, but we can learn, can't we girl?" He looked to Bonnie.

The child nodded vigorously.

"What would we put up here?" Anna asked.

"Whatever you want, but I was thinking of it as a playroom for us."

Anna thought of Murph's exercise equipment. It used to live in what was now Bonnie's room, but Murph had moved it out to make room for their foster child.

Now the treadmill took up space in their bedroom, the rowing machine was in a corner of the living room and the BowFlex dismantled and laying in bits. Although he never complained, she knew Murph missed his ready access to his fitness regime. Yes, she could see it up here.

"I wondered about a ping-pong table, maybe a pool table…".

Bonnie didn't react. Murph wondered if she knew what they were.

"Maybe some bean bag chairs and a reading corner." That got a smile out of Bonnie.

"How will we know how to do this?"

"YouTube. Or we can do it the old-fashioned way - books."

"Where do we start?"

"I thought that we'd paint first. If we paint the walls and ceiling now, then we don't have to worry about getting drips on anything. We might need to do some touch-ups later in case we make scratches or dents while we build, but we can do that. Then I thought that for maybe four feet out on the sloping sides, we'd square that off to make hidden storage space and a straight wall. I took a quick look on YouTube for ideas about finishing garage attics, and there are scads of videos. Want to go look at some?"

By the time the adults descended the stairs and made it to the living room, Bonnie had already turned on the large-screen television, called up the internet and had the search bar for YouTube ready.

$\sim$

LIFE WAS GOOD, thought Anna as she looked around her office. She had a job she found challenging yet fulfilling. She lived with a man she loved, a good man. She was looking after a little girl that she adored. While not used to furry creatures underfoot, she'd even come to dote on Sandy and Morgan, the dogs in their lives. Their house was in a beautiful setting, peaceful and private. As a kid visiting her grandmother in Ensenada, Mexico, she relished the beauty of the countryside, of taking a walk in solitude, without the intrusion of city noises or other people.

She tried not to dwell on the negative. Yes, she'd not had the most ideal of childhoods and yes, she'd had a rough decade in her twenties, but that was behind her now. She'd made a good life for herself. Many of the clients that she saw these days had it so much tougher. Unlike her, they'd not found a way to climb out of the mire of their past.

But a bane of her current job was paperwork. The court system seemed to have a form to account for every minute of her workday. There was no help for it. Anna slated the latter half of this afternoon to paperwork, determined to not leave the office until she was caught up.

ANNA, along with most of her co-workers, kept her door open unless she was with a client. Open doors led to open communication, with people feeling free to exchange ideas or just pass the time of day. They had an excellent team.

She looked up at the familiar snick of her door's latch finding its home in the jamb.

She had not heard him enter before he shut her door. In front of her stood Alejandro, arms crossed; he still moved like a panther. Now, he approached her desk, both muscular arms supporting him as he leaned on the furniture, towering over her. Anna resisted the temptation to slink back in her chair; he'd love that. He got off on power and intimidation.

He smiled. How could a smile convey such malevolence? Smiles were supposed to be friendly, inviting. This one made Anna want to shrink into herself, to become that frightened little girl/woman who was married off to him all those years ago.

But she was no longer eighteen, scared and powerless. She was a woman with skills, a free woman. She had paid her debt, her family's debt. Oh, how she had paid.

CHAPTER 17

Something jarred Carl from his sleep. There was the soft whoosh of silk on silk as Sally left their bed. Sally insisted on certain things. Only the finest bedsheets was one of them. Her lingerie and night attire were another. Even when they struggled to put food on the table, her undergarments came first. She said they made her feel sexy. He had to agree that the softness of the sheets was a turn-on, as was the sight of her clad in her lingerie. Despite the need to tighten their budget, she insisted she needed to look sexy for her man.

Lately, though, those glimpses of his wife's body had amounted to little. Partly that was his fault. Exhaustion was his constant companion these days, as was worry. He worried about money; he fought off feelings of being a loser, a failure since he'd lost his job. He worried about his little boys, their safety and well-being when he was not home. He worried about his stepdaughter, who suddenly was absent from their lives. He worried about what was becoming of his marriage.

"Go back to sleep," Sally told him. "I'm going to check on the boys."

Carl rolled onto his back, his eyes staring at the pattern of light and shadows the streetlights created on the ceiling. Right. When had Sally ever checked on the kids in the middle of the night? She left that up to him. If a child cried out in the middle of the night after having a bad dream, she would kick or nudge Carl to "go shut that kid up". He would. But sometimes when he got to the boys' room, his stepdaughter would already be there, comforting the little boy.

Repeatedly, he asked Sally where Lily was. A twelve-year-old girl didn't just walk out the door. Lily was not that kind of kid. She was a homebody and as attached to the little boys as he was. Every time he demanded to know where Lily was, Sally would freeze him with her look. "She's not your daughter, she's *mine*." It's not of your business.

It was, though. Carl had known Lily almost as long as he'd known Sally. Well, maybe not quite. He'd first met Sally at a pub. They'd shared a few dances, a few drinks, and things had progressed from there. A weekend in Las Vegas had morphed into a quickie at a wedding chapel, at Sally's insistence. Carl didn't mind, not really, although this was not quite the sort of wedding he'd thought about before. Still, it was time, he supposed, and they'd done the deed.

The day after they were back home, they headed over to pack up Sally's belongings so she could move in with him. She shared a house with three other women, and a child, apparently. It rocked his world to discover that two-year-old Lily belonged to Sally. The roommates had the child's belongings tied into a garbage bag. Sally's clothes were in a duffle bag outside the bedroom she called hers.

Apparently, Sally was behind in her rent and her roomies tired of coughing up her share. What ticked them off almost as much was the unexpected babysitting they had to do when the child's mother didn't come home. While each of them gave Lily a warm hug goodbye, their eyes were glacial when they turned to Sally.

Perhaps that should have sent a warning to Carl, but he was in the throes of love. To find that there was already a child involved was a surprise, but Carl liked kids. At least he thought he did, having never been that close to one before and hadn't contemplated what it would be like to have one of his own. Guess he'd find out now. And he did.

Most of the time, it was a delight. He tried again when each of the little boys was born, trying to convince Sally to let him adopt Lily, to have her take his name, to make her truly his daughter in every sense. No, she always told him. That wouldn't be fair to Lily's father. They needed to honor his name. Honor? In the last ten years the guy had never come around, never sent child support payments, never contacted them. It was as if the guy was dead. Or dead to them, at least.

· · ·

CARL HEARD a door down the hall open, then close. He rolled over, trying to get back to sleep. It would be better to be oblivious to what might happen next.

But sleep eluded him. Part of this brain wanted to shut down, but another part set his ears on high alert, attuned to any sound that would give him messages he didn't want to hear, to acknowledge.

Soon he heard soft giggles; he knew that tone. Not many years ago he'd been the recipient of them himself. He knew what could come next. There was the deeper rumble of a male voice, the more laughter. Next came the sound of bedsprings creaking rhythmically.

Carl pulled the pillow over his head, using an arm to smash it over his ears, trying to block out the sounds from down the hallway and the images flowing through his mind.

Why did he stay? What man would put up with being cuckolded? This kind of man, he thought. He would leave, leave in a heartbeat if it was just himself. Sally and his brother, Archie, deserved each other.

But it wasn't just himself. He had two little boys who depended on him. More and more Carl worried about their safety when he wasn't with them. He didn't think that Sally would physically beat the toddlers; she was mean and self-centered, but not deliberately cruel. Right? But neglect was another thing.

It used to be that the kids were not as clean as they should be. When he'd gather them into his arms, too often that little boy smell was not of shampoo, but the musky scent of skin and hair that had not been bathed in far too many days.

She was busy, Sally said. It was too much hassle to bathe them, and the kids made so much mess in the tub that it took forever to clean up the bathroom after them.

Yeah, they splashed around and made a mess, but it was just water, and they had so much fun doing it. Carl loved to play with them during bath time. Too often though, his temp jobs kept him out working until hours after supper time, and the kids were in bed asleep by the time he got home. Initially he'd assumed that Sally had kept to the nightly bath time routine, but it became clear that when he wasn't around, it didn't happen.

There was a time when Sally cooked. Not well, but there was food on the table, at sort of regular intervals. Not so much now. Only on rare occasions would he come home late to find the remains of supper in the fridge or left on the table. Spilled cereal boxes on the floor showed evidence of small children scrounging for themselves.

When she returned to the kitchen to refill her coffee cup or grab a beer, Sally would shriek at their sons when she spied the mess that they'd left. She'd holler for her daughter to come clean the place up. Since the girl disappeared, there was no one but Carl paying any attention to the upkeep of the place. Certainly not Sally, and definitely not Archie.

The squeaking of the bed springs stopped. Would Sally return, or spend the rest of the night with *him*? Carl didn't know which he dreaded more.

IT WAS SCARY, darned scary, thought Elizabeth. Yet, for the sake of her son, she had squashed down her fears and enrolled him in pre-kindergarten, the very one that Daniel attended the year before. The support of Cynthia and Keira had helped, and she didn't know what she would have done if these women weren't familiar with the school and entrusted the care of their own children to the staff.

Amy, well, Amy would fit in anywhere. A confident, bubbly little girl, capable and ready to tackle the world.

Daniel, though, was another story. He was more like Timothy; in fact, Keira was convinced that she saw many similarities between the two boys.

Just a year ago, Keira had been where Elizabeth stood now, terrified of leaving her son in the hands of these strangers who wouldn't understand him. One difference was that Daniel had a diagnosis of autism; had since just after his second birthday. That was something the school could understand, and they had strategies in place. They weren't flummoxed because Daniel didn't speak. According to Keira, his teachers focused more on communication skills than on trying to force the child to talk. That wouldn't work anyway, Keira said. She'd tried hard enough over the last few years to force her son to say words. Not that he didn't *want* to, but he couldn't.

At one time, Elizabeth would have said the same thing was true for Timothy, but he had spoken now. Oh, it was slow and seemed laborious for her little boy, but more and more often, words came out.

There were lots of plausible reasons for a language

delay, the speech/language pathologist said. Yes, like with Daniel, autism was a probable reason. But the onset of the seizure disorder could also be behind it. Intellectual disabilities were the reason sometimes. Then there were those kids who had idiopathic challenges with expressive language - no one knew the cause.

Elizabeth was fine with taking Timothy exactly as he was. But would these educators feel the same way?

THIS WAS her first formal meeting with the school. While she expected to meet with the pre-K teacher, Ms. Robinson, it startled Elizabeth to find two other women seated at the table. Mrs. Rose introduced herself as the special education teacher. Ms. Frey was the school administrator.

Right then, Elizabeth regretted not taking Keira up on her offer to come to the meeting with her. Even though Keira assured her that the school team was on her side, it was hard to not get her back up with these eyes watching her, eyes that probably found Timothy wanting.

Deep breath, she told herself. Calm yourself and give them a chance. Her earlier training came to her rescue. Her mother had been a stickler about maintaining outward appearances. Daddy said, "Never let them see you shake." She recalled him often saying to her brother, "It's a dog-eat-dog world and you gotta be tough." Mentally, she shook her head. Don't go there, she told herself. Don't think about your brother now.

Ms. Robinson leaned forward, spreading some sheets on the table. "I want to show you some of Timothy's drawings. He's quite talented, don't you think?"

Well, of course she thought so. She was his mother. But it was nice to see that someone else recognized his skill.

"He responds well to visuals," Ms. Robinson continued.

"His speech therapist says that as well."

"Yes, we've been through the speech/language pathologist's report you shared with us. We're following some of the strategies that she uses in therapy."

"I do at home, too."

Elizabeth waited for the 'but'. She knew there was one coming.

Ms. Robinson was not to be rushed. Next, she showed Elizabeth some photos of Timothy taking part in circle time. He, like many others, had his hand up. They took the photo from the back of the kids' heads, so she couldn't see her son's expression, but from the set of his shoulders, he wasn't upset.

Another picture showed the children in a semi-circle around the teacher as she held up a picture book for them to see. Except this time Timothy wasn't involved like the rest. While he remained part of the circle from the knees down, the rest of him was prone on his back, hands raised in the air, playing with his fingers.

Pointing to that picture, Elizabeth said, "He's done that since he was a baby."

"It's not uncommon at all for small children."

Elizabeth sensed the 'however', so she said it for them. "But none of the other kids still do that."

"I wouldn't say that it's unheard of with four- and five-year-olds, but no, it's not common."

Mrs. Rose spoke next. "While Timothy has settled in fairly well to the routine, we have noticed some differences between him and the other students."

"You mean he doesn't talk?"

"Yes, there's that, but I wouldn't say that he never talks. We're pretty sure that he's said the odd word here and there."

"I was in here the other day handing out snacks," offered Ms. Frey, the principal. "Timothy said a clear 'thank you' when I handed him his treat. Not all of our students show that courtesy."

Ms. Robinson explained more about their classroom routines. "Sometimes Timothy follows along well and joins in. There are other times, though, when he seems almost oblivious to what is going on around him."

"Based on what you told us about him before school started, we wondered if that was because of seizure activity that we just hadn't noticed. So we started watching more closely, keeping track of how he seemed before and during these episodes." Mrs. Rose's smile was rueful. "Maybe we're just not as experienced with seizures as you are, but we didn't see any signs of absence episodes or anything else we could pinpoint as likely being seizure-related. Are you seeing much at home?"

Elizabeth shook her head. "No, he's doing well.

We've had nothing for almost six weeks now, and the last one was minor compared to how they used to be."

"You're welcome to come observe in the class if you think we might be missing something."

"Thanks, I might do that. Is this what you mean by differences between my son and other kids?"

"Not exactly. Four- and five-year-olds are not exemplary social creatures. While they might want to be around each other, many don't have that give-and-take down pat yet. Cooperative games, waiting their turn, following the rules, and losing gracefully are in the early stages of developing." Ms. Robinson looked toward Mrs. Rose to better explain.

"Sometimes Timothy wants to play with other kids, and during those times he does so nicely. And at recess, he's inseparable from Daniel. Amy comes around often as well. In the classroom though, sometimes kids approach Timothy, wanting to play with him. At those times, it's as if he sees right through them. He doesn't turn his back on them, or lash out, it's more like he doesn't notice that they're there."

Ms. Robinson said, "This is especially true when he's concentrating intently. It's like he gets so focused on what he's doing that he doesn't notice anyone else. At other times, different things will catch his attention. Like his hands. Or leaves from that plant over there, swaying in the breeze from the open window. Other kids might notice that, but he seems entranced by the movement. To get his attention, we have to physically turn him around so he can't see it."

"What about his academics?" This concerned Elizabeth. After all, that's why her son was here.

"Pre-K lays the foundation for academics. It's all about language development, socialization, and exploration. Timothy's very good at the latter. His attention span is longer than that of many of his peers for things that interest him. Not so with things that don't take his fancy, though."

Mrs. Rose pulled out the copy of the speech/language pathologist's report that Elizabeth had brought to the school when she registered Timothy. The teacher flipped to the last page of the document and ran her finger down until she found the line she was looking for. "One recommendation here was to consider the possibility of an assessment, querying the possibility of autism."

CHAPTER 18

*a*nna took a sip from her coffee mug. It was bitter and cold, having sat there since morning, but she needed something to moisten her mouth, and something to do with her hands. Gripping the mug tightly, they could not shake. Swallowing with deceptive calmness, she peered at him over the rim. "What are you doing here?"

"What? No pleasantries? No 'how are you husband dear?' No, 'how's life been treating you?'"

"No."

"Why, my little Anna. How rude you've become. What would your abuela say about your behavior?"

She'd probably suggest I throw this coffee in your face, Anna thought. She'd reserve that for later if needed. "She never liked you."

Alejandro straightened and brought both hands to his chest with a fake grimace. "Oh, you wound me. How could you be so cruel?"

Cruel? He wrote the book on cruel. She held her

tongue. Experience taught her not to provoke him. "Why are you here?" she asked again.

"There's something I need from you."

He'd already taken everything from her.

"Ah, don't give me that look, little Anna. It was just business. You knew what you were getting into."

"No, I didn't."

"Well, your old man certainly did."

Anna was silent. She'd figured that out. But it had been a hard day when she realized just what her father had sold her into.

"It wasn't all bad, now was it querida?" Alejandro's tone was fake, almost wheedling.

Did he want something of her, truly?

"I can't give you any more children. You ruined that possibility."

"Did I? What about that girlie in your house? She looks about the right age. Is she mine? Were you holding out on me?"

"No! She's not yours! You know how many times you tried to get me pregnant after that. I *can't* ever get pregnant, thanks to you."

"Querida, *I* didn't do that. It's not my fault if the medico was not as skilled as he bragged."

"I nearly died, and you left me there!"

He shrugged. "I had business to attend to."

Anna set down the mug close to her right hand, the one farthest from Alejandro. She just might need it to throw at him. She gave a half-smile. She would enjoy seeing a half cup of old coffee running down his face.

"Tell me more about that girl. Who is she? How old is she?"

"I don't know."

His face darkened. "I asked you a question. Who is this child?"

As if she would ever tell slime like him anything about Bonnie, even if she had that information. Her turn to shrug. She half-turned away and opened her email program. Let him think she was dismissing him. She typed Betty's name into her To box. She emailed her secretary multiple times every day, so just by typing in the B, the email address populated itself. Three asterisks were all she typed into the subject line - a code in their office for help. If she hit Send now, Betty would have courthouse security there pronto. Her finger poised about the Send button.

"Don't ignore me," warned Alejandro. "You know that that doesn't end well for you."

"Alejandro," she tried to speak in a bored voice. "Spare me the theatrics. I'm not a scared little girl anymore. I'm not alone. You're here in *my* office, among *my* friends. Our secretary will have noticed my closed door. That only happens when I have a client in here and she has my schedule. She knows that I have no clients this afternoon."

"I don't care what your secretary knows." He paced. "I came here for one purpose, but now I have two."

Anna rolled her eyes. She felt like a bit player in a cheap movie, hamming it up. It worked; it irked him.

He leaned on her desk again. "That girl. I need to know who she is. She looks familiar." He studied Anna.

"She doesn't really resemble you, but there is something about her…".

Anna shrugged. "Beats me." She moved her hands over her keyboard. "Now, go. I have work to do."

"Ah, work. That brings me to the other reason I'm here." He made himself comfortable in a chair across from her desk, slouching and crossing one leg over the other knee. "Remember that little business I was in?"

"Business! Stealing and selling babies was a *business* to you?" She shook her head. "Of course it was. Trafficking in innocent human lives was how you made your living." She let all of her feelings about him shine through her dark brown eyes.

"Business is business, and it pays the bills." He narrowed his eyes. "It allowed you to live in comfort."

"You mean for the years that you held me prisoner?"

"Now, now, you're looking at it all wrong. Those were years we enjoyed each other as husband and wife. *I* recall parts of it fondly." He waggled his eyebrows leeringly.

Anna tried to hold back her shudder. She, too, remembered those times. They were seared into her brain, each and every rape holding its own separate, padlocked storage compartment.

"That's what I'm here for."

At the alarm on Anna's face, he waved a hand at her. "No worries, querida. You're a little long in the tooth for me now. No offense, but I prefer them younger and fresher than you. You're, shall we say, worn out, as I well know."

All the nothing Anna had stored up for this man, this beast, radiated from her eyes.

"Since we last shared, ah, time together, my business has expanded. Having to find girls like you took too long and a surprising number of them, like you, were disappointing. It took too long to bring them along before they produced anything useful." He shook his head at the foibles of the human reproduction cycle. "No, I've moved up. I now have a stable, an entire group of young women who are suitable for our purposes."

There was no way Anna could conceal the horror she felt for these women. She flexed her fingers over the keyboard, appearing to stretch. Her right baby finger hovered over the little microphone icon. Glancing at Alejandro, no, he was not watching her hands. She pressed the button, hoping that the machine would start recording their conversation. She had been experimenting with voice-to-text technology to speed up the never-ending paperwork required of her. She picked up her coffee mug, pretending to accidentally bump the monitor, turning it away, out of Alejandro's line of sight. She turned her chair toward the man who had once been her husband and her tormentor.

"Ah, I have your attention now. Did 'stable' do it? You always were a softie." He leaned forward, elbows on his knees. "Here's where you come in. Some of these women are, ah, young. They need someone older around, someone calm, a stabilizing influence. It's not good for the developing fetuses to have their mothers in a constant state of upset. You understand that, don't you?"

Anna gave a barely perceptible nod.

"You're coming back to Mexico with me, and you'll look after my girls."

Incredible! The gall of this man, first to think that he could steal young women and turn them into baby-makers for him. Then to think that she would assist him in this. Words would not come to her. Her eyes strained to see to the far right of her peripheral vision. Yep. Letters danced across the screen. She raised her mug to hide her smile.

"Of course, I will compensate you for this. I pay well. I saw that little hovel you called a home. My place is a mansion in comparison. You recall it, I'm sure."

Oh, she did. The opulence sickened her, especially knowing at what cost that money had come. How many hours had she spent in the gardens, inspecting every square inch of those twelve-foot-high concrete walls, looking for a way out?

Recognizing her revulsion, Alejandro brought out his bargaining chips.

"That little girl, *your* little girl. She would bring a fair price, don't you think? What is she, maybe twelve? Just ripe for some tastes."

Could any human being get any lower? Working in the courthouse, Anna saw plenty of low-lifes, but none were worse than this well-dressed man in front of her.

"But then, you're not living in that tiny place anymore, are you Anna? Don't think I didn't notice the packing boxes. You were moving out, not in. It wasn't hard to follow you and your well-meaning, uppity friends." He brushed imaginary lint off his trouser leg.

"You've moved up in the world, haven't you? That man you're shacking up with has a nice spread. Does he know that you're married?"

"I'm not married." Anna gritted her teeth. "I have an annulment paper."

"Oh, Anna, Anna. My, how naïve you are. Did you think those were real? Have you any idea how easy it is to buy such things? You wanted out, and I wanted to get rid of you. You were of no use to me anymore. It was a simple thing to have that paper drawn up. They made you leave quietly."

That stopped Anna cold. As a rule-follower, obeying the law meant a lot to her. She had believed that she was no longer married. She would never have allowed anything to continue with Murph if she thought she was still a married woman, no matter how despicable her husband.

"Hah. I can see that you had not considered that, my Anna. Now consider this. I want you."

At the look in her eyes, he continued. "No, not in that way, although," his eyes swept up and down the portion of her body that wasn't hidden behind her desk, "you're rather well-preserved. Maybe not pristine like that eighteen-year-old who first came to me, but not bad, not bad." He grinned at her, a menacing look. "We might still have some fun together, but I want you to look after my stable."

She pushed back from her desk, mostly trying to put more physical distance between herself and this devil incarnate.

"Before you decline my generous offer, think about

it. I know where you live. I know where your boyfriend works. I know where your friends live. All of them."

Anna's eyes widened.

"Yes, I followed each of them home. You guys get together so frequently that it wasn't hard." His eyes narrowed. "Since you knew me, my clientele has expanded. There's still a market for those couples desperate to have a child of their own. But, they prefer babies. I can supply those, but there's an even more lucrative market for older children. Some of my clients have tastes that might seem peculiar to you and me, but hey, who am I to judge? Those two little boys you see so much of might bring an acceptable price. And that little girl next door to your friend's house? What a charmer! My, wouldn't she make some people thrilled?"

Anna couldn't breathe.

Alejandro rose and stood with one hand on the door handle, preparing to leave. "I see that you're following my line of reason. Anna, my Anna. You always were the giving sort, sacrificing yourself for your family. Surely, you see that coming with me, building a new life taking care of these young women is the right thing to do? After all, you wouldn't want anything to happen to those nearest and dearest to you here, would you?"

He opened the door. Turning, he said, "I'll be in touch."

CHAPTER 19

ONE YEAR AGO IN TIJUANA, MEXICO

t wasn't working. She could not do this. To think that she used to complain about life at home. She and her girlfriends would talk about how tough they had it and how much better life would be once they were out on their own. All they needed to do was finish school, then save up a bit of money.

Yeah, well, that last part had not worked out. No matter what Evaline tried, there were just not enough pesos for survival. She allowed herself one meal a day. Any more than that and there'd be not enough money to buy a submarine sandwich at an all-night Subway. If she bought a foot-long sub late at night, then she could stay in that booth for a couple of hours. Twice she'd fallen asleep with her head on the table, only to be woken by the owner when he washed the floor early in the morning. He'd shaken his head at her, telling her she could not use his place as a bed. She was grateful that he'd allowed her to rest for a few hours. It was safer than on the streets.

Sometimes she slept sitting upright in a bus station, but had to be careful to rotate stations or they'd kick her out. She used a train station a couple of times as well.

She felt it again. There. That fluttering sort of sensation deep within her belly. It was unlike anything she'd experienced before in her life, but it was happening more and more often now.

She cradled her stomach. Her baby. Her resentment for this unborn child was huge at first; she saw it as the cause of all her problems. All it did was make her feel ill and got her kicked out of the only way of life she'd ever known. But now, as this new life started to move and make its presence known, her feelings changed. Glancing down at her swelling midsection, her face softened. Her baby. Hers.

Evaline knew that the life she was living was not good for a developing baby. She needed to get adequate rest so she could be strong for her baby. The child needed decent food to develop properly. Try as she might, Evaline could not find a job, other than one for a few hours here and there. Often, she did dishes in exchange for some food to eat. What would happen to her baby if it did not get the nutrients it needed?

CHECKING that no one seemed to pay her any attention, Evaline stretched out on the hard bench, dangling her legs over the narrow end. She brought one hand up to shield her eyes from the sun. Her other hand rested reassuringly on her protruding stomach. Exhausted, she drifted to sleep.

"Hey, are you all right?" A woman's voice penetrated Evaline's consciousness. A gentle hand shook her shoulder.

Startled, Evaline jerked upright. How awful to be caught in such a vulnerable position. Anything could have happened to her falling asleep in public like this. But this woman didn't look menacing.

"Is she all right, querida?" A man stood behind the woman.

"I don't know," was the reply. The woman sat on the bench beside Evaline.

THAT WAS the day that changed things for Evaline. This kind woman introduced herself and her husband. They told her they ran a home for unwed mothers. They took them in and took care of them - clean sheets, nutritious food and a safe place to stay.

The couple showed her pictures of the estate that housed these pregnant young women. They showed her pictures of the girls staying there, all in various stages of pregnancy. The girls smiled and looked like they were having a good time. They also looked healthy, too, every single one of them. When Evaline marvelled at that, the woman told her that their cook provided nutritious meals. It all sounded too good to be true.

A SOFT RAPPING on Anna's door had her looking up from her Friday afternoon date with paperwork.

Elizabeth stood there. "Got a minute?"

Anna composed her face. "Sure." She'd think about

her conversation with Alejandro later. She was good at compartmentalizing, had perfected it when she was at his mercy. "What's up?"

"I just had a meeting with Timothy's teachers. Driving home, you crossed my mind. I wasn't far away, so took the chance that you'd be in your office."

Anna went to the little machine on her credenza and poured them both a coffee. "Did the meeting not go well?"

"They were all very polite and all that, and said some nice things about Timothy. But they mentioned the 'A' word."

"Which is?" Anna had a good guess but wanted to hear Elizabeth's take on it.

"Autism."

"Does that surprise you?"

"It shouldn't, I guess, but hearing it from strangers, people new to Timothy, makes the possibility feel more real."

Anna and Murph had talked about this. Murph's opinion was that Timothy was coming along. As long as he continued to make progress and the supports for him seemed appropriate, then it was okay to let Elizabeth come to this at her own pace.

"I wish Murph would assess him."

"He can't," Anna explained. "You're friends. He was able to see Timothy a few times initially after the stuff with Dr. Mayberry because he felt he was in a suitable position to help, seeing as he had insights into Hanna Mayberry. But after we all became friends, it would no longer be appropriate. That's why he referred you to another therapist."

"I know. I get all that, but I trust him."

"Murph has that effect on people."

"He didn't say Timothy is autistic, wouldn't say one way or the other, but he thought it was worth looking into the possibility."

"You think that's psychiatrist-speak for 'don't rule it out'?"

"I could pass it off if he was the only one who'd ever mentioned it. But the speech therapist said she wonders as well. Dr. Muller, Timothy's neurologist, thinks there might be something other than just seizures. Then, there's Keira."

"Yes, there's Keira. She's sort of an expert in her own right, isn't she?"

"True. She may not have the paper credentials, but she's lived it for almost six years now."

"What's holding you back from finding out?"

Elizabeth puffed out a breath. "I don't know why I'm resisting the possibility. Maybe it's that we've been through so much already. Maybe I just don't want to deal with another diagnosis on top of what Timothy already has."

"What difference will it make?"

"Maybe none," Elizabeth admitted. "Keira says that a diagnosis gives you a lens through which to view your child, a window into seeing the world through his eyes. But I do that already! She says that it helps a school know which strategies to try. But they're already using those strategies with him at school."

"Does that tell you anything?"

"Yeah, I get it," admitted Elizabeth. "It's just that a formal diagnosis means admitting it. I struggled with his seizure diagnosis at first, but the evidence was pretty in my face as he kept seizing multiple times a day. There was always the hope that they'd get better, though, and they did. Autism isn't something that goes away."

"True. It's also true that even if he gets a diagnosis, he'll still be the same little boy you knew and loved prior to knowing this label."

~

"ESTHER, have you heard anything about Lily Ramirez?"

The school secretary turned to her computer. "I don't think so but let me check."

"I'm worried about her. It's been months since she's been in my class. Has another school requested her records?" Lily had been on Sue Bitman's mind more and more this last week.

"No, there's been no requests sent in. No activity at all since her last day in your room."

"Her attendance was never great, but she'd miss only a week at a time. No one's come to claim her things either; they're all still in her desk."

"Let's see. After she was absent the first week, our system sent the standard phone message to the number on record. No one returned the call. Then at the one month mark we sent our form letter. Again, at two months the same thing happened and at three. There's been no response from the family."

"And that's it? That's all we do when a kid disappears?"

"Frustrating, isn't it? Our hands are tied. Parents can choose to move their kids. They can even choose to homeschool or simply not send them."

"Homeschool. Did anyone file a homeschool plan for her?"

Esther shook her head. "That would be listed right here." She pointed to an empty slot on the spreadsheet. "There's nothing. She's such a sweet child, too."

"She is. Despite her sporadic attendance, she kept up well, too. Whenever she'd return, she seemed happy to be back. She'd never tell me, though, why she'd been away. Something about her little brothers was all I could get out of her."

"We know that nothing bad has happened to her. There have been no police inquiries."

"Should there be?"

"Only if she's reported missing."

"Can't we do that?"

Esther shook her head. "I don't think so."

"Why don't we have a police community liaison officer anymore? Maybe he could have helped."

"Budget cuts."

"Would you write down Lily's home address for me, please? I'm going to see what I can find out."

NOT THAT SHE wished to see her friend gone, but Anna was eager to inspect her email program. Had it captured Alejandro's words well?

First, she deleted Betty's name from the To box, replacing it with her own personal email address. Then, she put in her own work address as well. Wouldn't hurt to have a back-up.

Yes! Even though the voice-to-text program had not trained itself on Alejandro's voice, it still did a fair job of interpreting his words. There was the odd word substitution as it struggled for meaning, but the gist of it was there. Incriminating as heck.

Quickly, she typed "Alejandro 1" into the subject line and hit Send. Now she had a record of his words, even if her computer crashed. Thank goodness for cloud storage email services.

Going to her Sent folder, she pulled up the email that she had just sent and hit Reply. Now, while the visit was fresh in her mind, she typed out all that she could remember of the visit prior to thinking to record what he said. She then sent that message to both her work and personal email addresses.

There. Proof. Now, what to do with that proof?

CHAPTER 20

*A*nna's thoughts whirled as she drove home. Worst were the memories.

When Elizabeth had recounted to Anna the extent of how badly her husband had betrayed her, Anna felt for her friend. Not that Anna had ever expected any loyalty from her own husband, the one imposed on her, but she had expected some support and protection from her parents.

At first, she believed that her mother had been a helpless pawn in the scheme. But with age and wisdom, she realized that the woman who gave birth to her was complicit in sacrificing their daughter to an evil man to pay a debt. Her stepfather was the dominant one in the relationship, but her mother had not even tried to protect her. Although Tomar was the only father Anna had known, she was his stepdaughter, and he felt nothing for her. Her natural father was unknown, someone no one had ever been willing to talk about. Even with her abuela, it was a closed subject.

So that was the past. She had dealt with it, or so she told herself. But what to do about the present? Alejandro would not give up. At least he hadn't in the years that she had lived with him. It was doubtful that the years had softened him. Not likely, when he now talked about his stable of girls.

She pulled into their driveway, minus Bonnie. One phone call, and Elizabeth had agreed to keep Bonnie at her place for a few hours.

Murph was in the kitchen, chopping veggies for a stir-fry. He had skills with a knife, that man. For a second, Anna watched him chop with as much speed and accuracy as any top chef contestant on television. Sensing her presence, he set down the knife and turned. Wiping his hands on his apron, he came to gather her into his arms. Looking over her shoulder, he asked, "Where's Bonnie."

"I asked Elizabeth if she'd keep her until later this evening."

Arnold Murphy raised an eyebrow.

"I need to talk to you. Alone."

Removing his apron, Murph poured two glasses of chardonnay and settled them on the sofa facing the picture window. He loved this view and the solitary, noble tree that presided over the meadow. Near the tree he could see Morgan and Sandy pretend-fighting over a stick. He could imagine the grrrs coming from their mouths as they did mock battle, but both tails wagged furiously. All was right with their world. He could not help his smile as he glanced at the woman by his side. How'd he get so lucky?

BOTH OF ANNA'S hands entwined around the glass's stem. Although she swirled the liquid, she had yet to take a sip. How to begin? Where to begin? This was so not a story that she ever wanted to share.

Murph had told her over and over again that he loved her exactly as she was, warts and all, although no matter how hard he said he searched her body, he'd not yet found one wart. Well, he was about to learn of a big, fat, witch's wart, but this one was not on her nose, but on her soul.

She started, beginning with when she was seventeen and the whispered conversations she overheard between her parents, ones that cut off abruptly when she entered the room. The news, the big news the week before her birthday - news that not only would this be a party to celebrate her admittance into the adult world, but her marriage as well.

From there the story went downhill.

Murph's wine glass was drained, refilled and drained again. Anna's went untouched as she talked. Murph had to consciously tell his fingers to relax their grip on the stem of the glass before he snapped it in two. While that might feel good metaphorically, he'd rather it be the neck of the villain who had harmed Anna. Villains. Her parents were no better.

It was bad enough that this was Anna's past, that she'd had to suffer so much. She'd grown into a strong, independent, beautiful woman, despite all that had been done to her. But now that horrific past had intruded on her life, into their lives.

Not only did it involve him and Anna, but Bonnie had been threatened, as well as the children of their friends.

Was the threat serious?

WHILE ANNA CURLED up with her wine and a blanket, Murph made supper. They ate on the couch, this time facing the fireplace.

After leaving an exhausted Anna to relax, Murph went to collect Bonnie.

On the drive, he used his car's Bluetooth setup to call their friends. He'd tell Elizabeth in person, but first he'd need to stop over at Cynthia's house to warn her.

When he called Jake's cell, luckily Jake was at Keira's house. Putting Murph's call onto speaker phone, Murph conveyed just enough information to have them instantly agreeing to meet at his house tomorrow afternoon.

Jake said that he'd call Brendan to alert him. They both had the next day off, so it should be no problem.

Cynthia was an easy sell. Amy was happy any time she got to play with the boys, and she now loved Bonnie as well. Sensing how worried Murph was, she asked, "It's not about Elizabeth's ex, is it? He can't be getting out of prison so soon."

"No, no, nothing to do with Jackson or any of the

stuff that Elizabeth went through. No, this is about Anna's past and some of it haunts us now."

"I'm sorry. If you want us, we'll be there. What can I bring?"

"Nothing," he started to say. Then amended that. "You wouldn't have any of your peanut butter cookies, would you?"

HE LUCKED out at Elizabeth's home because Brendan's car was in her driveway.

"I just got off the phone with Jake," Brendan said. "I was filling Elizabeth in, but I don't really know what's going on."

"Neither do we for sure. But there's a chance that it could involve you, involve all of us. This is really hard on Anna, but she thinks you should hear the entire story, so you know what we might be up against." He looked away. "Let me warn you, it's not pretty."

"We'll be there. You know that we'll do anything we can for Anna." Elizabeth reassured him with a hand on his arm.

"It's not just about what you could do for her, but she's afraid that her past could affect you as well. All of you."

"Can you tell us what this is about?"

Murph shook his head. "This is Anna's story to tell. What she told me tonight is horrific, but there's more to it. I only wanted her to have to tell the whole thing once, so, we'll do it tomorrow after supper."

As he and Bonnie headed out, another thought

occurred to Murph, and he ducked back in. "Brendan, do you or Jake have any kind of recording device? I didn't think to run this by Anna, but it might help to have a recording of what she's going to tell us."

"Are you thinking legally?" asked Brendan.

"Let's just say that I'm glad that you and Jake are police officers."

As a parting thought, he added, "Keep an eye on the kids, will you? Same goes for Amy."

ELIZABETH WAS OFF, tearing through the house in search of Timothy.

He was where she had left him half an hour ago. Tucked into his Thomas the Tank Engine sheets, fast asleep. She left him be but kept his door ajar so she could hear if he stirred.

She phoned Cynthia. "Just checking that you and Amy are okay." She tried to keep the shakiness out of her voice.

"We're fine. But what's going on? Murph sounded mysterious. He's always so calm and collected; I've never seen him flapped like this."

"I have, just once before." Elizabeth remembered a devastated Dr. Arnold Murphy when he realized the perfidy of his former protégé, Dr. Mayberry, his worry over Timothy and how caring and helpful he had been in the aftermath of that debacle. "This is something to do with Anna, and it's shaken him badly. When I asked, he said that it's Anna's story to tell, and she wants to do it just once, to all of us." Then, she added, "You'll drive over there with us tomorrow?"

Hanging up, she collapsed into Brendan's arms. Any potential threat to her son brought back far too many memories.

"I'm staying the night," announced Brendan. "I'm not leaving you guys alone."

CHAPTER 21

*U*sually, their get-togethers felt relaxed and jovial. Not this time. A pall hung over the group, although they tried to pretend for the sake of the kids.

The little ones seemed oblivious to the tension in the air. But who knew with kids? Just because they didn't show it outwardly didn't mean that they didn't pick up on the odd atmosphere.

Bonnie was the exception. Her gaze travelled from adult to adult, as if she was trying to read the situation. She stayed closer to them more than usual and when she wasn't by an adult's side, she was keeping close track of the smaller children.

Supper was a picnic outside. The men grilled burgers and arranged picnic tables while Anna organized the kids. Each child had a chore, carrying out either plates, cutlery, salads or napkins. Yes, it would've been quicker to do it herself, but the effort to oversee

them took her mind off what was to come after
they ate.

Now, the kids and the dogs were playing, and
Bonnie had strict orders to make sure that the three
younger ones did not stray from the area between the
house and the tree. The adults arranged the chairs so
that they could all keep an eye on the children. Anna
was just as pleased that they sat in a rough line, staring
out. It was gonna be easier to tell her story without all
of their eyes fixed on her face.

MURPH LOOKED at her with a question. Yes, she was
ready to begin. He offered beer or wine to any takers,
then settled back into his chair, taking Anna's hand
in his.

"This will take a while," warned Anna. "And it's not
pretty. I'm afraid that it does not put me in a good light,
the things that I did and were done to me." With a
breath, she started in.

Brendan started the recorder, and so Anna began
her story, starting with her growing-up years.

I lived with my mother and stepfather. We spent our
time moving between various places in Southern
California and Ensenada, Mexico, where my stepfather
was from, and where his mother still lived.

While, the moves played havoc with my education,
academics came easily enough to me that I managed.
My stepfather was not unkind; he mostly ignored me.
That is, until I was 17. Then he looked at me more and

more, in ways that made me uncomfortable. But he did nothing improper.

While we were far from wealthy, I had no idea that the family was in financial trouble. I never knew what my stepfather did for a living, but there seemed to be times when he would flash money around. During other periods my parents would talk in hushed voices, and there would be no going out for dinner, no new clothes. I needed little, so it didn't matter to me.

As I approached my 18th birthday, several things were going to happen all at once. My birthday was in July, and I was graduating from high school in June. Whenever I tried talking to my parents about plans to go to college, they didn't want to hear it. They didn't tell me I couldn't go, but they didn't seem to share my excitement about the possibility.

Used to being ignored by my stepfather, it surprised me when he talked about having a party to celebrate me turning eighteen, my entrance into womanhood, as he called it. That seemed an odd way to put it but, whatever. Never keen on being the center of attention, a party didn't sound wonderful to me, but my parents had their hearts set on it. If it pleased them, I'd go along with it.

Anna felt Murph squeeze her hand. It was as if he was telling her here's another case of when you gave up your own preferences to make someone else happy. He was always telling her she did that too much.

Anna continued.

A week before my birthday, a guest came over for supper, Alejandro Sanchez. His attentiveness to me during the meal made me uncomfortable. As quickly as I could, I made excuses and went to the kitchen to clean up the dishes.

The next day my mother brought me into the salon and sat me down.

She asked me what I thought of Alejandro. I said I didn't know, he was just some friend of my stepdad's. He meant nothing to me.

"Well," mama had said, "Alejandro was quite taken with you. He and your papa talked, and it's decided. We'll combine your birthday with a wedding party. Alejandro and you will marry; it will be so exciting." Her mother gushed. "What a coup. Alejandro is so handsome and rich." She rambled on about what a lucky girl Anna was.

My mother couldn't understand my horror rather than feeling flattered. I did not know this man. I did not particularly like him when I met him. And I was only 18. Yes, I would have liked to get married one day probably, but I would find a man of my own choosing. First, I had things to do, like get a college degree, and then find a job.

My mother changed from excited to angry, saying I didn't understand. Mama wasn't asking me, she was telling me I would marry this man.

Apparently, Alejandro was a business associate of my stepdad. He was wealthy, and my stepfather, Roberto, was not. At one time he had had adequate money, but he was in debt now. Seriously in debt, life-threateningly in debt. The only way out for the family was for me to help. Alejandro wanted me. In exchange for my hand in marriage, he would write off the family's debt.

They needed me to do this. It was not an option. It was my obligation. Think of the little boys, mama said. My mother and stepfather had two small sons, ages four and six. They were innocent and knew nothing about any of this. Without my saving them by marrying Alejandro, the little boys would know hardship. Who knew? They might even lose their father, and then who would support them? With me doing this for the family, they would all be okay.

My mother talked about the wonderful estate where Alejandro lived and where I would be mistress. I would be well taken care of and not have to think about working, ever.

I protested that I wanted to work. I wanted to have a career. Mama dismissed that notion.

Over the next few days, the family prepared to travel to Ensenada where the wedding would take place. Several times along the way I thought of escaping. I could go out the back door of the restaurant and try to hop a ride with a passing truck driver. Normally, I wasn't into risky behavior but taking my chances with some stranger felt like it might be better than what I was getting into.

But then who would look out for my little brothers? What would become of them? While I was not fond of my stepfather; I was neutral toward him; I did not wish him any harm. And my mother was, well, my mother. I could not let them down.

My mother said that not all marriages last forever. I

knew that. While I had never thought that a divorce was something that would enter into my life, maybe if I stuck this out for just a couple years while my stepdad got back on his feet, then I could leave the marriage and begin my own life. Yes, it would not be that bad. I could stand this for the sake of my family.

Brendan stopped the recording; Anna needed a few minutes to collect herself before continuing.

* * *

A knock on the door broke Carl's peace. It was rare that he had the house to himself, with everyone else still asleep at nine in the morning.

The knock came again. He hurried to the door, hoping to stop that noise before it woke up the little boys. A woman stood there, a pleasant-looking woman of about his own age.

She asked, "Mr. Ramirez?"

"No, sorry. You have the wrong house." Carl started to close the door and return to his coffee.

The woman took a step forward, placing her foot in the doorway. She stuck out her hand. "Hello. I'm Sue Bitman. Maybe you can help me. I'm looking for Lily Ramirez. I'm her teacher. Do you know her?"

Carl straightened and opened the door wider. She had his interest now. "I'm Lily's stepfather. Have you seen her?"

Now, that was an odd question, Sue thought. Why would he think *she'd* seen his daughter if he hadn't? "Ah, no, not in several months. I'm worried about her. That's why I'm here, to see if she's all right and if she's coming back to school. We miss her."

"So do I," admitted Carl. He closed the door behind him and ventured out onto the step. He wasn't sure he wanted Sally to hear this conversation.

"What's going on?" Sue's suspicions were up.

Carl rubbed his forehead. "I don't know. Sally, my wife, considers Lily her daughter. Well, she is, of course, but she thinks of Lily as just her responsibility, not mine." At the look on the teacher's face, he hastened to explain. "I love Lily. She's a great kid and I wish she was mine, but Sally won't let me adopt her. Still, we're close. Or were close."

"What happened?"

"One day when I came home from work, Lily wasn't here. I kept asking, but Sally told me not to worry about it, that she'd take care of her daughter. No matter what I said, I couldn't get out of her where Lily was staying."

This was more than odd. "Does she have relatives she could be staying with?"

Carl shook his head. "No. As far as I know, there is no family, at least I've never heard of any. I don't know who Lily's birth father is or where he'd be."

"Could I come in and speak with your wife?"

"No, she's sleeping. She wouldn't tell you any more than she told me, anyway."

"Have you reported the child missing?"

"No. I've thought about it, but her mother assured me everything is fine. Our relationship is, ah, a little strained right now." Seeing the teacher's thoughts reflected on her face filled Carl with shame. He could have done better by Lily. He didn't trust Sally with the little boys. What made him believe her when she said that everything was fine with Lily? She was only a twelve-year-old girl. The world could be an awful place.

"I don't feel good about this. Not at all. I'm going to pass on my concerns to be police."

"Wait!" Carl stood. "I'll just leave a note for my wife, then I'll go with you." Having made this decision, he felt better than he had in months.

CHAPTER 22

*A*nna continued her story. Brendan clicked the record button on the device.

My abuela didn't like this. She'd prepared for my birthday party, but a wedding? No. It was not right. She had not met this man. She did not trust what her son was up to with her granddaughter.

The day of the wedding dawned sunny, as it often does in the mountains at that time of year. I spent the morning having spa treatments and my hair, nails and makeup done for me. These were new experiences, and I did not like strangers touching my body. My mother said to get used to it, this was my place in life now.

After lunch, cars rolled into the village. So many cars, so many strangers. I did not know this many people. There were more than had attended my whole high school. My mother said that these were business associates of my stepfather's and friends of Alejandro.

The wedding took place in the Catholic Church, the only church in the area, but not with our regular priest;

he was not around. I remember little of the service, other than looking once into the eyes of the man who would be my husband. During the whole ceremony, I could feel his eyes boring into mine, so I stared at the floor.

Although it must've been a big deal with all of those guests, I remember little about the reception or the dance afterward. I was too focused on what this meant for my life from then on.

Attending a Catholic girls' school, I had little experience with the boys. Because we moved so much, I had no close girlfriends, so I'd never been the recipient of their gossip about things that went on between men and women. But I was to find out that night.

Being underage and a rule follower type of kid, I never sampled alcohol before. My new husband insisted I drink champagne with him. It didn't matter if I liked it or not. I managed the first glass after sipping for a couple of hours. The second glass he made me drink had an aftertaste that I had not noticed with the first glass.

I had more and more trouble keeping my eyes open. My mother said it was all the excitement of the day. She helped Alejandro escort me from the banquet. It was a long drive to his estate, and I fell asleep in the car.

When I woke, he was carrying me into this darkened house. He put me on a bed and then put two hands to the neck of my dress and ripped it open. The rest was a blur. When I screamed from the pain and the fright, he tightened his hand over my mouth. I fought to get my nose free so that I could breathe. At some point, he must've noticed my struggles for air because he moved his hand slightly.

That pretty much sums up what my life became with him.

His goal was to get me pregnant. At least he was honest about that. It's not that he particularly liked me, he liked the fact that I would give him a child.

Sometimes there was a reprieve, and he might be away for a week at a time. Those were good days, or at least better days. When he was not with me, I was free to wander the house and the grounds.

While, the house was huge, cold and cavernous, the grounds were lush. A gardener and two groundskeepers maintained it. Sometimes they let me assist and those were even better days. But when I plead with them to help me escape, their eyes grew cold, and they withdrew. Their fear of Alejandro exceeded any sympathy they might have had for me.

On the days and nights when Alejandro was away, I explored the grounds. They'd encased the estate in 12-foot-high cement block walls with coils of razor wire along the top.

There were only three ways in or out. One was a walk-in door of heavy wood with wrought iron latticework. The padlock that barred it closed was larger than any I have ever seen. I searched the garden shed for any kind of tool that would help me get through that lock. There were no ladders. There were no bolt cutters. The shovels that the gardeners used were ones they brought in with them every day and took away with them so I could see no way that I could dig my way under the wall.

The other two entrances, and I called them entrances because to me they were how I had gotten in, but not a means of me getting out, had armed guards manned those portals 24 hours a day, two men at each gate. Those men would not look me in the eye, even though I said hola each time I passed them on my walks about the grounds. There was no help from them.

Anna twisted her hands and took a shaky breath. Murph put his arm around her shoulders and glanced at Brendan, who turned off the recorder.

* * *

Carl no longer had a car. He'd lost it when he could no longer make the payments after his factory closed.

After some hesitation on her part, Sue Bitman agreed Carl could ride to the police station with her. During the few minutes that Carl took to get himself ready, Sue phoned the precinct to say that she was coming in to file a missing child report. There. They had her contact information and an appointment time, just in case she didn't show up. She did not know this man who would share her car with her. She reasoned that anyone who could raise a child as nice as Lily could not be bad, but now she had some insurance that if she didn't make it to the police station, someone would look for her.

"You're the guardians of this Lily Ramirez?" The police officer seemed to have trouble understanding.

"I'm her stepfather," explained Carl. "She and her mom have lived with me since Lily's been two years old. But she's not my daughter legally." At the officer's look, he said, "I wanted to adopt her, but Sally, her mother, said it wouldn't be fair to the father."

"Who is this father?"

"No idea. Sally wouldn't ever say. I don't think she ever told Lily, either."

"Sally." The officer checked his notes and looked at Sue. "And you're not Sally?"

She shook her head and tried again. "I'm Sue Bitman, Lily's teacher. She hasn't been at school in months, so I went to her house to see where she was."

"You waited months to look into why a child wasn't at school."

Sue glared at him. "We have protocols in place for truant children. The day they're absent, we phone home to ask about it, or at least leave a message. This happens automatically for each day the student is missing without the parent having notified the school about the absence. According to the school secretary, the only number we have for Lily's parents was a mobile number. They blocked calls from the school after the first week."

"I know nothing about any calls," said Carl.

Sue ignored him and continued. "After the first week of absences, we send home a note, and that continues each week for the first month, then a different letter goes out monthly for three months. There has been no response from the family at all, and no requests from other schools for her records."

Sue and the officer turned to regard Carl.

He held up his hands. "This is all news to me. I've not seen any letters, but my wife is the one home during the day, so she brings in the mail."

"Where is your wife?" the officer wanted to know.

"When I left, she was still in bed."

"Shouldn't she be here with you, reporting her daughter missing?"

This sounded bad, Carl knew. "She always made it clear that Lily was *her* daughter, not mine. I asked where Lily was, of course, I did, but she wouldn't say, just that everything was taken care of. I presumed Lily is now with relatives."

"Who are these relatives?"

He hated to admit it. "I don't know. I've met none of Sally's family and she doesn't talk about them."

"Let's make sure I've got this straight," the office shuffled through his notes. "You are this child's grade six teacher and, after months of continuous absence, you decide to let us know she is missing."

Sue nodded.

"And you, sir," he looked at Carl, "have lived with this child most of her life. When one day she disappears from your home, you let it go months before wondering where she is?"

"That's not fair," protested Carl. "I wondered. I asked Sally all the time at first, but she refused to say. And she's right, I have no legal say over Lily."

Sue regarded him from the corner of her eye. "What about your moral obligation?"

"I'm here, aren't I?"

CHAPTER 23

The sun started making its way toward the western sky. The children played a game of tag with Bonnie.

Jake couldn't bear to hear any more. He needed a break. "Anyone want another beer?" He returned a moment later with the necks of three beer bottles hooked between the fingers of one hand and a wine bottle in the other. He topped up drinks all around, then returned to his seat, turning his palm upright, ready for the comfort of Keira's hand.

THEN I GOT PREGNANT, continued Anna. This was the beginning of better times. Alejandro insisted that I have plenty of fresh air and the best of meals. A doctor came out regularly to check up on me, a mostly silent doctor. He'd ask me questions, but would not respond to any of mine.

She took a sip of wine. "Best of all, Alejandra left me

alone during this time. His job done, so his interest in me waned, thank goodness. The compound would've been a beautiful place if I wasn't a prisoner there.

As the time for delivery grew closer, I thought more and more about what life would be like after the baby. Maybe Alejandro would change. Maybe now that he had gotten what he wanted, he would be a good father. Maybe the restrictions would ease up.

I asked if my mother could come for the birth. I was only 18 and scared. No, she wouldn't be here, I was told, but there would be a midwife. Even a woman I had never met would be much better than no friendly face. At least I assumed a midwife would be friendly.

I went into labor, not sure what to expect. But I was healthy and young, and women have been doing this for countless years so it shouldn't be a problem. I was wrong.

The first day of labor was worrying. After about 18 hours, the midwife realized the baby would not come easily. She said it was in breech position. She tried and tried to turn the baby but couldn't do it."

Anna looked at Elizabeth and Keira. You can imagine what it was like.

The pain came in relentless bands, made worse by her efforts to turn the baby. I fought her, but she hollered for two other people who held down me down.

By the second day I was exhausted, but it continued. Finally, she called for the doctor, the same one who visited me during my pregnancy. By that time, I hardly registered his presence in the room.

They put something over my mouth, and I breathed

in this stuff. That's all I remember until I woke up with this enormous pain in my abdomen, but an unfamiliar pain, different than I'd experienced during labor. And my stomach was flatter.

Overjoyed, I realized I had had the baby. I called out for them to bring him or her to me. After all that, I so wanted to see my child.

But they ignored me. I was alone in the bedroom, with my wrists tied to the top of the bed. When the midwife came to check on me, she said it was for my own protection so that I didn't hurt myself. She told me to just lay still. She ignored my cries to bring my baby to me."

Anna got up and paced the patio in front of her friends. She needed to move now as she told the rest of the story.

That's it. That was the end of my pregnancy and the end of my baby. I never saw my child. They took her. I know it was a girl, the midwife let that slip although I don't think she intended to.

Murph enfolded Anna in his arms. She rested her head on his shoulder, but no tears came. She shed a lifetime's supply way back then. Now these people, her friends, people she could trust, needed to know the rest of the story because the evil from her past might be about to touch them.

That was it. I was young and healthy and recovered fairly quickly, or I would have if not for the botched caesarean. The incision became badly infected. I had to cleanse the wound many times a day, trying to stem the sepsis that oozed out. Finally, the cook noticed how carefully I walked and told someone, because the doctor appeared the next week. He injected antibiotics and gave me pills that might've helped the infection, but I reacted too badly. It started with hives up and down my arms and then my legs and then my back and chest. I was so nauseated I could keep nothing down for days and days. I was dizzy and fell down the concrete steps, knocking myself out. The gardeners found me there; they noticed the blood down my front. My incision had opened up.

The next day I awakened, and the doctor was there. My abdomen was freshly bandaged and there was a new vial of medication on my bedside table.

It seemed that Alejandro did not want me dead. He still had use for me, so he wanted me to mend. I did. But there were many times when I wished that I had not.

Anna paused in her story, gathering her strength to tell the rest.

I had about a three-month reprieve where I hardly saw my husband. That made life more bearable. But then he returned, returned not just to the estate, but to my bed. The doctor told him I was healed, and Alejandro believed it was time to work on getting me pregnant again.

He was not pleased with how long it took. Maybe my body was not ready; my mind certainly was not ready. But it was another year and a half before I conceived again. This frustrated Alejandro, and he took it out on me.

. . .

THIS PREGNANCY WAS DIFFERENT. The nausea of morning sickness continued for all but the last few weeks of the pregnancy. For the first trimester, I lost weight. The cooks had orders to fatten me up, but I struggled to keep anything down. I wanted to, for the sake of the baby, but something in my body rebelled.

This labor started off more easily, and I heard no talk of a breech delivery. Still, it didn't progress the way it should. The doctor came and started a drip. He said it was oxytocin in the IV. And that it should hasten my labor. Two days later, it had not. The contractions were regular and intense, but they did not push the baby out. There was talk about the possibility that my cervix kinked. I think that was probably true.

Again, there was that cloth over my nose and mouth, and then I remembered no more. The baby was no more as well. I don't know for sure if she or he lived or died, but the child was dead to me. I never saw this baby either, and no one would tell me a thing about the child.

What I learned, though, was that the second caesarean had not gone well. There were some mistakes made, and I was damaged internally. I could never bear another child.

As bitter as that news was to me, it was to be a blessing. If I could not bear children for him to take, I was of no use to Alejandro.

He released me. He gave me 10,000 pesos and arranged a ride to the bus station.

From there, I took a bus to Ensenada, then walked the dusty trail up to my Abuela's house. She was no longer there. Other people were in her house, strangers.

They told me she had died. No one knew anything about my parents.

That night, I slept under a tree with some goats. They didn't mind me, and as the night grew cooler, we huddled together.

Come daylight, I walked back to town, bought breakfast, then a bus ticket to California. I would go back to my parents. I didn't know what else to do.

When I got home, or what I had thought of as home, there were strangers in the house. They didn't know my parents; they didn't know who I was talking about. Only then did I realize how much my family kept to themselves. I could think of no family friends to call on for help or to ask where my parents were.

There were a few rough years there, while I tried to figure things out, but I won't bore you with those details because they're not relevant.

"This brings us to where we are today."

CHAPTER 24

Brendan's phone rang. He checked the number and saw it was the station. "I think I'd better take this." He walked a little way from the group.

"Hey, Brendan, I think I have something that might interest you. Remember that kid you searched for, that girl with no name who no one was looking for? I think we might have a hit on her."

Brendan motioned for his partner, Jake, to come, and the two men walked around the side of the house. "It might be about Bonnie," Brendan said. He put the phone on speaker setting.

"This man and woman came into the station, a strange pair. The woman said that she's the kid's teacher. Her story checks out. She says that she worried when the kid never returned to school, so she went to her house. There she met the kid's stepfather, who said he didn't know where she was, that his wife had moved the girl somewhere, but wouldn't tell the guy where." He listened. "Yeah, yeah, I know. Sounds hinky, doesn't it, but the guy says that his wife was definite that the kid was hers and not his, so he needed to butt out."

"Where are they now?"

"They left. I've got their contact information for you. They call the kid Lily. Lily Ramirez."

***

TORN, Brendan and Jake decided that the news about Bonnie's possible identity could wait until after Anna finished her story. After all, Anna implied that her old history could impact their lives now.

ONCE THE MEN SAT AGAIN, Anna continued. "Elizabeth and Keira, you saw Alejandro at my place when we were packing. I do not know how he found me, had no idea that he was even looking. After I couldn't produce any more babies for him, his interest in me ended. Or so I thought."

"He looked like a grade A creep to me," said Keira.

"He came to my office yesterday," Anna told them. "At least now I know what he wants." She turned to Jake and Brendan. "I don't know how the law works on different sides of the border; hopefully you can figure this out."

Jake took out his notepad and waited.

"Alejandro has changed his game. I believe he was

selling babies. *My* babies back then, but who knows how many other women he was doing this to? Now, he's running in bigger leagues. He talked about his stable - a stable of women kept for breeding purposes."

Brendan and Jake exchanged looks. Brendan pulled out his phone. "Should I record this?"

Anna shook her head. "I don't think you need to, although you're welcome to record or share any of this with whoever you need to. I'm done hiding my shame; there are innocent women at risk here."

She opened a desk drawer and withdrew a folder. She'd made copies of the recording of Alejandro's talk in her office. While the voice recognition was far from perfect, it was reasonably accurate. She passed out copies to everyone. "While he was in my office, I pressed the recording feature on my email program. I wish I'd thought of it right away, but I still got enough information to incriminate him. At least, I think so."

She turned her back to them, looking at the children playing. "This stable, as he calls it. He wants me to go look after these women for him."

"Why ever would you do such a thing?" This made no sense to Elizabeth.

"He made some threats. My guess is that he followed some of us from my house when we packed, to here. We're all together often, so it wasn't easy for him to follow each of you home. He knows where you live. He knows you have children. He threatened your kids and Bonnie if I didn't do as he asked. I know he sold babies; I don't doubt he would also steal and sell children."

There. She'd said it. Now her friends would know just what she had brought down on their heads.

Anna's eyes filled with tears as she regarded Elizabeth. Her friend had already been through so much. Twice her son had been taken and put in danger. Now this on top of those horrors. "I'm sorry," she said. "So very, very sorry. If I could make this all go away, I would."

"It's not your fault," Elizabeth defended hotly. "You've been the victim in all of this."

"If I believed Alejandro would leave you all alone if I went with him, I'd do it. But I don't trust him. I'm not sure that you and your children would be safe, anyway."

"No!" Murph was on his feet. "There is absolutely no way that you are going anywhere near that man."

Jake and Brendan stood beside Murph. "He's right," Brendan agreed. "We're in his sights now. We won't be one hundred percent safe until he's stopped."

"Your sacrifice would mean nothing but pain for you and wouldn't do anything to ensure that Daniel, Timothy, Amy, and Bonnie are all right. No, there's another way," Jake assured her.

"Like what?" Anna wanted to know.

Jake didn't answer. He stared out the window in the distance, past the tree. There. There it was again. He nudged Brendan and pointed. "See that flash?"

The two men took off, racing toward the playing children. As he ran by, Brendan told Bonnie, "Get the kids into the house. Now! And stay there. Tell everyone not to move until we get back."

"And lock the doors," Jake added.

Once past the tree, the men saw no more of the light flashes, the sort made by binoculars reflecting sunlight.

The nearest road was a quarter mile away, on the other side of the meadow. Murph owned the land to just the other side of the gigantic tree; the rest of the grassy area was part of a nature preserve owned by the county.

As the gravel road came in sight, the sprinting men saw a silver Toyota RAV4 pull away from the curve and head west, back toward town. Too far to catch a glimpse of the license plate, Brendan and Jake stopped where the crumbling sidewalk met the long grass.

Examining the area, they saw evidence of trampled grass. Standing on the opposite side of that area and turning toward Murph's house, Jake had an unobstructed view of the tree and the home beyond. If he'd had binoculars, he could have clearly seen the four kids playing there only moments before.

Using his phone, Jake took several pictures of the trampled grass. Kneeling down, carefully spreading the tufts of weeds and wild meadow vegetation, he found a couple of footprints. Snapping shots of them, he exclaimed. "Wouldn't you know it? Look," he pointed at the ground, then held his own sole up for Brendan's inspection. "Nikes, like mine. Could you get anything more common?" Staring at the print, he estimated it was a about a size eleven, the same as his own shoe size. "So, a small, grey SUV and a Nike sneaker. There's about a million of each in this state."

Looking around, Brendan saw no one else. There were no homes or acreages out here, no reason for anyone to be parked here, no reason for anyone to be watching Murph's house. No good reason, that is.

***

WATCHFUL, the men split up and returned to Murph's house, taking different directions. But neither spied anything else suspicious. Suddenly, the isolation of Murph's acreage didn't seem so idyllic.

MURPH ANSWERED Jake's knock on the door. "Everything okay here?" Jake asked.

At Murph's nod, Jake rejoined Brendan outside and they inspected the perimeter of the house, before heading back inside.

"Whatever you said to her," Murph informed them, "caused Bonnie to speak. She said, 'Brendan said to lock the doors, and everyone has to stay in the house.' That's all we got out of her, but you must have impressed her for her to relay your message."

"Where are the kids?"

"Up playing in Bonnie's room," said Elizabeth. "Why did you take off like that?"

"I thought I saw a flash of something. It might have been sunlight reflection off binoculars, but I could be mistaken. A car took off shortly before we got there and there was no one else around."

"It's Alejandro." Anna spoke with certainty. "I know it."

"There's no proof," Jake said, although he suspected Anna was right.

"We need a plan."

"While the kids are upstairs, I should tell you about my phone call." He raised his hand in a halting motion. "Now, before you get your hopes up, this could be nothing, totally unrelated to Bonnie."

"What? You've found her parents?" This took Anna's mind away from Alejandro and the threat he represented.

"We don't know. The office calling me said that a couple came into the station to report a missing twelve-year-old girl, a Lily Ramirez."

"Her parents are just now looking for her?" Keira was estranged from her parents, but at age twelve, she couldn't imagine her parents deserting her.

"The woman was this Lily's teacher, and she was trying to find out why the student never returned to school. She went to Lily's house to find out what was going on. There she met Lily's stepfather, who said that he didn't know where the girl was. His wife, the girl's mother, sent her away and wouldn't say where."

"Sheesh. The kid's been gone for months, and he never looks for her?" Keira could not believe this.

Brendan asked Anna, "Do you have any recent pictures of Bonnie on your phone?"

"Sure."

"Would you text me a couple? I'll pass them on to the

station. A squad car is on the way to pick up Lily's mother and stepfather to bring them in for questioning." Then, he added, "This might not be Bonnie's family at all. It's sad but kids this age do go missing."

"Aren't you going to be there?" Anna thought that Jake or Brendan would best represent Bonnie's interest since they knew her.

"We would have been in on it, but we should stay here and sort this situation out first."

***

"I'M OFFICER HERNANDEZ, and this is Officer Boyd. Are you Sally Sykes?"

"Why are you asking?"

"Who is it, Sally?" The voice came from the interior of the house.

"We're police officers. We're looking for Sally and Carl Sykes."

Carl came to the door. "I'm Carl Sykes."

Hernandez looked him up and down. "We'll ask you to put some shoes on, sir, then come with us down to the station."

"Wait a minute," protested Sally. "I'm not going anywhere."

Carl was back with his sneakers in one hand. He wrapped his other palm around his wife's elbow. Putting his head back into the house, he yelled, "Keep an eye on the boys, will you Archie?" Taking his brother's consent for granted, he escorted his protesting wife down the steps.

Protesting was putting it mildly. She was yelling about mistaken identity, police brutality, but no one came to her rescue. Her head swivelled side to side, calling for Archie.

Carl smirked. As if Archie would stick his neck out for anybody, especially with the police involved. No, his big brother was hiding inside the house and would not venture out until there was no sign of anyone who upheld the law.

CHAPTER 25

*B*rendan and Jake packaged together the notes they'd taken while Anna talked, their recorder, and the transcript her email program recorded and took them to their captain.

Anna was a credible witness, known to many of them in law enforcement for her work as a courthouse social worker. That helped. The transcript did not, other than for informational purposes. There was no proof, other than Anna's statement, that these were words spoken by Alejandro Sanchez.

A search pulled up a number of men by that name, but none seemed to be about the right age of the man they'd seen that day at Anna's house. Border Security had no records of a man bearing those names on passports crossing the Mexican/American border.

When looking at just the individual bits, the story it pointed at was unpleasant. An unhappy ex-husband, wanting to re-connect with his former spouse, or wanting something from her. That happened countless times each week. And sadly, some of those exes acted threateningly. Jake and Brendan had witnessed that. But the man had left when ordered and, as far as they knew, he had not returned. Of course, Anna moved away the next day.

Next, there were the signs that someone may have been watching the house where Anna lived. There was no proof that there had been someone observing through binoculars, although Jake's gut told him that was the case. And that someone might have been Alejandro. Still, there was no proof that even if there was someone, it might not have been Alejandro.

Then there was Anna's tale, a tale of abuse and confinement. Was it confinement against her will? She had married the man, even though it was under some duress. But she'd agreed.

They'd need proof to back up her story. The Captain ordered a search for Anna's parents.

Anna's tales of her treatment at her husband's hands were despicable, but not likely indictable. Unless, and that was a big unless, they could find evidence that Anna had had children taken from her.

That was a story that would interest the Mexican federales. They did not look kindly on child abduction and child trafficking. If what Alejandro told Anna about his keeping a stable of women to be bred and their children sold, well, Mexican officials would be all over this.

The trouble was that they had little to go on. Anna had only a vague idea of the location of the compound where she had lived as Alejandro's wife. She didn't know for sure if the stable Alejandro referred to was the same building where she had lived. All she could tell them was a rough estimation of how long it took to drive from the compound to the bus station. It was at least something to give the federales.

Brendan and Jake had personal stakes in this, apart from being friends of Anna's. According to Anna, Alejandro asked about Keira, Elizabeth and Cynthia's children and implied that there was a market for them.

"Is there any other paperwork to back up her claims?" the Captain asked.

Jake left to make a call, returning ten minutes later with a paper. "She says that she never saw a copy of their marriage certificate, although she thinks she signed one during the ceremony. But she has this." He spread the paper Anna had scanned and emailed him. She said it was the marriage annulment Alejandro gave her.

Anna was raised Catholic. She understood they could annul an unconsummated marriage. She failed to see how her marriage to Alejandro could be construed as unconsummated. So, she was skeptical about the dissolution of her marriage. She kept the paper just in case, but didn't trust it. She had also avoided relationship with men, believing that she was not free to marry. That is, until Murph worked his way into her heart.

"Okay," said the Captain, gathering up their notes. "Let me take this higher up, then we'll be contacting our partners across the border." He rose. "In the meantime, I'd advise everyone involved to be wary."

. . .

***

BOYD AND HERNANDEZ watched through the one-way window. "We should have popcorn to enjoy with this," quipped Boyd.

"Why would a guy stay with a woman like that?" wondered his partner.

Inside the small interrogation room, Carl sat quietly, hunched forward, arms on his thighs, hands clasped and hanging together, while he stared at the grey, coffee-stained floor.

In front of him, Sally paced and raved and waved her hands and shouted. "How could you? You absolute idiot! You've ruined everything. I had it all taken care of and what did you go and do? How are we going to get out of this one? As if we don't have enough problems in our lives as it is!"

"Sally." He waited until there was a lull in her ranting, then tried again a little louder. "Sally. Your daughter is missing. We haven't seen her in months. She's only a child; anything could have happened to her."

"Oh, she's fine. That girl will land on her feet. She's her mother's daughter and has built-in street smarts."

"She's twelve."

"Twelve going on twenty."

That puzzled Carl. "She's a sweet girl, but just a little girl." Sure, she was responsible around the house, and good with the little ones, but no way was she a street-smart kid. Far from it. Carl and Archie had grown up in some tough areas, and Lily was no match for what she'd find on the streets.

"HEARD ENOUGH?" Hernandez asked Boyd.

"Yeah, let's do it." They gave one rap on the door, then entered the interrogation room.

Sally stopped mid-yell. Her expression instantly changed from that of a screaming maniac to a soft, frightened, helpless woman. "Oh, officers," if she could have gotten away with batting her eyes, she would have done it.

Behind her, Carl rolled his eyes.

"Officers, have you found my baby? We've been so worried."

"We don't know, Mrs. Sykes. We need more information."

"It's Ramirez-Sykes. My name was Ramirez before Carl and I married. I like to keep that name. It's a special bond that Lily and I have."

"Right." Boyd carefully kept his tone neutral. "Mrs. Ramirez-Sykes, then." He placed a folder on the table. When they were all seated, he opened the folder, taking out three sheets of paper, each facing down. Turning over the first one, he asked, "Have you ever seen this child?"

Sally's shriek echoed in the precinct parking lot. "Lily! Oh, my baby, my darling Lily. Where is she? Can I see my baby girl?"

Hernandez turned over the next photocopied snapshot.

Sally's reaction was slightly more subdued, but it was obvious she recognized the child.

Hernandez looked at Carl.

Carl nodded. "Yes, that's her. Is she all right?"

"We'll get to that shortly. When did you last see your stepdaughter, Mr. Sykes?"

"Probably one evening, maybe three months ago or so. She was okay when she went to bed. She was still sleeping when I left for work the next morning, but not there when I got home."

"Did you wonder where she was?"

Carl bristled. "Of course, I did. I asked Sally, and she said that Lily was fine, it was all taken care of."

"And you left it at that?"

"She's the child's mother, her guardian. She has the say."

"I see," Hernandez said, although he did not see at all.

Boyd tried with Mrs. Sykes, or rather, Mrs. Ramirez-Sykes. "When did you last see your daughter?"

"I'm not sure. I'm not very good with time. One day seems to blend into the other. You know how it is when you're home alone with kids, just one endless grind after another."

"Hmm." Boyd took over. "Do you think she ran away?"

"Oh, no, not my Lily. She's a good girl. She wouldn't do that, wouldn't worry her mama."

"Then how do you explain the fact that you have not seen your daughter in months?"

"I'm sure we would have heard if there was a problem," Sally explained.

"Pardon? How would you have heard? Who would have told you?"

"Oh, you know," said Sally. "There would have been something on the news, you know."

"Sally!" This was too much for even Carl. "What's going on?"

A shutter went over Sally's face, like she was trying on a new persona.

"Oh, for God's sake, if you must know, it was your brother. It's all his fault."

"Archie? What did he do?"

"Nothing, at least nothing yet. But he was going to." Sally looked to the officers for understanding. "Archie is Carl's brother. He moved in to help us out with the rent and stuff after Carl lost his job. He's been a lifesaver, really. I don't know how we would have managed without Archie."

Carl flushed and studied the floor. Yep, that same coffee stain was still there.

"But Archie is Archie. He's a man, with a man's needs. It was okay for a while, but then Lily started to, you know..." she lowered her voice to a whisper, "develop. Archie noticed. I could see him watching her out of the corner of his eye when she went by, when she bent over to pick up one of her little brothers, when she, well, you know how girls are. Lily was realizing the power she could have over men."

"Sally!" What he heard horrified Carl. "What the hell are you saying? That's not Lily at all." Archie, maybe, yes, but not Lily.

"Oh, Carl, you're sometimes like a child yourself. You need to wise up to what's going on around you. Yes, Archie was looking at Lily *that* way and it would not have been long before he acted on it."

Sally rested her elbows on the table, placed her chin in her hands and leaned forward, allowing her blouse to gape at the neck. "I was protecting Lily. She's young yet for that sort of stuff, and I wanted to spare her. Plus, we needed Archie. We need his money. So far, I've been keeping him happy, keeping him with us. Until Carl can find a permanent job, we can't exist on just the odd job he picks up. We need Archie to support us, so I keep him happy. If his attention turned to Lily, who knows if he'd stay?"

Boyd schooled his face to remain neutral. In police work, he thought he'd seen it all. But just possibly, this woman's depravity topped all that he'd experienced before. "So, what did you do then?"

"I did the only thing I could to keep her safe. I thought about bringing her here, or to another police station, but you know that there are lowlifes in such places, and I didn't want my little girl to run into any of them." Sally smiled as if she was clever. "I came up with a much better plan. I took her to the courthouse. It's safe there, with all the guards and lawyers and judges." She stopped.

"And then," encouraged Boyd.

"I told her to keep quiet. That wasn't hard for Lily.

She was always a quiet, little thing, but in the last years, she's been even shyer. Sometimes days will go by without hearing a peep out of her. Oh, except for with her brothers. She's great with them, my Jordy and Benjie. She talks to them and plays with them, letting me get a few minutes of peace here and there."

"You told her to keep quiet," prompted Boyd.

"Yes, I knew that someone would notice her, a girl alone, and they'd look after her."

"Why did you tell her to keep quiet?"

"So we wouldn't get in trouble."

"We?" Carl wanted no part of this.

"Yes, darling, we. I didn't want anyone to know that you'd lost your job, how bad our finances were, and that you weren't providing for us anymore. The world shouldn't have to know that we live off of your brother. And no one needed to know about Archie and Lily."

"Ma'am, did anything inappropriate go on between your brother-in-law and your daughter?"

"No, nothing. I stopped things before anything could happen and got Lily out of there. She'd be somewhere safe, and there'd be no competition in the house."

All three men stared at Sally.

"Will you excuse us?" Boyd and Hernandez left the room, heading for their captain's office.

CHAPTER 26

*I*n the meantime, Anna, Murph and Bonnie needed a patch of normalcy in their lives. They worked on their garage attic renovations. They began by painting the sloping ceiling and took turns using the two long-handled rollers, splattering paint in their hair, on their faces and on their clothes. It was impossible not to, at least for inexperienced painters, as they tilted their heads back to watch the progress of the roller on the walls and ceiling. The primer sealed the yellowing drywall. The next day they began with the colors that Anna and Bonnie chose. They steered the child away from the wilder options, promising her she could use any splashes of any color she wanted with the furnishings they'd buy. The entire back wall was something different. That received three coats of blackboard paint. As soon as it was dry, Bonnie spent hours with the colored chalk, creating designs.

With a pale ecru on the other walls, the place already looked warmer. Next, they considered how they'd use the space. The way the walls sloped to meet the floor meant that they could end up with a lot of wasted space. So, they built cupboards along the two walls, each about twenty-one inches high and maybe two feet out from the wall. This would provide both storage room, plus some seating. With cushions on top, it would be a cozy place, especially when their friends' kids came over..

Bringing home a truckload of two by fours and plywood, they set up saws and worked. Bonnie was not bad with a hammer and soon caught on to using the cordless drill. They made some mistakes and had to backtrack. For instance, they forgot to leave room for the heating ducts and blocked them off. Bonnie patiently undid screws until they came across the vents, so that they could extend the ducting out into the room and attach new grills.

Not a bad family project and something to keep their minds off the possibility of Alejandro lurking about, while they waited to hear how Jake's and Brendan's captain planned to proceed.

***

USUALLY, Anna was the supervising social worker in instances like this. It felt funny to have a different role.

At twelve, Bonnie needed some autonomy. If the child had been utterly opposed to seeing her mother, Murph and Anna prepared to make a case to the judge, but Bonnie's eyes lit up at the chance to visit her mom.

This first meeting took place in the courthouse, the very building where Anna first spied Bonnie, wandering the hallways alone and abandoned. Anger burned inside Anna at the thought of anyone dropping off this precious child, then leaving, just leaving her, hoping that the fates would be kind.

As Murph said, the fates *were* kind, and Bonnie landed on her feet with them. Still, the child went through some agonizing hours not knowing what to do, then uncertainty about living in her temporary home. She seemed settled now, but Anna knew how being reunited with the family that gave you up could wreck a child's newfound contentment. She also knew that the bond of the nuclear family was strong.

Anna wondered who was more nervous - she or Bonnie. Lily, she corrected herself. The child's name was Lily, although Bonnie suited her. As Murph reminded her, Bonnie was not theirs, just on loan so that they could enjoy her while she was with them.

IT WAS LATE. Their appointment was for ten, but they'd been waiting in this room for half an hour now, waiting for the social worker to tell them that Sally Ramirez-Sykes was here and ready to see her daughter.

Would Sally show? Anna had spent too many sad hours with children who eagerly awaited a visit with their parent, only to have that parent not show up. She so hoped Bonnie didn't experience that disappointment and rejection today.

. . .

FINALLY, at forty-seven minutes after the appointed time, the knock came. Sally had arrived. Sadly, there was only about ten minutes of their time left. They'd booked the room for another family at the top of the hour.

"Oh, my baby, my baby!" Sally gushed and drew Lily/Bonnie to her bosom. Bonnie's eyes met Anna's as the child peered over her mother's shoulder. Her eyes asked for help. Anna pasted on a smile and nodded. She tried to convey "It'll be okay" with her facial expression. Still, Bonnie's eyes didn't leave hers until her mother released her to hold her shoulders at arm's length. "Look at you! My, how you've grown." She pulled the girl back in for an uncomfortable hug.

Grown? Really? Anna wondered just how much a twelve-year-old grows in a few months. She looked over to find the social worker's eyes on hers. They exchanged a glance, likely sharing the same thoughts as they watched this scene.

Sally led Lily to the couch. They sat knee-to-knee, Sally grasping both of her daughter's limp hands. Now that there was less emoting going on, Lily/Bonnie's shoulders relaxed some and she gave her mother a small smile. That was all the encouragement Sally needed to bring the girl in close for another hug. Although Sally mopped at her eyes, neither Anna nor the social worker noted any actual tears. "How have they been treating you? Are you all right, my darling?"

Anna was biased. She could not help being skeptical about Sally's concern when this was the first question about the child's welfare in over a quarter of a year.

Sally continued. "We've missed you so much. Your brothers ask about you all the time. We really miss you around the house. Have you missed us?"

Lily/Bonnie looked at her mother.

"Lily," Sally's voice was sharper. "Answer me!"

Lily/Bonnie face was stone. The only thing that moved were her eyes as they sought Anna's.

Sally tugged on her daughter's chin. "Your mother asked you a question, Lily. You must respond when I speak to you. We've been over this before." She took a deep breath, glancing at the social worker. "Now, tell me. Have you missed us?" She gave Lily/Bonnie's closed fists a shake.

Silence.

Sally spoke to the social worker. "Sometimes she can be a stubborn child. I suppose it's her age, but we didn't raise her this way."

Again, the social worker's eyes met Anna's. The social worker held up her wrist and pointed to her watch. "Five minutes left."

"Oh, surely that can't be right," protested Sally. "I just got to see my darling girl."

"Your time was from ten to eleven o'clock, Mrs. Ramirez-Sykes."

"But I just got here!"

"That is true. We had this room reserved for you for an hour. Another family needs it at eleven."

"That's fine, we'll go somewhere else."

The social worker shook her head. "No. You heard what the judge said. This first visit was to take place here and for one hour."

Sally turned back to Lily and pulled the child's head to her shoulder. She stroked her daughter's hair, while Lily/Bonnie slumped awkwardly. "Poor baby. This mean lady says we'll have to say goodbye, after just a few minutes together." She moved Lily back and held her shoulders. "But we'll see other again soon. I promise."

The social worker made no such promise. "The courts will decide after I give my report."

CHAPTER 27

*J*udge Bursey approved another visit. Often, despite an obvious lack of parenting skills, there was still a bond, and it was harder on the child to not see the mother or father.

For the next family visit, Anna took Bonnie to the cafe across the street from the courthouse. Again, the visit was to be one hour long. Again, Sally was late, but this time by only a half hour.

Once the woman arrived, Anna and the social worker moved to an adjoining table to give the mother and daughter some privacy. But the women remained near enough to hear every word; neither trusted Sally, and were ready to fly to Lily/Bonnie's defense if needed.

BOTH HAD severe misgivings about Sally Ramirez-Sykes and her fitness as a mother to Lily. When discussing it in the judge's chambers, Judge Bursey stated that if Lily was a younger child, then he would proceed with more caution. But, given her age, and that she agreed to seeing her mother, he would grant one more supervised visit off premises, then a supervised family visit in a similar place, then they'd move to family visits without supervision, but in a neutral location. He still wasn't confident that Lily should spend time in her family home. Not yet, at least.

SALLY AND LILY'S half-hour in the cafe was stilted, with Sally doing all the talking. It was obvious that Sally grew increasingly annoyed at the lack of response from her daughter.

Anna explained that selective mutism, an anxiety disorder, was the diagnosis that Murph felt most accurately reflected what they saw in Lily/Bonnie. The child could talk; they had heard her infrequently, and those instances seemed to increase, but only within Anna and Murph's home.

Selective mutism is an anxiety disorder. At first, the child may be nervous about speaking in certain situations or with certain people. As her anxiety increased, so did the array of times when she felt too uncomfortable to speak. Not that she was being defiant or stubborn. She was frightened, frightened of saying the wrong thing, frightened of being put on the spot. Murph said that likely inside her mind was whirling a hundred miles an hour, tearing through all the plausible scenarios, all the things that could go wrong, the things she could say or do that would bring displeasure. He also suspected that her mother had warned her to keep her mouth shut.

THE NEXT MEETING involved the family. Again, Anna, Lily/Bonnie and the social worker were there just a little ahead of the appointed time. Twenty minutes later, Sally arrived in a flurry, gushing over seeing her beautiful little girl again. A while later Carl entered, carrying one son and leading the other by the hand. Jordy, the three-year-old, looked confused until he spotted Lily. He screamed her name and raced to throw himself at her. She met him by the booth, scooping him into her arms. The little boy hung on tight as Lily rocked him from side to side.

When the younger boy spied his stepsister, he squirmed to get out of his dad's arms and ran to Lily. She set down Jordy and picked up Benjie, closing her eyes as she held him tight. This was a real family reunion.

Carl stood patiently by, giving the children time to enjoy their embrace. When Lily set Jordy on his feet, Carl moved in for his hug. He squeezed his eyes tight, but not before Anna could see the sheen of tears. Carl kissed the top of her head, whispering, "I love you Lily. We all miss you."

If that was true, then the cynic in Anna wondered why he'd not tried to see her in over four months?

"Touching as this is, we need to order our food." Sally's tone stopped all conversation.

Anna wondered if it miffed Sally that the attention was not on her.

Sally patted the bench beside her. "Come sit by your momma, precious girl."

With her eyes still on the little boys, Lily/Bonnie obeyed and took her place beside her mother. Carl slid into the booth across from them. Jordy climbed up beside Lily. Benjie struggled to climb onto the bench by his dad. Seeing his struggles, Lily/Bonnie brushed by Jordy to lift Benjie onto the seat, then settled herself beside him. Immediately, he crawled into her lap.

Sally spoke to Carl. "Will you look at that? The princess is at it again, hogging all the attention."

Anna wasn't sure if Sally realized that she and the social worker could hear her comments.

That left only fifteen minutes of the visit. Sally half-raised herself out of the booth, searching for a server. Catching the eye of a woman wearing an apron, she said, "*Now*, if you don't mind. We'd like to order." Consulting none of her family, she ordered a large latte and pie for herself, a coffee for Carl and one strawberry milkshake with three glasses that the children were to share. When the food arrived, she admonished, "Lily, be careful how you pour that. It's expensive and I don't want any wasted or a mess on the table. I'm wearing white pants, you know."

CHAPTER 28

This was to be Bonnie's first unsupervised visit with her mother. Anna was nervous; Bonnie seemed indifferent. Used to asking her foster daughter questions, then gauging the answer by Bonnie's expression and body language, Anna remained uneasy. While Bonnie agreed she wanted to go, when asked if she was excited to see her mother, all Anna or Murph got was a shrug. They exchanged expressions in the front seat while Bonnie stared out the window in the back.

The agreed upon location this time was a park. Murph was familiar with it, having walked his dogs there when he lived in a previous house. He liked the social worker's choice of locale. It was quiet and open, a serene place to spend some time together, but he shared Anna's misgivings. It was one thing to have a visit while another adult was present, someone to run interference if something untoward was said to Bonnie/Lily.

Despite now knowing her actual name, they

continued to call her Bonnie at home. That had been Bonnie's choice. They'd asked her several times if she preferred they call her Lily or Bonnie. When he said, "Lily", Murph held out his right hand. When he said, "Bonnie," he extended his left hand. Each time they gave her the option, Bonnie touched the "Bonnie" hand. They'd checked in again just this morning, running through the same procedure. This time, the girl responded by speaking. She clearly said, "Bonnie." So, Bonnie it was.

Traffic was heavier than usual, with a detour around road construction. So, they arrived just a few minutes before their meeting time. Glancing around the parking lot, they saw no one walking or waiting around.

"Bonnie, do you see your mom's car?"

After checking in all directions, Bonnie shook her head and settled back to wait. Murph wondered just how much waiting this child had done in her life. Ten minutes of sitting in the car with the airconditioning running grew old. Murph shut off the car and suggested they go for a walk, keeping the parking lot in sight.

The day was pleasant, sunny and warm, the kind made for a stroll in the park. They walked up and down this side of the paved walkway three times before Bonnie stopped and pointed. Turning into the parking lot was a vehicle she recognized.

The three hurried to meet the car as Sally parked. Expecting just the mother, it surprised them when Bonnie ignored her mother and rushed to open the back door. With practiced hands, she undid her brothers' car seats. She lifted Benjie into her arms as

Jordy clambered out on his own, then clasping his big sister's legs. Bonnie tried to set Benjie on his feet, but he was having none of it. He clung to Bonnie's neck, not letting go for anything.

"Ungrateful kids," complained Sally. "Sure, no time for their mother now after all the work I did to get them here."

Turning, Bonnie gave her mother a half-smile, while keeping one arm around each of her brothers.

Sally reached into the car to rummage around in her purse. She brought out a package of cigarettes and a lighter. She put one in her mouth and lit it, while putting the rest of the pack into her roomy jacket pocket. She pressed the button on her key fob to lock the car doors and pocketed the keys. "Well, are we going to stand around here all day? I've got better things to do than to huddle in some parking lot."

Neither Murph nor Anna wanted to leave yet. As much as they'd tried to be understanding, they had not warmed up to Bonnie's mother. Nor did they trust her.

Murph went over the rules the judge had laid out. "We'll leave you guys and be back here at three o'clock for Bonnie. You are to remain in the park." He pointed to the left. "There are swings, slides, a sandbox and some climbing structures over there." He tried to sound optimistic. "The kids will have a great time."

He checked with Anna. Her eyes said that she was still uneasy.

"Bonnie, take this, please." He handed her his mobile phone. "Put it in your pocket. If you need us for anything at all, call Anna and we'll be right here."

Bonnie nodded. She'd used his phone before and knew that Anna's number was speed dial one. She slipped the phone into her back pocket.

Jordy jumped up and down at the mention of slides. He'd loved it the one time he got to try one out. He tugged on his sister's arm, urging her in the direction Murph had pointed. Bonnie shifted Benjie to her hip and went with her brother.

Shrugging, Sally followed behind, blowing smoke out of the side of her mouth.

Murph and Anna remained in place, watching until the quartet made it to the play area. Sally immediately sat herself on a bench some distance from the swings and slides. It was hard to tell from where Murph and Anna sat, but Anna felt Sally wore a bored expression.

"I know a little coffee shop only a few blocks from here. What do you think about waiting there, rather than going home?"

"The closer we stay to Bonnie, the better I'll feel," replied Anna. "I don't like this."

Murph grinned and put his arm around her. "You mean you don't like *her*."

THEIR TIME at the coffee shop dragged. Not that they didn't enjoy each other's company. They did, they really did, but thoughts of Bonnie wore heavily on their minds. Each kept checking their watches for the time.

The judge's orders were for this to be a private visit between Sally and Lily/Bonnie, without the watchful eyes of any social worker types. He hoped that only the two would be closer and show more of a typical mother-daughter bond.

Hmph, thought Anna. Doubtful. But she kept those thoughts to herself.

Because the judge stipulated that this was an unsupervised visit, Murph and Anna timed their return to be as close to the three o'clock hour as they could get. They did not want to be accused of sitting in the parking lot staring at Sally and her daughter.

As they pulled into the parking lot, their eyes widened, and they looked at one another before swivelling their heads in all directions. Murph pulled into their previous spot. That was easy to do because the parking lot was empty. Entirely empty.

Panic filled Anna. Had Sally taken off with Bonnie? Had they lost her?

Already out of the car, Murph took her arm and pointed. Off to the left, they could see a girl with shiny black hair pushing a much smaller child on the swings. Checking his watch, Murph saw it was now five minutes past the hour when the visit should have been over. Taking Anna's hand, they walked as quickly as they could to the play area.

"I see him," said Anna. "Jordy's sitting in the sandbox. The kids are all here." What a relief. But where was Sally?

Near to the swings was a cinderblock building that housed the washrooms. "Anna, would you go check the women's washroom? Maybe Sally stepped in there."

Murph waited, one eye on the children, the other on the direction Anna had gone.

She returned minutes later, shaking her head. "It's empty," she said. "No sign of Sally."

Worry mixed with anger. True, Bonnie was legally old enough to babysit, and she was a responsible girl, but this was to be a visit between her and her mother.

Pasting smiles on their faces, Anna and Murph approached.

Jordy saw them and ran to them from the sandbox. He had on just one shoe. Calling to Lily, he said, "Your mom and dad are here."

Exchanging glances at the little boy's choice of words, Murph and Anna continued to Bonnie's side. Murph put one arm around her and gave a sideways hug. "Hi! Where's your mom?"

Silence. Bonnie's face was a mask, the type of hidden expression she hadn't worn since her first few weeks with them.

There was movement beside Bonnie. Looking down, he saw Jordy. He pantomimed bringing his first two fingers to his mouth, sucking in, holding his arm stiffly to his side, then blowing out. He did it twice.

He couldn't mean what Anna thought he meant, could he?

Murph asked again. "Where is your mother?"

"Gone for a smo…". Bonnie's hand clamped over Jordy's face, halting the rest of his sentence.

Hmm.

"You kids keep playing for a bit longer. Murph and I'll sit on that bench over there." Anna pointed at the nearest wood and wrought iron park bench.

Murph's shoulders were stiff as they made their

way to sit down and watch the children. "She left them," he said. "Just left three kids alone in a strange park. Sure, Bonnie's twelve and some people might think she's of babysitting age, but this visit was supposed to be about Bonnie. *Not* about Sally."

"Or about finding someone to take the boys off her hands."

"Look at those poor kids. I wonder how much of Bonnie's life has been spent taking care of them?"

"Mostly when she's not in school, I'd suspect." Another thought struck her. "I wonder if that's why she used to miss so much school?"

"Is that considered abandonment? That woman left three kids alone here."

"It's a grey area, I'd say," was Anna's guess. "Grey because of Bonnie's age. Legally, Sally might have not broken the letter of the law, but she certainly broke the intent of the visit Jude Bursey mandated. Then there's the morality of it."

"How do you think Bonnie feels about it?" Murph asked.

"Who knows for sure? My guess is that that girl has learned to bury her emotions down deep. She doesn't appear traumatized or terrified. I wonder if this has been a regular occurrence in her life." She watched Bonnie's radiant smile as Benjie giggled as she pushed him higher on the swing. "Damn that woman." She hurt for Bonnie.

"So, what do we do?"

"Our options, as I see them, are to wait here for

Sally's return, or to call Child Protective Services and report the boys as abandoned."

"Is this a police matter?"

"I'm not sure. She has broken Judge Bursey's order for a family visit, but we don't know how long she's been gone. My guess is that Bonnie won't tattle on her mom."

"Do we call the police?"

CHAPTER 29

"Kind of nice to have friendly police on speed-dial," Murph said as he dialed Brendan's mobile phone. "Got a minute? We have a bit of a situation here."

"When don't you guys have a bit of a situation? I used to think that I lived a quiet life until I met all of you," he joked. "What's up?"

"It's about Bonnie."

Brendan threw a balled-up piece of paper at Jake's head. When his partner glared at him, he pointed to his phone, then motioned Jake over. "Jake's here, too, now. I'll put you on speaker." He checked his phone. "Hey, isn't this Anna's number?"

"Yeah, long story. Here's what's happened. Today was the day for Bonnie's first unsupervised visit with her mother here at Windower Park, over on the east side. The woman showed up, late, of course, but not alone. She brought her sons with her. We're not sure if that was supposed to be part of the plan, but it made

Bonnie happy to see her brothers, so we went along with it. The deal was that this was an unsupervised visit, so we went to have coffee for the rest of the hour. When we got back, there was no sign of the mother. Bonnie was here alone with the little boys." In answer to Brendan's interruption, he said, "No, they're all fine. But we don't know if they should have been left alone. And we don't know where the mother is. The visitation should have ended half-an-hour ago, but she's not here."

Muffled curses came through the speaker to Murph's ear. "Yeah. Double that. What are we supposed to do? We can't take Bonnie and leave the boys here alone. It doesn't feel right to pack up the boys in our car and take them home, either." He watched the youngest boy as he struggled up the rope ladder that led to the slides. "Is this classed as abandonment? Should we call the police? Child Protective Services?"

"You just called the police, buddy. Hang tight. Jake and I are on our way, but it will take us a while to get there. I'll send a cruiser your way. There's a precinct nearby, so one should be there in about five minutes. In the meantime, have Anna call CPS. She has contacts there. My guess is that they'll send someone over, or have the police take the kids into their care until CPS can take over."

Jake was on the phone making arrangements.

Brendan warned. "Don't let Bonnie's mother take off with the kids. Stall her if you can, but it might not be possible. If she's already left, the police will take your statement, then take over from there."

Murph clicked off the phone and returned it to Anna. "How's Bonnie going to take this, do you think?"

"I hope she doesn't feel like we're ganging up on her mother."

"Someone needs to!"

"Too true. But I don't want Bonnie to lose trust in us."

"She's been with us for months now. She must know our intentions."

"Let's hope so, but those nuclear family bonds are tight. And I get the feeling that she's used to being the adult in the room, protecting her mother, and protecting the boys as well."

In the distance, they could hear sirens getting closer.

Bonnie's hyper vigilance came out. Her head tilted toward the approaching noise. She quickly checked that her brothers were nearby and called them to come to her. Called them. Anna actually saw her open her mouth and the boys ran to her.

Thankfully, Bonnie led the little boys toward Anna and Murph. They rose to meet the kids, just as the siren shut off and a police car came to a stop beside Murph's truck.

"I'll go," said Anna, and she went to meet the officers. Murph followed more slowly with the three children. He tried to give Bonnie a reassuring smile. "It'll be fine," he said. He led the children slowly toward the parking lot.

Bonnie's look said that she didn't believe him. Likely things had all too often not been fine in her young life.

Having finished her story, Anna and the officers waited for the other four to arrive.

"Look," Jordy tugged at Bonnie's hand. His eyes shone. "A real police car. Maybe I can sit in it. Look at the lights!"

Murph thought that there was a very good chance that the child would have a ride in that car.

Between the information that dispatch had relayed and Anna's information, the officers were at least partly prepared for what might happen next.

Bonnie halted about thirty feet from the vehicles. She looked around her. Anna watched her tighten her grip on Benjie's left hand and Jordy's right. Then she turned and sprinted toward the nearest bushes.

Prepared, the officers caught up with her before they had gone far. Anna and Murph were right behind them. One police officer hefted a little boy into each of his arms. The other officer stood in front of Bonnie, blocking her way. The child's eyes darted to the left, then the right, as if seeking escape. Anna was there by then, putting her arm around Bonnie's shoulders.

"It's all right, Bonnie, you're safe." She pulled her in for a hug, then turned her around. "See, your brothers are fine." Benjie had his mouth around the corner of the officer's shoulder microphone. He giggled when a crackling came over the transmitter.

The group began walking back toward the vehicles. When they were almost there, Murph and Anna turned to Bonnie, forming a trio. Time to tell Bonnie what was going on. She deserved answers.

Anna began. "Sweetie, there's a problem. You know

that. Your mother was supposed to stay here, to be with you and the boys. She was not supposed to leave."

Bonnie spoke. "It's okay. I looked after them."

Anna hugged her again. "Yes, you did, you took fine care of them. But that's not the point. The judge said that your mom was supposed to be here from two to three o'clock. You mom broke that ruling."

Murph took over. "We should have left here at three o'clock - you, me and Anna. But we couldn't. We could not leave the boys alone."

Bonnie looked at Murph's truck. Her eyes seemed to say that there was room.

"The judge gave us permission to be foster parents to you. We don't have permission to take the boys with us. They belong with your mom, but she isn't here. That's called abandonment. We're not allowed to take the boys with us. In a few minutes, people from Child Protective Services will be here to take the boys to a safe place until we find your mother. Or these police officers will take the boys to Child Protective Services. They'll be fine, just like you were fine when you stayed with Janice and Kevin."

Bonnie's eyes flickered around, as if she was trying desperately to form plans. "But..." she started. She didn't finish her sentence as another car roared into the parking lot, screeching to a halt, far too close to where the group stood.

Sally threw open her door, tossing her still-smoldering cigarette onto the grass. "My babies! Are they hurt? Are they all right?" She reached for Benjie.

"Let go of my son. He's not done anything wrong. You can't arrest him."

"No, ma'am. We are not arresting your children. We are taking them into protective care."

"Why? Their mother is right here."

"What is your name, please ma'am? May I see your driver's license and registration?"

"Oh, for God's sake. You're not going to give me a speeding ticket."

"No, ma'am." He held open the back door of his cruiser. "Please have a seat here and we'll get this straightened out."

"I will not! Let me have my babies."

The office gently took Sally's left arm, escorted her into the back seat, then shut the door. Through the closed windows they could hear the rumble of her yells, but the words were muffled.

At first startled by their mother's appearance and screaming, Jordy and Benjie went silent. But when the officer jiggled them up and down and twirled in a circle, they were soon laughing. Maybe their mother's rants were common and easily forgotten.

Opening the driver's door of his car, one of the officers stuck his head in to talk to Sally. "Ma'am. Ma'am." He had to wait for a lull in her tirade to be heard. "Is your license and registration in the glove box of your car?"

Somewhere in the cursing and howls of outrage, there must have been an assent. Before anything further transpired, two cars joined them. One contained Jake and Brendan; the other belonged to social workers from Child Protective Services.

Bonnie gave the two men a half-smile. Jake ruffled her hair while Brendan gave her shoulders a squeeze.

"Things are under control here, I see," stated Brendan. Everyone looked composed except for the banshee in the back of the squad car.

The social workers introduced themselves. One was an acquaintance of Anna's. Anna took her aside and quickly filled her in on what was going on. The woman nodded. That jived with the information given to her and her partner. They pulled child seats from the trunk of their car and secured them into the back seats. They had done this all too many times before.

Bonnie tensed, guessing what was about to happen.

"It's okay," reassured Anna. "The boys will be safe."

Brendan squatted down in front of Bonnie. "Here's what's going to happen. You'll go home with Murph and Anna, like usual. I will take your brothers to a safe house, like the one where you stayed before you moved in with Anna and Murph."

Bonnie's eyes roved to her mother, yelling and kicking in the back seat of the police car.

"Your mom will be safe, too," Brendan assured her. "They will take her to the police station to get this straightened out. They'll call Carl to come, too." His eyes went to Anna's. When she nodded, he continued. "Your mom made a mistake. She shouldn't have left you guys alone. That was against the judge's orders. Then she was not here to take her sons home with her when she was supposed to. That was wrong. She'll need to answer why she did that. Do you understand?"

Bonnie nodded, but her eyes were on her mother.

Sally's face was a grotesque caricature with her nose mashed against the window, her hair askew, and her mouth smeared with lipstick. They could hear Lily's name coming from the woman's maw, mingled with cuss words.

Lily/Bonnie winced.

Brendan squeezed her hand. "You did nothing wrong. You did everything right. You looked after your brothers, kept them safe, and they had a good time playing with you."

"None of this is your fault," Anna said. "Brendan's right. You did nothing wrong. Your mom made a mistake, and she did something wrong, not you."

The social workers motioned they were ready. The one officer carried the little boys to their car, relinquishing Benjie first. Seeing the strange woman, the little boy cried. He called out for Lily. Sensing a turn of events, Jordy also began to cry. He squirmed to get out of the officer's arms, reaching for his sister and calling for Lily.

Bonnie/Lily's eyes filled with tears and she took a step forward.

Anna restrained her. "Shh. They'll be fine. They're just scared. Remember how you felt before you got to Janice and Kevin's house? Then you saw it was all right there. Your brothers will be fine. They'll be fed and taken care of. You'll see them again."

With the little boys safely strapped in and one social

worker sitting in between them, their car drove out of the parking lot.

One officer got into Sally's still-running car. He turned off the ignition, picked up Sally's purse to take to her, then locked Sally's car doors.

As both officers got into their cruiser, through their open doors Sally's screams came clearly. They involved repeated words - her daughter's name, profanity and "all your fault". Then the doors shut, and that car left the parking lot.

CHAPTER 30

$\mathcal{I}$t was late when Carl and Sally got home. It actually could have been earlier, but the interview with the police kept getting sidetracked when Sally went into a rant. Reining her in was never easy at the best of times, but it was especially bad when she'd been thwarted. The interview with the police went on and on and on.

There were several reminders that the interview was being recorded. That did not deter Sally in her venting about the injustices she'd suffered.

She had nothing good to say about her daughter, Lily. As Sally told the police, it was all that little b….'s fault for calling the cops on her and for no good reason, too. Despite repeated reassurances that no, Lily had made no calls at all, Sally's belief held firm.

She could not see that any blame for the situation rested at her feet.

Sally believed Lily to be ungrateful, after all the things her mother had done for her.

Carl dared to interrupt. "She's a good kid. Look how much time she spends with the boys." At Sally's curled lip, he added, "Sometimes I think she spends more time with them than you do."

"Well, naturally," was the retort. "She's closer to their own age. And she has no other responsibilities."

Looking for just such an opening, one officer brought up Lily's poor attendance record at school. "Why is that?" he asked.

"I do not know why these people haven't been sending her to school. It is shocking. A young woman needs her education."

"Ma'am, I was referring to her attendance record when she resided with you."

"Oh." The officers swore they could see the wheels turning in Sally's head. "Sometimes she needed to help her family and take care of her brothers. We've been under stressful situations. Carl here lost his job and things have been tough since then. If not for his brother, we'd have been out on the street."

"Yes. Now back to your children. We have a copy of the judge's orders about your visits with your daughter. The times are stipulated right here." He turned the paper around so Sally could read it. "You have a copy?"

Sally nodded.

"Did you note the timeframe?"

"Yes, but you know how things are, especially with kids. They never run on a schedule. I'm sure the judge understands that."

The police officer continued. "You left the park, leaving your children alone there."

"No, I mean yes. It wasn't how you're making it sound. The kids were fine. No one else was around to bother them. And Lily watched them. They love her and the kids had a great time playing together." She looked at Carl. "It's not like it's the first time Lily's taken care of them."

"You can say that again."

"Do you feel your daughter is old enough to be in charge of her brothers?" This time it was the second officer asking.

"Of course. She's done it for years," assured Sally.

The officer pretended to check his papers. "Can you tell me again how old she is?"

"Twelve. She's twelve."

Gathering up their papers, the officers excused themselves to make calls.

RETURNING, they set an appointment card in front of Sally. "You're to be in Judge Bursey's office at nine o'clock tomorrow morning."

"Nine in the morning!" Sally protested. "No way."

"She'll never make it out of bed by then," Carl muttered.

"He'll need to talk to you about abandoning your sons and whether visitations with your daughter should continue."

Sally leaned forward. "I. Did. Not. Abandon. My. Sons." She rose. "My kids were fine. They were with Lily. I'm a wonderful mother, you can ask anyone who knows me."

.   .   .

***

ELIZABETH AND TIMOTHY sat in the waiting room, about to see Dr. Hancock. This was their third appointment. It brought back memories of the frequent appointments Elizabeth had had to take Timothy to when his seizures were out of control. Now they only saw the pediatric neurologist once every three months, and hopefully they'd soon be down to semi-annual check-ups. The fears of a more serious seizure disorder were lessening as Timothy seemed to head toward a seizure-free state. Dr. Muller even talked about cutting back on the meds if things continued along this path.

But this, this was different. As scary as the seizures were, facing the prospect of another diagnosis was daunting. While there was the hope that the seizures would lessen and then stop altogether, if Timothy was autistic, that was something that would never go away.

Keira had helped put this into perspective. "Your kid is your kid. This is the way he is. Whether you have a label to put on it changes nothing about that kid. What a diagnosis would mean is that you and the school know where to look for strategies that might help him. The goal is for him to function as comfortably as possible. Who cares what the label is? He's still Timmy."

"Timothy," Elizabeth had corrected.

Keira grinned. "Sure thing, Liz."

Elizabeth threw a napkin at her friend.

. . .

THE ASSESSMENT TEAM let Elizabeth watch through a two-way mirror. After what she and Timothy had been through, she had trouble trusting him with strangers, including recommended professionals. Her heart stuttered, recalling almost losing her son at the hands of the psychologist, Dr. Mayberry.

This way, she was just one room away and could watch everything that went on and hear every word through the speaker system. He had already had appointments with the occupational therapist and then a speech/language pathologist, a different one than he saw for therapy.

Today, he was with a child psychologist. They were doing something they called an ADOS, an Autism Diagnostic Observation Schedule. Timothy was cooperating, mostly. Some things he refused to respond to, yet Elizabeth was positive he knew the correct answer. Other times he responded in ways that surprised his mother. This same psychologist had done an Autism Diagnostic Interview with her, while the occupational therapist played with Timothy in the other room. These professionals were sensitive to Elizabeth's reluctance to leave her son alone with a stranger, so all interactions took place where Elizabeth could watch through the two-way mirror. She would have preferred remaining in the room with him at all times but accepted their explanations as to how this might taint the assessment results. Still, she'd be happy when this was all over.

.　.　.

***

"Want to tell me your take on the mother?" Judge Bursey asked.

Anna regarded him steadily.

The judge grinned. "If you can't say anything nice, don't say anything at all. Is that it?"

"I think she struggles to put her children's needs ahead of her own."

"I'm reluctant to cancel visitations."

"I see that. Bonnie, I mean Lily, is attached to her mother and most certainly to her little brothers."

"I'm curious about her name. Now that you know she is Lily Ramirez, have you dropped the 'Bonnie'?"

Anna shook her head. "We asked Bonnie, and she preferred we continue to call her Bonnie."

"That's telling." The judge leaned forward on his desk. "There is a tight bond with these siblings, or rather, step-siblings. I'd hate to break that. I'm reluctant to allow more unsupervised visits, but the child and her mother still need contact. Anna, I know that this is intrusive, but would you and Dr. Murphy consider holding the next few visits in your home with one of you present?"

Anna thought for a few minutes. "I'll talk with Murph and let you know, but my guess is that we'll agree."

CHAPTER 31

"You landed on your feet here," Sally told her daughter. "I told you you'd be fine." Her glance took in the deck with the outdoor kitchen and the huge patio doors leading into Anna's and Murph's living room. "Better than fine." She wondered how she could use this to her advantage. These people obviously had more than they needed. As Lily's mother, she deserved some of this, too. After all, she was sharing her daughter with them. They owed her. She placed an arm around Lily.

The girl stiffened, not used to physical affection from her mother.

From nearby came a wail as Benjie tripped and fell.

"Better go see to your brother," Sally directed. She settled herself in one of the lounge chairs. She could get used to this way of living.

.   .   .

THROUGH THE WINDOW, Anna watched. Bonnie/Lily was great with the little boys. Their mother, not so much. She quickly stifled that thought. No need to be unkind, and she really didn't know the woman well.

Anna diced more onions and added them to the pan to begin caramelizing. There would be eleven of them for supper tonight and she planned to simmer a large pot of chili all afternoon.

The sliding door opened, and Sally came in. "Smells good in here." Best to keep on the right side of this woman, Sally thought, even if the bitch had called the police on her at the park. Maybe that had worked out for the best, if it brought her into this house. Some good would come of this. She reached into the purse she'd left by the front door. "Forgot my smokes." She flicked a lighter.

"Sorry. No smoking in the house, please," Anna warned.

"Okay." Stuffy people, Sally thought. "I'll go to the patio then."

Stooping to reach into a bottom cupboard, Anna pulled out a foil pie plate, then hurried after Sally. "You can use this for an ashtray."

Sally looked from the pie plate to Anna and back. "Right."

EVEN TO SALLY'S urban mind, it was quite pleasant sitting here in the sun, with a mild breeze. It would be better if the yard wasn't so noisy with hollering and laughing children. Why Lily couldn't keep her brothers quieter, she'd never know. Especially since Lily rarely talked herself, you'd think that she'd encourage the boys to be quieter. But no, if anything, she seemed to egg them to race around and yell.

Jordy came trotting by her, the little Corgi mutt running full tilt behind him. One of the dog's paws stepped on the edge of the pie plate, flipping it, the ashes and butts it held onto the patio pavers. Oh well, Sally said to herself. It was their dog that did it. She watched as the breeze swirled some ash into the air and two butts tumbled head over heels into the grass.

Next, Benjie came screaming up to her, wrapping his grubby little hands around her legs. She was sure that he'd get something on her skirt, but glad that her legs were bare, so no little boy handprints remained. She brushed him away, and he ran as fast as his little legs could carry him, back to where Lily sat under that one, enormous tree.

Sally's peace fractured. Besides, she was restless. She'd never been one to be satisfied for long with her own company. She needed things to be moving and shaking, she told herself. This quiet life was not for her. How had she settled into such a mundane existence? She knew, just knew, she was destined for better things than this.

Rising, she strolled down the driveway to the sidewalk that wound around the meadow. There were other homes on this street, although few, since each owned five-acre lots.

The road curved up and to the right, following the edge of the Murphy property. A nice place, if you were into birds and grass and isolation. Might be okay for an afternoon, but Sally needed more out of life than this.

Just up ahead, she could see a silver SUV parked at the curb. Maybe a Toyota of some kind. As she got closer, she could see the back of a man's head. He was in the driver's seat, looking at a map. He paid her no heed when she walked by.

She walked as far as the sidewalk went; no way was she wearing these sandals through the meadow grass or the dirt path. Who knew what creepy crawlies might touch her toes? She turned around to retrace her steps back to the house.

Approaching that SUV again, she was curious. Why was it parked here in the middle of the boonies? It was about halfway between Murph's property and the next acreage. The driver held the map against his steering wheel but wasn't looking at it. Instead, he was watching the three children playing in the meadow. Staring at them, actually. Every few moments his attention veered between the house, then back to the kids. Weird.

Sally slowed as she neared the vehicle. That was one fine looking specimen of manhood and all she could see were his shoulders and head. She put a little more hip movement into her stride. Yes, now he noticed her, although he seemed to divide his attention between the playing kids and her. Well, she could fix that.

She strolled around the front of the car to the driver's side window. Leaning down, she peered in at him. "Hey, there."

The window rolled half-way down. The man eyed the bosom that was in front of his face.

"Are you looking for someone?" Sally wiggled just a little as she said that. Yes, she had his attention now, firmly fixed on a part of her anatomy of which she was particularly proud.

"I'm always on the lookout for that special someone," replied Alejandro. He gave her a knowing smile. "Are you special?"

"So they tell me."

"What are you doing way out here?"

"I'm doing a visitation thing with my kid." She pointed out the window. "See that girl out there? That's my Lily." She looked coyly at Alejandro. "Do you think I'm old enough to have a daughter that age?"

Alejandro laughed. He hit the automatic unlock button. "Are you finding it hot in the sun? Why not sit in here and enjoy the air conditioning?"

"Don't mind if I do." Sally got in, making sure that her skirt rose to just the right height on her legs. Then she put one knee over the other.

Alejandro's look said that he appreciated the sight. His attention turned again toward the kids as an especially loud giggle reached them.

Sally noticed that his eyes mostly followed Lily. "She's beautiful, isn't she? Takes after her mother."

Alejandro's hand brushed over Sally's thighs as he reached into the glove box, pulling out a pair of binoculars. He raised them to his eyes and adjusted the focus. "Yes, she's a good-looking girl. In some circles she'd be highly sought after."

Sally eyed him. Alejandro was watching Lily in an assessing way, but not with the same leers that Archie had given her. No, Sally did not think that Lily was her rival with Alejandro. But he was definitely interested in her. Why?

A LARGE TRUCK DROVE BY, slowing as it approached, the driver taking in every detail of Alejandro's SUV. The truck kept going, turning into Anna and Murph's driveway. The man opened his door, holding a phone to his ear and talking. His eyes didn't leave the silver RAV4. A woman got out of the truck's passenger side and opened the back door, leaning in. She soon emerged with a small boy. As soon as he climbed out, he raced to meet the other children playing in the field. While the woman went into the house, the man started toward Alejandro's car.

"Babe, I think it's time for me to get out of here. You coming?" He started the car.

"Sure." Sally reached for her seatbelt and snapped it in place. "This place is too tame for me."

Alejandro gave her knee a squeeze, then pulled away from the curb, heading away from the man. Alejandro wasn't sure, but he thought the man had just snapped a picture of the back of his car.

Alejandro grinned at Sally. Maybe this day was not a lost cause. This woman looked a little old, a little saggy, and a little sad. But she still had potential and the right attitude. "Are you up for a little fun?"

"Sure. Always." Sally's reply held no hesitation.

CHAPTER 32

*J*ake joined Keira and Anna in the house.
"Did you notice that car?" he asked their
hostess.

"That grey SUV? Yeah, it's been here for about a half
hour, just sitting there."

"Hard to say, but it might be that same car Brendan
and I chased last week. Could be my imagination,
though. The guy took off as I started toward him. I got a
shot of the license plate though and just sent that off to
Brendan. He's not off for another hour."

He stood watching at the patio doors. "Kids look like
they're having a good time."

Keira joined him. "I don't know if Daniel likes the
little boys or the dogs better." She turned to Anna.
"Speaking of little boys, where's their mother?"

Anna looked up from stirring the pot on the stove.
"Out on the patio. Not playing with the kids much, but
at least she's watching them."

"Ah, not so much," contradicted Keira. "She's not here."

"Maybe she got tired of sitting and went for a stroll." Anna was confident that the woman would stick around for the entire visit this time. Sally had not been pleased to have the police called on her after abandoning the kids at the park. Plus, the judge had been clear that any more instances like that and she'd lose her visitation privileges.

"Do you think she could have been the woman in that guy's car that Jake and I saw? If so, she left with him."

THEY SAT on the same side of the plush, upholstered bench in the hotel's lounge. This time of day there were few customers and the corner booth felt private.

Alejandro was getting a good feeling about this woman. While Anna had not fallen in with his plans as easily as he had hoped, he might have just found a replacement. He wasn't that picky; he simply needed someone to keep the girls in line.

This first stage of the dance though required some effort on his part. He could exude charm when he tried, of that he was confident. So far, it seemed to work. Now to see what would lure her in.

Reaching into his back pocket, he pretended his phone had vibrated, and he checked the message. "It's nothing," he said to Sally. "Nothing as important as you." He smiled.

Sally simpered, or at least Alejandro was pretty sure that was the word to describe her reaction to his compliment. Yes, she would be easy to manipulate.

Sliding his finger up on his iPhone, he had an idea of what might reel her in. "Want to see some pictures of my place?"

"Of course." Sally leaned closer, her chest resting on his upper arm.

"I have a little place in the hills." He knew his estate was impressive by almost anyone's standards. This woman hanging on his arm didn't look like she had much acquaintance with wealth or class. Turning his phone to landscape view to better see the pictures, he showed her the perfectly landscaped grounds with the flower beds, fountains, cabana and pool, flagstone patio and sheltered gazebo.

Her eyes got larger with each one. Alejandro didn't tell her how cheap the labor was to maintain the place in this pristine condition. The photos didn't show the high concrete block walls, nor the razor wire along the top.

"Where *is* this place?" Sally asked.

"In Mexico, not too far from the border. It's in the mountains, and the climate is perfect." He opened another album on his phone. He'd done this many, many times. It always worked; women fell for the place and came willingly. "Want to see the inside?"

"Ooo, yes, of course."

If Sally had thought the grounds were something, she was in awe of the high ceilings, the tiled floors, and the sheer size of the place. "How many bedrooms?"

"Ten, although only three of them are suites."

"Who cleans the place?"

"I have an excellent staff. The head maid and the cook run the place, really. They keep the rest of the staff in line."

"Staff? How many are there?"

Alejandro shrugged. "I'm not sure. I've never counted. Juana and Josefina run things for me. They do the hiring. I have a bookkeeper who keeps track of payroll." Among other stuff, he thought to himself.

"What I wouldn't give to see a place like this."

"Maybe you will someday, maybe you will." He finished the last of his whiskey and soda. The noise level in the lounge rose as the after-work crowd came in. "Would you like to go upstairs? I have a nice suite."

∽

IN ENSENADA, MEXICO

"Is it time?"

Oh, she hoped not. Evaline tried straightening, tried to school her expression so that the cramping pain didn't show. She wanted to hang on to this baby as long as she could. Even if she couldn't physically hold it in her arms yet, their lives intertwined. Labor and birth would change that, and she'd lose the bond forever.

But Juana had seen this too often not to recognize the signs. She tapped on her mobile phone. "We have another one ready." She put away her phone and gently took Evaline's arm, steering her toward the room permanently at the ready

- the birthing room. Juana took care to make it pleasant. After all, these girls were frightened and in pain. Always. For most, it was their first pregnancy. Having a calming room with soothing colors, fresh flowers and a comfortable birthing chair was the least they could do for them. Hopefully, all went well, and this was the only room they'd need. Next door was a room outfitted as a medical clinic where more drastic procedures happened, but thankfully, rarely needed. For that, Juana was grateful. She trusted the skills of the midwife, well, mostly, but the doctor was a different matter. His instructions were to save the baby at all costs. He was an obedient man.

This time Evaline could not hold back the groan. By Juana's estimation, the pains were coming more quickly now. This might not take as many hours as it usually did with first-time births.

Nurse Manez, as she liked to be called, arrived within the hour. Juana doubted that the woman actually had credentials to back up her title of nurse, but if it pleased her to be called nurse, then so be it. The woman was hard enough to get along with as it was. Warm and fuzzy she was not. If a young girl thought that she'd get handholding from the midwife, she was sadly mistaken. Juana tried to step in and do that part when she could. A little hand patting, a damp cloth on the forehead, a few ice chips pressed to the lips, the little things she could do to ease the torment these young women went through.

Juana thought back to her own experiences with childbirth decades ago. Four births, resulting in three children. Was the death of a babe any harder than struggling through hours of agony pushing out a child, only to have that child taken from you?

But these women knew what they were getting into. Oh, the first ones hadn't, back then when this operation was working out its kinks. Some even believed that they'd been randomly rescued by an organization whose aim was to help pregnant women with nowhere else to turn.

They did. They helped them. For some, that meant escaping the dangers of the streets to spend the rest of their pregnancy in the luxury of this estate. They were well-fed. They received excellent, well, adequate medical care. They were safe here. None of that would have happened had they remained on the streets. The fates of their babies might have been worse than the children born on the estate would experience. Anyone willing to pay big pesos for an infant must want to be parents awfully badly and would take care of the child they had bought.

EVALINE CRIED OUT. The stoical stage was over, and the signs of panic rose in the girl's face. Soon the midwife would knock her out. While Juana would have preferred other methods, she wasn't in charge, but she had to agree that it was easier to do what had to be done without a screaming and writhing body to contend with. It wouldn't be long now.

CHAPTER 33

*E*lizabeth checked caller ID and saw that it was Brendan from his work number. Odd. She thought that he'd be nearly at her house by now. "Hi. Did something come up?"

"Yeah. It might be nothing, but I need to check it out. Hang on a sec." He held the phone away and answered a question from his captain. "Jake and Keira are already at Anna and Murph's place. Jake spied a vehicle idling nearby, and he thought it might be the same one we saw hanging out there last week. The car drove off before Jake got to it, but he snapped a picture with his phone. It's only a partial plate, but we're checking it out."

"Are you still coming to pick us up?"

"Not sure. If this vehicle belongs to someone on the street and there's nothing suspicious about it, then yeah, I'll be over. But if it is this Alejandro guy again, then I'd better stay on this. Until we know for sure, I think that you and Timothy should stay in your house with everything locked up tight. And tell Cynthia and Amy to do the same thing. The captain and the Mexican officials are sharing information. They're far from figuring this out yet, but they've heard rumours. He's not a nice guy."

"Okay. I'll call Cynthia and we'll wait to hear from you. Should I let Anna know?"

"I'm talking to Jake as soon as I hang up with you, so he'll tell her."

THE ROBES WERE the most luxurious ones Sally had ever seen, let alone tried on. Gorgeous things. She almost hated to remove hers to get into the jetted tub. But Alejandro's welcoming smile convinced her. Round two, or was this three?

SHE WAS PLIABLE ENOUGH, thought Alejandro. And she was greedy for nice things. He looked her up and down from the corner of his eye. She might have a few more baby-making years in her. Not many, but maybe she could pop out one or two. She was certainly an enthusiastic partner, so it wasn't a hardship. Not that any of them were, really. He was careful in his selection; they only wanted good-looking babies. No one wanted to buy a homely kid. He reached for the champagne in the ice bucket stand and topped up their glasses.

Tilting his head back, he blew out smoke from his cigarillo. Sally had never had one before but was game to try. He sensed that she'd be game to try anything.

"You like this?" He motioned around the room.

"Of course," she said, snuggling into his side. "Who wouldn't?"

"Could you get used to this kind of life?"

"In a heartbeat." She didn't have to think twice. This was what she was meant for.

Casually, Alejandro threw out the bait. "I might have a job. I'm looking for a woman to act as my assistant."

That got her attention.

"But the job comes with responsibility. I'm not around all the time, so I'd need this person to take charge when I'm away."

Sally sat up. That calculating gleam was back in her eyes.

"I initially came up here to offer the job to Anna Sanchez."

"Anna! What would you want with her?"

"I knew her years ago. But now that I've talked to her again, I'm not so sure that she'd be right for the job."

"I'm sure she's not." Trying not to appear too eager, she probed for more details. "Where is this job? In town here?"

"No. You know those pictures I showed you on my phone? The ones of my estate? It's there."

"In Mexico?"

"That's right. But it would not be solely at the estate. There is some travel involved."

"Travel?" She'd always wanted to travel.

"Yes. With me. Mainly around Mexico, but sometimes in other countries." He checked around the spacious bathroom. No, no clothes, except for the hotel robes. Still, best to make sure. He got out of the tub and picked up their robes from the floor. Surreptitiously, he shook each, but nothing dropped out. He'd already checked the clothes Sally had been wearing and her purse. No wires.

"Where ya going?"

"Nowhere. Just wanted these off the floor so they don't get wet in case we have activities that create waves."

Sally almost purred. But as pleasant as she expected the next minutes to be, she kept her eye on the prize. She was more about the long term than simply this moment of pleasure.

"What's this job about?"

"There are young women at my estate. We take them in. They're young and pregnant. We give them a place to stay, healthy meals and a safe environment until they've had their babies."

"Then they leave?"

"Some do. Some stay on."

"What do they do?"

This was the tricky part, but if Alejandro read her right, moral standards were not this woman's strong suit. Besides, they were providing a service, a much-needed one if his profits and the waiting list were any proof. "We run an adoption service. These are young, single women with no means to care for a child. Some don't want a child, but found themselves pregnant. We take care of these women, then after the birth, find homes for their babies. Good homes, often wealthy homes. These children will grow up in far better circumstances than did their mothers." He watched Sally's reaction. She didn't blink.

"What's the job, again?"

"Ah, I didn't explain that very well. As I said, these are young women, not experienced with life. They require someone a bit older, more mature to guide them. Someone who is calm and won't get in a flap about an approaching birth. Being upset is not good for the woman or for her babe. Plus, it ruins the atmosphere of the estate if there is discord."

Sally shook her head. "No one likes discord," she echoed.

"At times it might require a firm hand organizing the girls. Some are quite young and still act like children. They need to get along."

"You don't want cat fights."

He grinned. "Ah, you understand."

Sally grew up with three sisters, all close in age, all competing for the same lone bathroom at the same time and all wanting to borrow the same clothes. It was often not pretty.

"This job. Where would the person live?"

"On the estate. In your own separate suite of rooms, of course. There's a bedroom, sitting room and bathroom reserved for this employee. And free room and board, of course."

"And a salary?"

"Oh, of course. Did I not mention that?" The starting wage he mentioned was more than both Carl and Archie brought into the house together. And there would be no expenses to come out of that.

Sally tried to think of the negatives. "Would I, I mean the person have to cook for all these girls?" She hated cooking.

"No, no, definitely, no. I have a cook for that. And a housekeeper who looks after the place. They each have helpers they are in charge of." He sipped his champagne. "This job is more of a management position, not labor." He liked that glint in Sally's greedy eyes. "Is this the type of job that might interest you?"

The first words in Sally's mind were, "You bet!" But she was savvy enough to believe that there was benefit to playing hard to get. She pretended to hesitate.

"What is it? Is the salary not in the range you were expecting?" He waited. "We might be able to go a little higher if that would seal the deal." He named a figure twenty percent higher. He thought he had her now.

"What about the travel that you mentioned?"

"From time to time, when we have room to take in new girls, we would need to travel. I'd want my assistant to be good at finding the right girls, ones who were healthy, but in need of rescue. It would mean befriending them, helping them, and getting them to trust you, then staying with them in a hotel until we were ready to travel back to the estate." He motioned around the room with his glass. "Of course, we would stay in hotels like this. We'd treat the girls right, too, just not in suites such as this."

"Of course not." She thought a minute. "You cover travel costs as part of the job?"

"Yes, that's definitely included, as is getting from here to the estate. I have a jet that takes me where I want to go." He believed he'd baited the hook well. Now to just give a little yank. He'd see if he could remove any of her last hesitations. "But you are married, no?"

"Sort of."

"How can one be sort of married?"

"I'm not sure I'll be married much longer. It's not working out. Irreconcilable differences, you know?"

Yes, he knew, He'd bet that the differences were between the amount of money the poor sap brought in and the amount that Sally wanted to spend. One last hurdle. "You have children?"

"Ye-es." Sally hesitated. This was a guy who might understand. "I have two little boys. They weren't really my idea. I never saw myself as a mother - too much to do, you know?"

Alejandro nodded.

"Carl really wanted kids and they sort of just happened. And before that, I had another kid. A girl, the one you saw. I was young and stupid and got pregnant when I didn't mean to. Sort of like the girls you help. Back then, I would have thanked anyone who looked after me, then found a suitable home for the baby." She made a face. "Babies are messy things. Noisy and dirty and always wanting something." That made her think. "These girls, do we have to look after the babies until they're adopted?"

He shook his head. "We have a system. There is quite a waiting list. As it's coming time for the birth, we pair the waiting adoptive parents with the soon-to-be-born child. The new parents often get the baby the day it's born; they prefer it that way. That's another reason I need a jet ready at all times."

"Sounds like a perfect setup."

"It is. Interested?"

BRENDAN LOOKED across the desk at his captain. Progress had been slow, excruciatingly slow.

Not that the Mexican police weren't concerned, they were. Very. They didn't like human trafficking, especially when infants were involved. But finding information on Alejandro was difficult. No one knew much about him; those who did know weren't talking. The federales assumed that Alejandro paid well and bought loyalty.

EVALINE'S INERT form offered no resistance as the midwife cleaned her. The placenta had delivered nicely. The babe was already bathed and dressed and swaddled. They were just waiting for the chopper to land to take him on the first leg of his journey to his new home. The awaiting parents had been notified with the exact minute the child made his existence into this world, his weight, healthy state, footprints and photos. They were thrilled that by late tonight the child would be theirs. They had already wired the second half of their payment. To them, fifty thousand in US currency was nothing to finally have a child of their own. This couple even had a wet nurse installed at the house already.

Together, Juana and the midwife hoisted the frail form of Evaline onto a trolley then wheeled her into the room she shared with one other girl. It would be a while before Evaline woke up. Giving birth was hard work, plus she'd need to work the drugs out of her system.

CHAPTER 34

There were a few more details Alejandro needed to get straight. He decided to be blunt. "What about your kids?"

Yes, that thought had crossed Sally's mind. She kept trying to shove it away. This was *her* time. She'd spent enough years devoting herself to kids. Carl was the one who wanted children. Let him look after them.

"How old is your daughter?" Alejandro made sure his voice sounded casual.

"Twelve." While the girl was useful in looking after the little boys and around the house, Sally didn't enjoy having a teen in her house, or an almost teen. She hated that people would think she was old enough to have a kid of that age. When Lily was young, people made such a fuss over how pretty she was. But now, the kid rivalled Sally herself. Especially with Archie. Ah, but she'd not have to worry about that anymore if she went with Alejandro. Archie could do what he wanted.

"Twelve. That's a little young for baby-making, no?"

"Yeah, a bit, although some girls have kids when they're in their early teens." Sally eyed the man beside her. "Why?"

"Just wondering. If she was a little older, maybe she might have joined our stable. You know, had a pleasant life with us and produced some babies. Girls have them so easily when they're young and nubile."

Sally was catching on to something. "These adoptions. Do they pay a lot?"

Looking directly at her, Alejandro confirmed it. "Yes. A lot."

"Is it only babies they pay for?"

"In the past, yes, but we are thinking of branching out. There are other ah, markets and families looking for older children." He left it hanging.

"What kind of people?"

"Wealthy people, very wealthy people. Ones who hand over cash and can well provide for a child."

Sally thought of the way she'd grown up. The life her children were experiencing was not much different. What if, in exchange for some nice money, she could guarantee that each of her kids could grow up in luxury? "What kind of money?"

"This is a new venture for us, so I am not as certain about the price as I am for newborns. If I had to guess, I'd say somewhere in the nature of fifty thousand for a healthy child."

A swift thought flittered through Sally's brain - too bad she hadn't had more kids. "So I'd get fifty grand and my kid would get a good home and a grand life."

"*We'd* get fifty grand. There are expenses I'd need to take out of that sum and a finder's fee."

"Yes, of course."

"And once the money changes hands, we cannot guarantee what happens. But then, you had no guarantee when you had a baby just what kind of life he would have. All I can guarantee is that it would be a wealthy home."

"Money matters."

"Yes, it does."

"My Lily. I have a worry about her. She is, ah, blossoming, becoming a woman. She's a very pretty girl. Her stepfather's brother, Archie, stays with us. He's taken an interest in Lily and not an uncle kind of interest, if you know what I mean. That's why I had to get her out of the house, for her own protection. That's why she's staying with Anna right now. If I left and Lily went back home, I would worry for her safety."

"A mother would worry about her child. By all means, bring her with you, if that would make you feel better. We'll find a place for her."

As MUCH AS Sally hated to leave the luxurious comfort of this hotel room, a niggling worry bothered her.

"You know what that bitch, Anna, did to me? The last time I was just a few minutes late collecting the boys, she called the cops on me. Can you believe it?"

Wary, this got Alejandro's attention. "Cops? We don't need them."

"No, no one does."

"When are you supposed to get your sons?"

"Ah, well, we didn't exactly say. I mean, the judge had talked about two-hour visits, but you know how kids are."

"How long has it been?"

Sally reached for Alejandro's wrist and pulled his watch toward her. "Almost three hours, give or take a bit."

"Get dressed."

Sally slid the robe slowly off her shoulders, smiling at Alejandro.

Tempting, but with Alejandro money came first. Always. "We can play this three ways," he explained. "We can stay here and have some more fun."

Sally smiled and approached.

"But, if we do that, the cops will probably look for you. That will make it harder to get away, if you are coming with me to Mexico. You're fun and all that, but I'm not getting caught, not for you or anyone. I might have to leave without you."

Sally pouted.

"Or, we could leave now for my plane, just the two of us. You'd work for me."

"The third way?"

"We could go back for your kids. If you think you could grab them quickly, we could leave on my jet tonight with them." He waited. "Your choice."

While Sally might seem like a gal all about the moment and having fun, that wasn't really her. Sure, she needed to squeeze as much enjoyment as she could out

of her miserable life, but she was a planner. Or liked to
think of herself as one. The promise of future colossal
sums of money sounded good to her. And I'd be buying
my kids a better life, she told herself.

When she told him her choice, Alejandro smiled that
smile that women in his stable feared. Yes, this Sally
would fit into his organization well. He could use her
for a while.

They formed a plan.

"Hi, Anna. This is Sally. Would you believe it? I had a
flat tire."

"But your car's here. I can see it in my driveway and
the tires look fine."

"Not that car. I mean the one I'm in. But this nice
man came along to help, and it's all fixed now. I'll be
there in ten minutes for the boys." She hung up before
Anna could ask any more nosey questions.

ALEJANDRO PARKED some ways from Murph and Anna's
house. He got out and disappeared through the trees.
Sally came around and got in the driver's seat. She liked
that Alejandro was always thinking. He was not like
Carl or even Archie, who seemed to drift through their
days. Alejandro thought things through. He came up
with two plans.

If there were signs of police around looking for her,
Sally was to let them see the silver RAV4, then lead
them away. She'd go to the parking garage of the hotel

they just used and climb to the fifth level. Parking the car, she'd take the stairs up to the penthouse and let herself into their suite. She'd stay there until Alejandro called. Then she'd follow step B of their plan.

If there was no police presence, then Sally would go in and collect her sons. Nice and simple. She'd wait for Alejandro's call, then drive to the small local airport where the jet waited.

They doubted that Anna and Murph would hand over Lily. No, they needed another plan for that.

Alejandro would make his way through the woods and come out behind the house. In his pocket were the keys to Sally's car.

In a bag were two hamburger patties liberally laced with Benadryl. He'd seen the dogs hanging around Anna's place and needed them out of the way.

EVALINE STIRRED. The phrase 'run over by a truck' came to her mind. Everything ached. How was that possible? Her eyes pulsed in time with the pounding pain behind her forehead. She squeezed them tightly shut. No, that didn't help. It took such effort, but she raised her hands and pressed them over her eyes. She brushed her matted hair from her face. How did she get in such a mess? Evaline prided herself on her hair - long, straight, and glossy. The only time it had not been her pride and joy was during those times on the street. Not eating or sleeping had taken a toll on her locks. But once Loreen and Alejandro rescued her, her health had returned, and with it her beautiful hair.

Alejandro. That brought it all flooding back, why she was here, what she had experienced.

Her hands explored her stomach. Flatter, but not flat now. She wondered if it would ever be flat again, then chided herself for being so shallow.

Her baby was gone. She remembered part of what had happened, the pains that gripped her midsection, trying to tear her apart, and Juana telling her it would be all right. It had gone on for hours, then nothing.

Her eyes scanned the room, searching for a crib, a bassinet, any sign that her child was here. Nothing.

CHAPTER 35

Standing at the patio doors, Jake saw it.
"There's that car again. I'm going after it." He
planted a quick kiss on the top of Keira's head. "Better
get the kids in the house." With his truck keys in one
hand, he called Brendan to let him know he was about
to approach the vehicle. Once again, he only got so
close when it slowly drove off. Jake sprinted back to his
truck. He would not lose the guy this time. He sent a
text to Brendan. "It's on the move. I'm going after it."

RESTLESS AND HUNGRY after having their play
interrupted, Daniel, Jordy, and Benjie milled around.
Bonnie, more savvy than the boys, picked up on the
atmosphere among the adults. She kept looking
between Anna and Keira as if looking for answers to her
unasked questions.

Daniel saved the moment. Following Anna into the
kitchen, he asked, "Cake?"

At the rare sound of his voice, Anna turned quickly, crouching down in front of the little boy. "You'd like some cake? Sure." She raised her eyes to Keira's making sure it was okay.

Keira nodded through a glistening of tears.

Rising and taking Daniel's hand, Anna led him toward the kitchen counter where she had a frosted cake ready for their dessert.

Daniel shook his head and pulled his hand from Anna's. "Cake. Ice cream cake."

Ah. The last time they'd been here, Anna served them ice cream cake. But she had none now. Daniel, the child who rarely spoke, asked for something and she could not grant his request. "I'm sorry. I have none. This is all I have today."

Anna and Keira communicated with only their eyes. Keira nodded and reached for her satchel handbag. "Are you okay with the kids if I go get one?" Then she remembered that she'd ridden here with Jake and he'd just left with his truck. Anna offered her car keys. It would not take long to run to the nearest Dairy Queen. "Daniel, do you want to stay here with Anna and play, or do you want to come with me and help pick out the ice cream cake?"

Without speaking, he went to the door and waited for his mom.

❧

"I LOST HIM," Jake reported to Brendan. "Except I'm not sure it was the same guy. The driver seemed shorter this time, but we weren't really close to him before. The vehicle turned into the parking lot of the Hyatt. I can see the entrance and exit from here and it hasn't come out."

They arranged for officers to join him and they'd search floor by floor for the silver RAV4 with license plate 6TR J24.

SHE DIDN'T HEAR the soft snick of the door latch above the sounds of the little boys running their toy cars around the living room floor. Anna checked her watch. It was hours after the time in which Sally's visitation should end. Where was she? Anna hated to report her to the police again, but the judge would not be pleased. Would this mean an end to Sally's visits? How would that affect Bonnie? Although she didn't seem that attached to her mother, the girl adored her little brothers. Still, the nuclear family bond was strong, even if the mother didn't always deserve to be called that.

"Hello, Anna, love."

She whirled at the sound of that voice. Her eyes went to the open door, then the man standing not three feet in front of her. He always moved like a panther.

The back of the couch obscured the boys' view of his presence, but Bonnie saw him. Perched on the raised hearth of the fireplace, her wary eyes watched what was about to unfold.

Anna's first thought was for Bonnie. This child had been through enough.

"What? Not happy to see me?"

Anna remembered how Alejandro loved to taunt. He enjoyed the power.

"What do you want?" How had he gotten in here so easily? Keira must have not shut the door tightly when she and Daniel left. Anna should have checked and set the alarm system. She really should have. Now, the wolf was here, and it was her fault.

"You, my dear. I want you, of course. My job offer still stands." He half-turned to look at the three children in the living room. "But I want them, too." He gave that grin she remembered all too well. "I won't play favorites. No one has to feel left out. You will all come with me."

Anna signalled Bonnie with her eyes. She made her gaze go repeatedly from Bonnie to the stairs leading above the garage and back again.

Bonnie got it. She nodded and started toward her little brothers. Crouching, she took their hands.

Anna opened the cutlery drawer, pretending to search for something. She tried to make as much noise as possible, trying to cover the sound of the three children sneaking out of the room behind Alejandro. Slamming it shut, she then opened another drawer, reaching for the first thing that came to mind. She pulled out a rolling pin, holding it behind her back. With her hip, she shut the drawer.

Alejandro laughed. "What do you think you can do with that?" He approached. A noise caught his attention. Benjie missed a step as he climbed the stairs, but his sister's firm grip on his hand prevented his fall. Still, he yelped. Bonnie reached down and hefted him to her hip as she ran the rest of the way up the stairs, shepherding Jordy in front of her.

Anna took her one chance. While Alejandro looked the other way, she raised the rolling pin to attack.

Alejandra turned at the flash of movement. With one hand, he caught the descending piece of wood. "Anna, Anna. You're feistier than you used to be. I like that in a woman." He set the rolling pin on the counter. "We don't need this."

Anna tried to make a run for it, scooting between Alejandro and the far side of the table.

He slammed the table towards the wall, pinning Anna. She gasped with the pain as the table edge cut into her hip.

Keeping pressure on the table to keep Anna in place, Alejandro rounded the table. It was easy for him to reach around and grab her by the hair. Only then did he ease up on the table's pressure. "Anna. Calm yourself. We don't want damaged goods, do we?"

Despite the pain in her scalp, Anna fought. She knew the results would not be good if this man had his way. Not good for her or for the children. She fought. In retrospect, all those classes in Tai Chi might not have been the best option. Why didn't she study karate instead? Or kickboxing?

The table was now askew. Chairs tumbled over, but still she fought.

Alejandro grabbed her from behind, wrapping both arms around Anna and squeezing her to him.

She tried stomping on his feet, but he lifted her off

the floor. Held aloft this way, she couldn't get any purchase. Still, she wiggled, furious at how easily he had captured her. Being this close to him brought back memories. First was the scent. She remembered his smell as he lay over top of her, thrusting. The pain, the pressure, the fear and the loathing for what was happening to her. She fought the images racing through her mind. She fought being thrust back into those times, the helplessness, the futility of struggling. No! She was not there. This was now, not those times.

Alejandro carried Anna toward the sink. Grabbing the damp dishrag, he stuffed it into Anna's mouth as she panted in an effort to breathe.

Now a new stench filled her senses. Why had she not thrown that into the wash and brought out a new dishrag? Putrid food tastes filled her mouth. She gagged and shook her head. No. No more. If it stuffed in any farther, she'd suffocate.

Alejandro threw her to the floor. Keeping a knee on her back, he reached for a dish towel. Pulling on her hair, he raised Anna's head, shoved the towel under her face, then dropped her head. Her nose hit with a crunch. His knee keeping her pinned in place, he tied the dish towel around her head, keeping the filthy dishrag in place. With her arms trapped under her, she was helpless. Raising himself up a bit, he surveyed the appliances lined up on the counter. One hand dragged over the toaster until it fell to the floor. It banged into one side of Anna's head. "Oops, sorry," Alejandro said.

He yanked the cord from the toaster. One by one, he pulled Anna's arms behind her back. Using the electrical cord, he tied her wrists together. He tested the tightness. Yes, they were secure. "Ah, look at that. You have crumbs in your hair now." Gently, he brushed off some crumbs that the toaster deposited on Anna's head, then righted the toaster. "You really should clean this thing out more, you know. It's a fire hazard."

The bread machine made it to the floor next, the plastic cracking and splintering off from the impact. Its cord tied Anna's ankles together. "Now, shall we go check on those kids?" Alejandro hefted Anna over his shoulder and started up the stairs.

CHAPTER 36

*B*onnie's instincts were honed from living in a house where you never knew if you'd be safe. Life was somewhat better with Carl, but before that, she'd spent some rocky years with her mother and her mother's boyfriends. Then, when Archie moved in with them, things got tense again.

Bonnie could live with the money problems. Although only twelve, she overheard a lot and understood even more. Sometimes she thought she worried more about making the rent on time than did her mother. She understood about not having enough food in the house. From a very young age, she'd learned to accept whatever there was without complaint. It was harder for her little brothers. They didn't understand when their stomachs hurt and there was nothing to eat. But those were normal problems. It was when Archie's breath smelled in that bad way and he walked funny that his eyes got mean. Meaner than usual. Sometimes he hurt her mom. Sometimes he her hurt too, but Bonnie knew to stay away as much as she could.

This man here, though, was scary in a different way. Maybe because she didn't know him, but maybe there was something else. She'd felt it when he showed up at Anna's other house, before they'd moved. Bonnie knew that Elizabeth and Keira sensed it too from the way they'd picked up weapons and moved to defend Anna.

Now that bad man had Anna. She loved Anna, but Anna wanted her to protect her little brothers. But how? Although she'd grown a lot this past year, she was no match for a man. She'd try, oh, she'd try, but how? She looked around the room. Yes, there were lots of tools lying around. There were two cordless drills, a step ladder, cartons of screws, a box of nails, a set of screwdrivers and drill bits, pencils and squares and levels. None seemed like suitable weapons. Maybe the level, the long one. She hefted it.

From the kitchen she heard banging and crashing. Oh, Anna!

She needed to get back there to help her, but first she had to see to her brothers. There was no furniture up here, just one old metal stool. Maybe she could pick that up and bash him with it. She lifted it to test its weight. Yeah, she could lift it but didn't think she could throw it very far.

Along the one wall was the bench seat they were building. Eventually it would run the length of the left wall, but they hadn't gotten that far with it. Part was still just framed in two by fours. The rest of its length was covered with plywood. They couldn't decide whether they should make cupboard doors for storage, or lift-up lids. So, they'd just screwed on the plywood, planning to decide later. The three of them. Bonnie liked how Murph and Anna included her in their discussions as if her opinions mattered, as if she was a part of the family.

The bench area was the only place Bonnie could see to hide her brothers. Jordy first. He looked scared by all the noises from downstairs. Bonnie was too. Jordy understood about hiding and knew that sometimes it was safest to keep quiet.

Bonnie motioned to the enclosed plywood space. "In there, Jordy. Crawl in and hide."

He got the idea. He'd hidden under his bed many times.

Benjie was harder. Jordy, wise for a three-year-old, stopped his crawling, turned and called to his little brother, encouraging him to join him. That was enough to get Benjie started.

Bonnie stayed by the opening until the boys were twenty feet in, far enough from the opening that no one could see them, even if they poked their heads in the opening. It was dark back there. Benjie didn't like the dark; Bonnie hoped that he'd keep quiet. She turned to go back down the stairs to help Anna, when she heard heavy treads coming up the steps.

$\approx$

ALEJANDRO LOOKED around the attic space that was still under construction. "You don't keep a very tidy house, do you, Anna?"

She squirmed, perched over his shoulder, her head hanging down his back. She said something, but the dishrag muffled any words she tried to make.

"Let's see. What can I do with you?" He plunked her onto the old metal stool, the back support scraping her shoulder blades. "Stay," he warned her.

Anna tried to get off the high stool, but it was difficult with her ankles tied together.

"I said stay." More forceful this time. "Do not try my patience. You know what happens." He pushed her back onto the stool, then slid it and Anna towards the plywood atop two sawhorses that they used as a makeshift table. He picked up the dull, grey roll of duct tape, testing its stickiness. "Excellent."

Loosening one end, he wrapped it around Anna's chest and back again, time after time after time, securing her to the back of the stool.

It was tight, very tight. Anna couldn't take in a deep breath. Maybe it's because I'm panicking, she told herself. He won't tie me so tightly that I can't breathe. I'm useful to him.

Around and around the tape went, each tearing sound etching itself into her brain as the tape parted from the strands underneath it on the roll. Alejandro lowered himself to wrap the tape around her lower limbs and the chair legs.

Good. While his attention was elsewhere, Anna chanced getting a message to Bonnie. Yes, the child was in her stockings; they'd be quieter than shoes. Anna motioned Bonnie with her eyes toward the door. Many times she and Murph had laughed at Bonnie's preferred method of descending the stairs. She'd sling one leg over the wooden banister and slide down. They called it Bonnie's swoosh. Frantically, Anna tried to motion with her head toward the open doorway that led to the stairs, then put her head back and try to simulate the swoosh with her chin. Please, Bonnie, please understand. Sneak out of here and go silently down the stairs. Run, run out of here and hide somewhere safe.

The child got it. In a flash, she was out the door. Anna saw the back of Bonnie's leg as it lifted high to scale the banister. Moments later, there, she thought she could hear the soft thud of Bonnie's landing. Anna hoped that the sound of the tape Alejandro was unwinding had covered it.

Alejandro rose and inspected his work. Satisfied, he looked around. No kids. He wasn't worried about Lily or Bonnie or whatever they called her. He doubted she'd go far from her brothers. He'd seen her type before. Duty was stronger than self-preservation. He could work with that.

He pulled his mobile phone from his pocket and called Sally. "I'm ready for you. Go to the top drawer of the desk." He waited until she opened the drawer. "Take those keys in the folder. It tells you which vehicle they're for. It's a grey Escalade, parked on the third level of the parkade. Drive it here. I need your help to pick up your kids."

Sally pressed the off button on her phone. She

looked sadly at the robe she wore, reluctant to take it off. Her own clothes were in a heap on the floor. Sighing, she let the robe fall and dressed. Maybe she'd take the robe with her.

CHAPTER 37

Sally had no trouble finding the Escalade. Thank goodness he parked it facing out, as she wasn't sure how she would fare at backing a thing this big out of the parking spot. It was off in an isolated area anyway, with no immediate neighbors.

Nice, she thought. She'd never been in a vehicle with such soft leather. She took a minute to figure out the basic controls, then she was off. The SUV purred. It had that new car smell, and everything was spotless. Yes, this was the sort of vehicle she should be driving.

Winding her way through the parkade gave Sally time to adjust to driving something this size. She made it to the ground floor, smiling and smug. She had this.

Then she stiffened. There was a cop car and two police officers between the entrance and the exit. They were not letting any cars into the parkade. Sally had no choice but to join the lineup waiting to leave. They now wedged her in. But, she noticed that the cops just waved each car out, that is, except for one. Some poor chump drove a silver RAV4, and they were all over him. They made him pull over to the side, while the other cars drove on out.

Sally smiled and waved at the nearest cop, who gave her a small salute.

WITHIN TEN MINUTES Sally was back at Anna and Murph's house. Had it only been early this afternoon that she'd last been here? It felt like so much had changed in just a few hours. Her life had taken a major turn for the better. She gave an appreciative glance at the robe taking up space in the passenger seat. Yes, she was meant for the finer things in life.

Sally parked, reluctant to vacate the luxury of the Escalade. She patted the steering wheel. "I'll be back soon," she promised.

The front door was ajar. She slipped inside, shutting it behind her. Turning, she surveyed the mess in the kitchen, the signs of a struggle. She tensed, that feeling of panic bubbling up inside of her. She'd been in situations like this, turning over chairs to get away, dodging and pleading.

Deep breath, deep breath, she told herself. No one's after you. You're in charge now. You're with Alejandro and he has the power. Power was important.

Footsteps came down the stairs. Alejandro. "Sally, there you are. Come on. We need to get moving." Motioning for her to follow, he turned his back and went back up the stairs.

Seeing Anna trussed up in tape at first startled Sally,

then it caused her to grin. The high and mighty Anna. Look where she was now. Sally smirked.

"Get your boys," ordered Alejandro.

Sally didn't see them.

"Listen. It sounds like there's rats in here." Alejandro pointed to the boxed-in length against the wall. "They won't come out for me and I can't reach them in there."

Sally bent down to peer in the opening. It was too dark to see. "Jordy? Benjie?"

The shuffling sounds increased, and soft crying started.

"Come to momma, boys."

They didn't come.

"We don't have time for this." Alejandro picked up the circular saw and an extension cord, looking for a place to plug it in.

"What are you doing?"

"If they won't come out voluntarily, I'll have to cut them out."

"What? And risk damaged goods?" Sally wedged her head and shoulders in as far as she could. "Benjie, come to mommy. I'm here. We're going to have a treat. Are you hungry?" That kid was always hungry, always whining for something. Carl thought he must have worms.

The crying stopped, then there were scuffling noises as a small body began the long crawl out. When Benjie could see his mother, he crawled faster, grinning at her. She may not be much of a mother, but she was all he knew.

"Jordy, you come too."

More crawling sounds. Soon two dirty, sweaty young boys stood in front of her.

"Where's your sister?" Sally asked.

Jordy shrugged.

"We need to go." Alejandro lifted one boy under each arm, grimacing at the smells the kids emitted, and started down the stairs.

"What about her?" Sally pointed to Anna.

"Leave her. She's not going anywhere."

None too gently, Alejandro deposited the small boys in the back seat of the Escalade with a stern, "Stay!" The kids cowered.

"Now where's your daughter? I searched the house while I waited for you, and she was not around. But she was here when I called you."

Sally glanced around the room, trying to guess what would be in Lily's head. When there was violence around the house, the child made herself scarce, but always saw to her brothers. She'd stashed the boys away but was probably too big to fit in that hiding spot herself.

Glancing outside, the tree caught Sally's attention. The kids were always playing around it, and Bonnie was the one who led them there. Maybe…. "Come on," she told Alejandro. It felt good to boss someone else around. She headed off, reassured to hear his footsteps following her. Good. Alejandro acted like he was in charge, but Sally would turn that around, little by little.

.   .   .

THE LEAVES WERE thick and lush, so it took a few minutes to spot the toe of a white sock perched high in the branches. There was no way Sally was climbing up there to bring the girl down, so she'd just have to rely on talking. After all, Lily had been obeying her mother all of her life.

"Lily, honey, what are you doing up there?"

No answer. Well, Sally had not really expected one. The kid rarely spoke.

"Time to come down. We need to get going."

Other than the breeze rustling the leaves, there was nothing. Sally's patience, scarce at the best of times, was waning. She had an idea. She said quietly, "Alejandro, go wait in the car. Let me speak to Lily alone."

"With the kids? You've got to be kidding me."

"It's just for a few minutes, then we'll be along."

With a sigh, he turned and left, muttering in Spanish as he went.

What, did he think she didn't speak the language as well? Perhaps she'd keep that knowledge to herself for now.

"Lily, honey, I need you to come down. Your brothers are all alone with that man. Do you think that is a good idea?"

A branch creaked.

"Here's the truth, Lily. You're old enough to know. We have to do some things. We are going to go live in a wonderful estate where there is always plenty of food." That should do it. Lily was always trying to rustle up something for the boys to eat. "It's a beautiful place, with plenty of room for your brothers to run and play.

They'll be healthy and happy there, but there's a problem."

Lily climbed down a bit so that she could hear better.

This was working. Sally lowered her voice a bit more. "The problem is that I'll have to work while we're there. The boys are too little to be left on their own; that is why we need you to come with us. You know how they love you and we rely on you. You are mommy's big girl. I need you."

Now Sally could see her daughter from the knees down.

"There's another thing. If I leave without you, you'll get me in trouble. Big trouble. The police might even take me away. Then what would happen to your brothers? Do you want them left with Alejandro?"

"No!" Lily's word was quiet but forceful.

"Then come down here and help me. If you're with us, I'm not in trouble and the boys will be fine."

Lily climbed the rest of the way down, landing lightly in her stockinged feet. Conflict warred all over her face. She glanced toward the window of the room over the garage.

"Oh, she's fine," said Sally. "I was just there talking to her. She said she's expecting Murph any minute. The two of them have plans, plans that involved just the two of them. It was nice of them to let you stay with them for a little while, but it's over now."

CHAPTER 38

This was a bad day, as far as Jake was concerned. Even with two officers monitoring every vehicle that came in or out of the parkade, and two of them crawling each level of the parking lot. They didn't find a silver RAV4 with the correct license plate.

They found two SUVs fitting the RAV's description. One was an innocent guy here on a business trip. The other matched the vehicle description, but had the wrong plate. When they ran the plate, just in case, it belonged to an older woman who drove a Nissan Sentra. Stolen.

Running the RAV4's VIN led them to a Hertz rental agency. Yes, they had rented that car to a Hugo Bossman for a week. The rental period was almost up, with the option to extend it with a phone call.

There was no one registered at the hotel by the name Alejandro. Or Hugo Bossman.

Dead ends. He let Brendan know.

Neither of them had heard from Keira or Anna in a while. He'd better check in.

～

PARKING IN THE DRIVEWAY, Keira helped Daniel out of his booster seat, and then reached into the trunk for the ice cream cake. Balancing it carefully, she opened the walk-in garage door. That was closer than walking around to the front or kitchen doors.

Walking through the garage, she heard scraping noises overhead. "Sounds like the kids are up there playing, Daniel. Do you want to go join them?"

Nodding, he ran inside and disappeared from sight.

Keira opened the door that led to the utility room, and then walked down the hallway to the kitchen. "It's just us," she called to Anna. As she walked, she apologized for the cake. "You would not believe the color combinations that Daniel chose. They used whichever ones he pointed to, and I can't be held responsible for how it…". Her voice trailed off. "Anna?"

She'd been so intent on carefully carrying the cake that she didn't take in her surroundings at first. Now, nothing else filled her consciousness. Good thing she was near the table, because the cake slipped from her fingers. She took in the overturned chairs, the crooked table, the appliances on the floor. And the blood. There was blood on the floor near the sink. Oh, god, what had happened here? Quietly, she called again, "Anna?" She searched for signs of a body in the great room. Nothing.

Daniel! Had she just sent him off on his own?

Shoving the cake the rest of the way onto the table, she raced to the stairs that led to the garage's attic room. She met her son coming down the stairs and hugged him to her. Then she held him at arm's length, checking him over. "Are you all right?"

He nodded. "Anna," he said and started back up the stairs.

Keira pushed him behind her. "Stay here." Maybe there was something there that a little boy shouldn't see.

That same shuffling noise came again, the one she and Daniel had heard from the garage. Two steps more and she was in the room.

"Anna!" There was her friend, tied to a chair, rocking it back and forth. "Careful! You'll topple over." Anna was duct-taped to the high-backed stool, an old metal one with paint splatters all over it. She tried to pull some of the tape off of Anna's face. Prying gently with her fingernail, she got only a tiny piece free. This stuff had some sticking power. She needed a tool. Looking around, she didn't see any scissors.

Anna made frantic head motions toward the table saw. On the saw's platform sat a utility knife.

Bringing up the blade, Keira approached Anna's face. Anna's eyes told her to go ahead, but Keira couldn't. She just couldn't. Instead, she went behind Anna, crouched down and started sawing through some of the tape that bound her friend to the chair. Once she freed Anna from the bands holding her arms and back to the chair, Keira then sawed through the electric cord that bound Anna's wrists.

There. Her arms were free. Now Anna could work at

her own face. To make it easier, Keira slowly and carefully cut the tape behind Anna's ears. The sticky stuff wound many times around her head, badly matted in Anna's hair. But at least now Anna had some ends free so she could ease the tape from her face. Keira knelt and worked at the tape binding Anna's legs to the chair. Thank goodness her friend wore pants that prevented the tape from sticking to the skin of her legs.

The left corner of Anna's mouth was now free. Although her words were muffled, Keira heard the word she dreaded.

"Alejandro."

IT WASN'T OFTEN that Murph had to go into the office on Saturdays, but today was one of those days. That came with the territory, being a psychiatrist. Sometimes the level of a patient's distress didn't coincide with the optimal days of the week. This time the call from the patient's wife had been spot on. Things had deteriorated and Murph helped get him admitted into the hospital.

Turning into his driveway, Murph groaned. Sally's car was still here. Not that he minded having their visits here at the house, but the woman was a bit much. Her little boys were cute, but they were, well, little boys. A twelve-year-old girl was one thing, but toddlers were something else. They were on the hyper side, not at all like Bonnie. Or Lily, as her family called her. Funny that when they asked Bonnie, the girl preferred they continue to call her that. Lots of psychological implications there. Murph noticed that when the little boys were here, they seemed to slip into calling their sister Bonnie sometimes as well.

A lot had changed in Murph's life over the past year. He'd met and wooed Anna, a woman like no other. He could hardly believe his luck that she had agreed to move in with him. He'd like something more permanent, but Anna was adamant against any kind of legal commitment. He could wait.

The addition of Bonnie, a delightful young girl, had also enriched his life. He enjoyed having a family. Because Sally was Bonnie's mother, he'd plaster on a smile and be cordial to her. He had been looking forward to a few minutes alone with Anna, then dinner with their friends, but if that had to include Sally and her sons, so be it.

He had his key out to unlock the front door, but it pushed open without him turning the lock. Odd. Anna was usually strict about keeping things locked up, especially since that Alejandro had shown up at her place. Thank goodness that Brendan and Jake had arrived that time and warned Alejandro off. He'd not been back since.

Murph toed off his loafers on the boot tray, hung his keys on the rack by the door and turned.

Destruction! Murph's heart stopped. So did his lungs. He went utterly still. A thousand thoughts flooded his brain, none of them good. With effort, he forced in a deep breath, then another. He fought for control of his mind. Something had happened and Anna needed him, needed him to be clear thinking. He spied the blood on the floor. All his good intentions skyrocketed away with his blood pressure. He opened his mouth and roared, "Anna!"

UPSTAIRS, Keira and Anna ceased their efforts with the duct tape. From the corner of her mouth that was free, Anna told Keira to go downstairs and get Murph. Anna could not imagine what was going through his mind when he saw evidence of the struggle that had taken place in the kitchen.

Murph beat Keira upstairs, taking the steps three at a time. He stopped momentarily in the doorway, drinking in the sight of a disheveled, but alive Anna. Then his medical training took over. "Are you all right? Where are you hurt?" He began patting her down from head to toe.

Anna tried to grab his hands with hers to stop their movement. "I'm okay," she tried to get out. She knew that he would have noticed the blood. "Nosebleed. It's all right now." She threw her arms around his neck and just let him hold her, swaying them back and forth.

Finally, Murph pushed her away from him, far enough to look her over. "Who did this to you?" He feared he knew the answer.

"Alejandro."

"How did he get in here?"

"Sally brought him."

"Sally?"

Anna nodded.

Murph brought Anna's hands down to her sides and

gently continued working at the tape firmly stuck to her face, her lovely face.

"Just yank it," Anna told him.

"Can't do that, babe. It would hurt too much."

Keira joined them and continued to work at the tape bound to Anna's hair. She'd firmly grip a small patch of hair close to the scalp, then with her other hand, gently pull off the tape. She'd already cut the tape into smaller sections and was making some progress.

"Where are the kids?" Murph felt bad that this was an afterthought. He prepared himself for the worst.

"They took them."

"Bonnie, too?"

"I think so," said Anna, "at least that was their plan. Bonnie hid the little boys under the benches. They came out when Sally called to them. Then they left to find Bonnie.

"Why would they want Bonnie?" Keira asked. "Her mother already tried to dump her. Why would she want her now?"

Anna and Murph's eyes met. There was no good reason that they could think of.

CHAPTER 39

*A*nna tensed at the noises downstairs.

"It's okay," said Keira. "I called Jake. It sounds like he and Brendan are here."

While Jake used his phone to snap pictures of the carnage in the kitchen, Brendan was on his mobile. Still talking, he responded to Murph's yell and made his way upstairs.

Upon seeing Anna, he bellowed for Jake. They needed pictures of this as well.

Both men gave Anna a hug, relieved she wasn't hurt worse.

While Brendan updated their captain of what had transpired this afternoon, Jake put in a call to the officers who had picked up Sally a week ago.

To the best of Anna's knowledge, Sally had been about an hour-and-a-half late picking up the boys and had only spent maybe ten minutes of the two-hour visit anywhere near Bonnie. Judge Bursey would need to have these facts and, most importantly, know that Sally had taken off with Bonnie.

At least Anna assumed that Sally and Alejandro had the girl. Jake and Murph arranged for officers to search the grounds and the surrounding forest. But Sally's intent had been quite clear - she was taking all three of her children with her.

Meanwhile, a tow truck hitched up to the silver RAV4 with the switched license plates and hauled to the police compound to search for evidence. Sally's car got a tow to there as well. If Sally had been in Alejandro's vehicle, then maybe he had been in hers as well and left evidence.

Surely Alejandro had a record in this country. If not, the Mexican police would be interested in his prints.

Jake's and Brendan's captain and law enforcement on the other side of the border continued to share information, but so far, they could not find the estate Alejandro talked about, although they did not doubt its existence or that there was human trafficking going on.

A THOUGHT OCCURRED TO KEIRA. "Hey, where are the dogs?" She spied Anna's cat, Tomlins, peeking out from under the sofa.

Brendan's phone rang. "Yeah?"

"Do these people have a dog?" It was one of the officer's searching the grounds for Bonnie or evidence. "There's a German Shepherd here. He's pretty dopey."

"We'll be right there."

When Murph hesitated, Anna said, "Go, go. I'll feel

better knowing they're all right. I'm fine and Jake's here."

It didn't take long for Jake's phone to ring. It was Brendan. "Can you bring your truck? We found both dogs, but they need to go to the vet's. Looks like they've been poisoned."

THROUGHOUT ALL THIS, the slow cooker did its thing and Anna's chili cooked to perfection. The same could not be said for the ice cream cake that remained on the edge of the table. Enough of it was salvageable for two little boys and one small girl to have their fill.

While the crime scene techs did their jobs, the friends took their meal to Elizabeth's house. Cynthia and Amy joined them, but it was a subdued party. They put Anna's quietness down to the shock of her attack.

Brendan walked Cynthia to her home to pack a bag for herself and Amy. Those two would spend the night at Elizabeth's house. So would Brendan.

There would be a periodic police patrol passing that house all night, as well as Keira's where she, Daniel and Jake slept, and at Murph and Anna's.

Although welcome to spend the night at any of their homes, Anna insisted she needed to get home.

CHAPTER 40

*L*ying in bed that night, Anna had time to think. Under the cover of darkness, with Murph's soft snores beside her, there was no need for pretense.

It was all her fault. None of this would have happened if not for her. Anna's very presence had put her friends at risk, and now there were children involved.

There were always children involved. Since the start of this, innocent children had been at the heart of it.

As bad as it had been when children were just abstract concepts, just the possibility of a life and personality, it was so much worse when she actually knew and loved the child.

They had Bonnie. As much as the optimistic side of Anna wished to believe that the child's mother would keep her safe, the realistic Anna, the one who had seen too much of life, knew better. After all, hadn't Anna's parents sold her? Despite putting a prettier spin on it, that was what they had done. Was there any evidence that Sally would be any different? None.

She was grateful to Jake and Brendan and the local police for their efforts to work with their Mexican counterparts. But in all this time they were no closer to finding Alejandro or where he kept his stable. Anna had given them as much descriptive information as she could recall, but it had been over a dozen years since she had been there. And even then, she mostly saw only the inside of the compound. Yes, she had been on the road when she arrived and when she departed that final time, but both journeys had been in darkness.

Without a location, the police were unable to perform a rescue or even investigate. Their willingness to help meant nothing to those poor trapped young women.

There was only one person who had a chance of finding the location. Only one person who might be able to find Bonnie.

She watched Murph, his face relaxed in sleep. She knew what he would say. He would be opposed at her putting herself at risk in order to try to save Bonnie and her brothers. He'd say that she'd been through enough, that she didn't have the skills or the power, to leave this to the police. He'd want her to protect herself and she knew that he would try to protect her, to stop her from doing what she knew she must.

As silently as possible, she pulled back the covers.

～

ANNA LEANED her head against the window of the bus and watched the nighttime scenery go by. There were long stretches of just darkness, then the lights of some little hamlet, then black again.

This felt so wrong. Everything Anna had fought to escape. Yet here she was, returning to that which she had vowed never to see again.

With her counseling background, Anna knew the perils of suppressing memories. Yes, but there was a fine line between that and pulling them out, letting the images endlessly parade through her mind until she drowned in the pain.

As the bus slowly neared her destination, Anna could feel those memories creeping up, like slowly rising bile. Memories that she tried to believe belonged to another Anna, one that was young and naïve and trusting and weak. One who had things done to her, oh, so many things.

She felt for that young girl she had been. One who loved her family and believed that they loved her. That first year was bitter as the realization slowly sank in just what they had done to her. Would she have sacrificed herself to help them? Maybe. No, yes, she probably would have, if they have given her a choice.

Instead, they had sold her, that's what it was, a transaction. She was a means to solve the problem her stepfather had gotten himself into. She was expendable, a pawn, useful to help them build a new life. A life without her.

The sorrow came flooding back. Well, she remembered that day when she had finally made her way back to their family home. The gruelling trip had taken days and days of walking and riding dirty, crowded busses, but finally, she made it.

Walking up the driveway, she expected to be welcomed with hugs and tears and gratitude. After all, Anna had given up several years of her life for them, and too many assaults on her body to count.

But they weren't there. They'd left. No one knew where they had gone; no one knew of any messages they'd left for their only daughter. Her mother, father and two younger brothers vanished.

Had Alejandro known? Surely he was still in touch with her father. Had Alejandro told them that their daughter had left his estate? Did they care?

They sold Anna and allowed her body to be used, their grandchildren forcibly stolen. No, Anna didn't need people like that in her life. Anyone who could do that to their own flesh and blood was evil and deserved nothing from her. After that day, Anna had never tried to find her family again. She vowed to make her own way.

And she had. Anna was proud of the life she created for herself. She was educated. She had a rewarding career where her work was respected and valued. She did well in a world that had not been kind to her. She turned her back on her family, and did her best to erase from her mind the effects of those years when she was Alejandro's chattel, to do with what he wanted.

Anna rarely allowed herself to think of the children who had been removed from her body and taken. It was too painful. When she saw the endless stream of neglected and mistreated children who came through the court system, she prayed that the children her body had produced lived good lives. Surely anyone willing to pay that much to buy a baby would provide them with love and care. She had to believe that.

The buyers were not the evil ones, she kept telling herself. The evil lay in those collecting and selling human infants for profit. And in men like Alejandro who thought nothing of lying with vulnerable young women, whose only goal was to impregnate them so there would be another baby to sell. It was like a puppy mill for humans.

Never would Anna put herself into their hands again. Never!

But they had Bonnie. Bonnie/Lily, whichever name they should use, they had her. If there was any chance of rescuing Bonnie from the life that Anna had experienced there, it was up to Anna to do what she must.

The bus climbed into the hills of Ensenada.

CHAPTER 41

*M*urph rolled over, automatically feeling for Anna to pull her toward him. Mostly asleep still, he squirmed closer, his arm searching for the warmth of his lover, his partner. Sweeping his arm across the covers produced nothing.

He sat up. The door to their ensuite bathroom was open, with no sounds or light. Maybe she was downstairs. It had been a very rough evening for her; maybe she couldn't sleep. She should have woken him. Throwing back the covers, he went to look for Anna.

It didn't take long to search the house. There was no sign of her. Turning on the exterior lights, he could see that she wasn't on the patio or anywhere around the outside of the house.

He had a bad feeling. Heading to the garage, he saw her car was missing. Where would she go at this time of night? It was almost four in the morning.

He called her cell phone. Faintly, he could hear the jazz tune that Anna used to signal incoming calls. He followed the direction of the sound, but it stopped. He dialed again, this time getting a better lead on where the ringing came from. Upstairs, above the garage. The same room Alejandro had been in. Was it only yesterday?

He ran up the stairs. There was Anna's phone, sitting on the table saw. Had she been unable to sleep and thought to do some work up here, setting the phone down then forgetting it? He looked around. No, the project didn't look like anything had changed recently. Why would Anna's phone be here and not with her in her car?

That bad feeling intensified. No. Oh, no, she wouldn't. She couldn't. After all they knew about this bastard, she wouldn't go after him herself, would she? Two of their best friends were cops, guys who knew what they were doing, guys who had resources to call on, guys who were not vulnerable women who'd been brutalized by Alejandro before.

After searching everywhere to see if Anna had left him a note or any sign of where she was, he sat down at the kitchen table. It was four thirty-five in the morning. Close enough to five. He dialed.

"Brendan, we need your help."

THE BUS STATION in Ensenada had changed little since Anna last saw it. Maybe the seats had been replaced. But the weary ticket seller looked like he had not been. Who knew if he was the same person who had sold her her ticket out of there over a decade ago?

Anna bought a ticket to the town of El Refugio. That was as close as transportation could take her to the estate.

Anna paid in pesos. Before leaving her car in her office parking lot at home, she had stopped at an ATM, withdrawing as much cash as her daily limit allowed, then taking out more money as an advance on her credit card. An Uber took her to the bus station.

Once across the border, she had exchanged some of her dollars for pesos. She wore a small purse attached to her belt. Apart from that, all she carried with her was a backpack of Bonnie's. She packed only a small change of clothes, not wanting to awaken Murph. And she needed to travel light.

She was older and stronger now, but not necessarily in better shape. She remembered the long, long, winding, dirt mountain road to get from the estate to El Refugio. They had driven her the last time. Today, she would have to walk it. She wore jeans and sneakers, prepared for her hike. She just hoped that she could do it in the daytime. She also hoped that she'd make it there and back out.

"ALL RIGHT, I'M COMING." Carl thrust his legs into the jeans thrown beside the bed. The knocking on the door started up again. Wiping the sleep out of his eyes, Carl pulled open the door to find two police officers glaring at him. The same two he met before, Hernandez and Boyd.

"Is Lily Ramirez here?" While Hernandez remained on the steps asking questions, Boyd stuck his head in the door, shouting out Lily's name. Silence greeted him.

"No one's home but me," explained Carl.

"Where is your daughter?"

"She's not my daughter; she's my wife's daughter. And she's living in foster care."

"Where is your wife, sir?"

"I don't know."

"You don't know where your wife is?"

"I worked the night shift yesterday. When I got home, I could hear my brother snoring in his room, but no one else was around."

"Is it unusual for your wife to not be home at night?"

Carl squirmed. He hated airing that his marriage was not the ideal partnership he'd hoped for. "Sometimes," he mumbled.

"What about your sons?"

"They're usually here."

The officers regarded him steadily.

"Sally's a stay-at-home mom, so I assumed the kids were with her."

"Just not at home."

"Sally's like that sometimes."

"Mr. Skyes, do we have your permission to look for the child in your home?"

Carl stepped back and motioned with his arm for them to come in.

While Boyd began a search, Hernandez detained

Carl in the entryway asking questions. "Are you aware that your wife took the girl Lily away from her foster home without permission?"

"No, why would she do that? She dumped her off to get rid of her. Why would she take her back?"

"That's what we want to know. Let's continue this down at the station."

"WE CAN'T JUST head to Mexico and hope that we'll run into Anna. It only works that way in movies."

"I'm not staying here," Murph said. "I'm going after her."

"Yes, and we're with you, but we can't just go running to the border." Brendan tried to be reasonable. "We need a plan."

"My plan is I'm going and I'm bringing her back."

Brendan and Jake looked at each other. Brendan's phone rang.

"We might have a lead," his captain told him.

"Jake's here, too. I'm going to put you on speaker phone."

They'd been working on finding Anna's parents, hoping they might leave a trail to Alejandro's operation. It was all they had so far. "The problem was, they'd changed their name. Several times, in fact. Her father is not a nice man, but his gambling problems made him worse." The captain explained the scams they knew this guy and his wife ran. Plus their sons. These two young men might just be the lead they needed. "One is eighteen, the other twenty. They're close to their mother, so keep in touch with her. We're trying to access their mobile phone records, but there are jurisdictional problems, and we don't have enough probable cause. We're watching the mother and may get at things from that end."

"Anything we can do to help?" asked Jake.

"Not yet. I've got people looking into the father. From time to time, he goes to Mexico. When he comes back, his debtors seem to ease up on him. We don't know yet just what he does south of the border."

CHAPTER 42

"*M*urph, you can't just go off half-cocked." Jake tried to reason with him. "We don't know where Anna went."

"Yes, we do. She's gone to Alejandro's, that place where he held her and raped her."

"Yeah, I agree, but we don't know where that is. Mexico's a big country. Are you just hoping you'll come across her?"

Murph glared at the man. "Every time Anna has been in trouble, I've not been around. I arrived too late both times. She needs me now, I know it."

"I get that. But if she needs you, you don't want to be in the wrong place. Just give us a bit more time."

"Time isn't something Anna has."

"You don't know that. Look, we have bumped this up to priority. This is now kidnapping, and possible trafficking. The FBI is involved. The Violent Crimes Against Children International Task Force, too. They're on this right now."

Jake's phone vibrated, and he put it to his ear. "That was Brendan. Some news at last. They're still working on locations but have a general idea of where to look. Brendan will be here in a minute to pick us up. We'll head to Tijuana and wait to hear where to go from there. Early this morning, Anna's passport registered at that border crossing."

ANNA HAD FORGOTTEN what the dry heat was like. It was one thing within the walls of the compound with its greenery and shade trees. Out here there was just dust. Oh, and iguanas, she'd forgotten about them as well. Mostly they just regarded her with their tongues flicking in and out, wondering what she was doing here, trudging along this dirt road. Anna wondered about that, too.

She'd forgotten to bring a hat. The Southern California sun didn't seem quite this intense. She stopped to take a swig from the one of the water bottles she'd bought from the OXXO service station before starting on her walk. This *felt* like the right road, but who knew? She took just a small drink. One bottle was already empty, and she didn't know how long she'd need to make this one last. If she'd chosen the wrong road, it would be a long walk back to town so that she could try again.

It was almost thirty minutes later that she heard the sounds of a vehicle. Knowing what could go on in some of these isolated, rural areas, Anna got herself off the road. She lay down behind some rock outcroppings to watch.

Two men in a jeep drove by, windows down, music blaring, a shotgun in a rack on the back window. Funny. Something about the passenger's head looked familiar. Maybe that was a good sign, and he was a guard she'd known back when she lived here. No, that wasn't right; this guy was too young to have worked there a dozen years ago.

As the sound died away, Anna dusted herself off and continued, sticking to the side of the road and alert for sounds of approaching vehicles.

Around a few more bends, she saw it. She'd remember those gates forever. Imposing, fortified, and guarded.

At the side of the road was the jeep, that same jeep, now empty of its occupants. Four men stood conversing and laughing in front of the gate. Four at once. Well, she had not thought this would be easy. Taking a deep breath, she approached, watching the men intently.

One in particular caught her attention. This was the guy in the jeep.

No, it couldn't be. She had not seen him since he was a child, but surely this wasn't… "Danny?" The word was out of her mouth before she could stop it. So much for a surreptitious approach.

The men stopped talking. One whipped his head around to stare at her. After an intense look, a slow smirk broke out.

"Anna, big sister. It is you. Alejandro said you'd be

back." He laughed and nudged a younger man. "Hey recognize sister dear?"

As the other man turned, Anna could see in his face the little boy he had been. Manuel. As a small child he'd followed his brother around, looking at him with adoration. Looked like that hadn't changed. But why were they here?

"Alejandro said that you wouldn't be able to resist the money he offered, especially when he increased the incentive. He told us about the tiny place you lived in, compared to all of this." He swept his hand toward the gates.

This was not the family reunion Anna had hoped for all of those years ago. There was no warm and fuzzy feeling coming from Danny. Manuel looked uncertain.

"Go ahead, little brother," directed Danny. "Open the gates. I'll radio Alejandro that she's here."

IGNORING the leering gazes of the other men and the mocking one of Danny, Anna entered through the imposing gates. She winced as she heard them lock behind her. All those images of being trapped flooded her brain, the desperation to get out, the bird in a gilded cage feelings, and now she was back.

Well, it was done now. Murph came to mind. He would be furious at her. And hurt; she hated to hurt him, but there was no choice. Without her, Bonnie's fate was sealed. Anna continued up the winding driveway to the haughty building ahead.

A woman waited for her on the front steps of the estate house, a woman Anna had never met. Although the physical place remained familiar, it made sense that in over a decade, the staff changed.

The woman, wearing a weary smile, came down the steps with her hand extended. "Buenas dias. You must be Anna. We've been expecting you."

Anna's innate courtesy made her smile in return, but she did not know yet if this woman would be friend or foe. After all, Alejandro could charm when it suited his purpose.

"Come in. Alejandro insisted that you have your same old room."

Anna could not prevent the dismay from showing on her face. That lizard. He knew just how to twist the knife.

The woman squeezed her arm. "It'll be all right. Things are different here than you might remember."

Yeah, Anna just bet. Could they be worse? Alejandro was now stealing twelve-year-old girls. They entered the bedroom of Anna's nightmares.

"Alejandro had me buy you a new wardrobe. He was specific about what he said you'd like." She opened the closet to show Anna a colorful array of clothing on hangers. These were far from the muted and pastel colors Anna preferred. It would be just like Alejandro to have stipulated these colors and revealing styles on purpose to taunt her.

"Anna!"

Before Anna fully turned toward the sound, a tight hug engulfed her as Bonnie buried her face in Anna's shoulder. She wrapped her arms around the girl, holding her tightly, rocking her slightly from side to side. Then, holding her at arm's length, she brushed the child's hair from her face. "Are you okay?"

Bonnie nodded.

"Of course, she's fine. Why wouldn't she be?" Alejandro's grinning voice came from the doorway. He entered and stroked Bonnie's head.

Bonnie shrank against Anna's side.

MURPH PACED THEIR HOTEL ROOM. Jake lay on one of the beds, channel-surfing, while Brendan scrolled through messages on his phone. They'd been through surveillance jobs too many times to let their nerves show. Much of police work was a waiting game. This was especially frustrating since it was out of their hands.

They were here as observers and advisors, offering what they knew about the operation on the American side of the border. Out of courtesy and cooperation, the Mexican law enforcement team kept in contact.

Brendan's phone vibrated. Murph's pacing stopped as he saw Brendan raise his mobile to his ear.

Ending the call, Brendan stood. "They think they have a location. We can go, as long as we remain at the back and keep out of the way." Used to being at the heart of the action, this was tough for him and Jake, but better than nothing.

Murph was already at the door.

"Ah, Murph," said Jake. "We're not walking there, but do you think you should put on your shoes?" He picked up the two small duffle bags they'd packed for Anna and Bonnie. If they found the two of them, they might want to change into familiar clothes. *When* they found them, Jake corrected himself.

CHAPTER 43

*a*nna shifted so that her body was between that of Bonnie and Alejandro.

Alejandro laughed.

Behind him appeared Sally. "What's *she* doing here?" She looked Anna up and down. Yeah, Anna was definitely wanting, she thought. Not nearly as attractive. She smiled up at Alejandro, wrapping a hand around his bicep.

"She's come to look after my girls."

Sally scowled. "I thought that was *my* job."

"It was, but now that Anna has graced us with her presence, it's not. Anna's the one I wanted. She has just the right nature for my needs."

This was not going the way Sally planned. "*I* meet your needs, don't I?"

He patted her hand. Best keep these women calm and doing his bidding. "Of course you do, darling. Anna meets *different* needs than you." He waggled his eyebrows at her and watched as Sally's shoulders relaxed. Keeping women mellow was a lot of work. That's why he wanted Anna here. She played no games, and her calmness would help keep the peace. As his stable grew, this was more and more of a problem. Dios, these women fussed and squabbled like children.

IN THE DISTANCE, a sound grew louder. "Ah, it's almost here," Alejandro said. He gestured to the hallway. "Shall we, my dear?" He led Sally away.

BONNIE LOOKED AT ANNA QUESTIONINGLY. Anna knew that sound. It was ground into her bones from all those years ago. The helicopter. That meant it was coming to take away someone's baby.

Could she stop it? How?

"Wait here," she told Bonnie.

She took the right corridors by instinct, the layout of the mansion coming back to her. How often had she searched these halls looking for a way out, a place to hide? There were none, she knew that, but still she had tried.

Footsteps sounded behind her. Looking over her shoulder, she saw Bonnie. The child had not obeyed. Would Anna have in her position? Likely not. She held out her hand for the girl, then they hurried on.

Opening a side door into the broad patch of lawn area, Anna saw the helicopter had already landed, its rotor still moving. Climbing into the machine was a woman. In her arms was a wrapped bundle. Two men, each holding rifles, helped her into the front passenger seat.

Two other armed men stood on the other side of the chopper, while a further pair faced outward, scanning the garden.

This was new. There'd never been guards inside the estate before. Had some of the women tried to fight? The gates were barred, so the opposition had not come from outside the compound. Anna admired the courage of the young mothers who had fought for their babies. She doubted they'd been successful.

She turned as excited little voices came from the side of the house. There was Sally, each hand firmly clasped around one of her son's. They'd dressed the little boys in identical miniature navy suits, with white shirts, and shiny patent leather shoes, their hair wet and slicked down. The boys pointed at the helicopter, their feet dancing as they went with their mom toward the huge, noisy machine.

"Yes, you get to go for a ride." Sally's voice bubbled with enthusiasm. "Won't that be fun?"

About ten feet away, Benjie's free hand went into his mouth and he tried to hang back.

Sally shook his hand. "Come on!"

Alejandro stepped out of the shadows, his strides rapidly taking him to the trio. He swooped the child into his arms, then sat him atop his shoulders. With his free hand, he tickled the child, making him giggle, forgetting his momentary fear.

· · ·

DREAD FILLED ANNA'S SOUL. No, just no! She could not be witnessing this. It could not be what she thought it was. No mother would willingly give her children up to who knows what. Not even Sally, surely.

Anna's instinct was to rush forward, grab the boys and run. But to where? She well knew that there were no hiding places here and no escape. The armed guards would not let her through.

And what about Bonnie? Right now, no one seemed to have noticed them. Were they planning to secure the boys, then come back for Bonnie? She needed to hide her before she could think about trying to save the boys.

Bonnie tugged on Anna's arm. She pointed at the helicopter with an enormous smile. Her brothers were going for a ride. Couldn't she?

"No, no, child. It's not what you think," warned Anna. She pushed Bonnie behind the base of a bougainvillea. "Stay here. Keep quiet. I'll be back for you."

Without checking to see that Bonnie obeyed her instructions, Anna raced across the wide expanse of lawn toward the helicopter. Ahead of her, a burly man in the chopper reached out as they passed each child to him. He strapped them into seats, then placed himself between them. He handed first Jordy, then Benjie a small paper cup of liquid, helping Benjie to drink his.

No, thought Anna. Don't drink the Kool-Aid. She watched as Jordy smiled, then handed his empty cup to the man.

Anna's motion caught the attention of guards. Weapons no longer at their sides, they pointed at Anna.

Alejandro stepped forward, raising his hand to his men. "It's okay, I've got this," he hollered to them. He wrapped his hand around Anna's upper arm and gave a shake.

"Quit it," he told her. "You can't stop this, you know that." He pointed at Sally. "See? A mother letting her boys have a ride. What could be better?"

XB-ARO. Anna said the aircraft's call letters over and over in her mind. She watched helplessly as the helicopter lifted into the air.

CHAPTER 44

*D*inner was bizarre. Anna was so tempted to skip it and cloister herself in her room with Bonnie, but she needed to eat. Her stomach rebelled at the thought of stuffing it with food, but she might need the nutrients for what was ahead.

Eighteen young women, in various stages of pregnancy, ate in two sittings in the huge dining room. Alejandro, Sally, Bonnie and Anna shared a smaller, more elegant dining room that had once been Alejandro's office.

Sally seemed over her pique about Anna taking the job she felt Alejandro had promised her. Who knew what the man had given to appease her? Smug was the only word to describe her now.

As their soup bowls were removed to make way for the entrée, Alejandro motioned for Anna to rise and join him in the other room. Chatter in the main dining room ceased as Alejandro's shoulders filled the doorway.

"Evening, ladies," he said. "There's someone I'd like you to meet." He pulled Anna from behind him, placing her close to his chest. Too close. With one hand on each of her shoulders, he squeezed. "This is Anna. She'll be your main go-to person. She was once one of you." He paused, pleased at their gasps. "Yes, she was. She went away and got herself educated. Now, she's chosen to come back and help us out. She'll be an asset to our household."

Anna held herself stiffly, determined not to flinch at the pressure on her shoulders. Never show weakness with this man.

She looked into the eyes of the young women seated around the highly polished table. One by one, as instructed by Alejandro, they gave their first name, their expressions ranging from smirking to pleading. They looked healthy, every one of them but for one smaller member with her chair slightly distanced from the others. Her dark eyes pierced Anna's; in them Anna saw her younger self.

Twisting from Alejandro's grasp, Anna whirled, heading for the kitchen. Passing the open door to the small, private eating area, she nodded her head sideways to Bonnie. The child understood and followed Anna. Sally, engrossed in pouring herself another glass of champagne, didn't seem to notice. Or care, thought Anna.

She pushed through the swinging door into the kitchen where several people worked. Juana looked up.

"We'll take our plates to my room, please," Anna told her.

Juana hesitated, glancing toward where Alejandro and Sally waited. Then she nodded, giving instructions in Spanish to an older teenager.

As Anna and Bonnie carried their covered trays down the hallway, they could hear Sally giggling and the lower rumble of Alejandro's responses. They deserved one another, Anna thought. Then she looked at Bonnie guiltily. Sally was still the child's mother. But Bonnie appeared to take no notice as she walked beside Anna.

LOUNGING on the couch in Anna's suite, Bonnie watched a DVD. Bonnie had sought Anna's input on which movie to play. Anna pretended interest, but her mind was miles away. It kept going to Murph and what he must think of her for skulking away. Had she ruined things between them forever? Still, if she had to do it again, her choice would have been the same. What else could she have done when Bonnie was at risk?

Well, she was here now, and Bonnie was still at risk. In her mind, Anna went over the layout of this building, all the rooms that she had inspected so long ago, including Alejandro's private suite. Although that area was off-limits to all but him and the cleaning staff, twice he'd taken Anna there. She believed he did it to isolate her further from the other girls, seeming to give her special privileges. Anna wanted none of it. If someone wanted to lie with Alejandro, they were welcome to him. She hated that he called her his wife.

A soft rap on the door interrupted Anna's reverie. She tensed, then realized that Alejandro would never knock tentatively. The rap came again, then the doorknob slowly turned.

The upper half of a face peeked through - the young woman who had sat apart from the other girls at the dining table. After checking the hallway behind her, she opened the door further, slipped in, then closed it behind her. She pressed the lock.

Anna knew from experience that that lock meant nothing. Alejandro could get in anytime he wanted.

"I'm Evaline," the waif of a woman said. She would probably have been beautiful if not so pale.

Anna gestured to a chair.

Nervously, Evaline fidgeted with the hem of her shirt. Then she got up her courage, her gaze directly on Anna's. "They say that you got away from here."

Anna nodded.

Evaline sat forward, perching on the edge of her chair. "How? How did you get out of here? I can't find a way."

"Neither could I. He let me go, said I was of no further use to him."

"How? How do I get to be of no use?"

"They destroyed me enough that I could no longer have children." Shoot, Anna thought. She should not have said that in front of Bonnie, but the child seemed engrossed in the movie.

Evaline seemed to fold in on herself.

"Don't give up. There has to be a way." Anna didn't want to disclose that her friends must surely be looking for her and that law enforcement agencies on both sides of the border were investigating this operation.

Although Evaline looked sincere, there was always the possibility that Alejandro had sent her here to find out information.

The only sounds filling the room then were those from the television set. Evaline stared at it; who knew if she was following the plot or lost in her own thoughts?

Anna thought about the building they were in and the changes over the years. Before, sizeable areas were vacant. Although not locked, they were unused. Anna had explored each one.

But things were different now. The scope of Alejandro's operation was much larger, plus it looked like he'd expanded his business to include more than just selling babies. Her heart ached for Jordy and Benjie and the fates that might befall those boys. She wondered if Sally gave a thought to what might become of her sons.

With his operation being so much larger, Alejandro had more at stake. He was all about what was best for himself. Surely with more to risk, he would have escape plans built in. How quickly could he summon a helicopter to take him away? It was hard to bring in a copter stealthily. What contingency plan would he devise?

$\mathcal{G}$unshots in the distance. The noise instantly woke Anna from where she dozed on the bed. Through the open door into her sitting room, she could see Bonnie asleep on the couch. The child had not wanted to return to the room she shared with her mother, opting to remain with Anna, even if that meant sleeping in her clothes.

More noises outside, past the walls. Anna went to the window, but the sun was just thinking about rising, so shadows still bathed the compound. The shots did not seem to come from inside the enclosure; they were too muffled to be that close.

A spark of something hopeful flared in Anna's chest. Could it mean that the good guys had found Alejandro's location and rescue was on the way? Ah, but it could also mean a dispute between drug cartels that sequestered themselves in these mountains.

Bonnie stirred on the couch. Her worried head poked out from the covers.

Tired of being passive, Anna heeded the urge to move.

Knowing Alejandro, he'd protect his hide. Just because she'd not found an escape route on her previous searches, did not mean that he had not had one built in the ensuing years.

She doubted it would be a general plan for everyone to get out. No, that was not his way. He would protect Alejandro, and that's it.

The most logical place would be for him to have one built in a place where only he had access. His personal suite had expanded, taking over the bedroom beside it, which was now his office.

Holding Bonnie's hand and motioning for her to keep quiet, they crept through the hallways toward Alejandro's suite. Anna could not believe she was voluntarily entering that room. Suck it up, she told herself. Push down those encroaching memories and the feelings of being a helpless girl at his mercy. She was not that woman anymore.

The door was ajar. Was this a trap? It was one thing to risk herself, but what about Bonnie? She glanced at the child, wondering if she should return her to her room, and explore on her own.

Bonnie's gaze seemed to say, "No way," almost as if she read Anna's mind. Very well. They'd try this together.

With a deep breath, she gently pushed on the door, just enough that she could see inside, closing it behind her. The room was deserted, at least the sitting room was. She listened, ears alert for the tiniest sound.

Nothing. Maybe he was sleeping, although she doubted it. If the gunshots had woken her, they would surely have alerted Alejandro. Wary as a panther, he was always on guard, even when putting on an aura of relaxation.

Grateful for the plush carpet, they tiptoed across the outer room. To the right was the office; an opened door on the left led to the sleeping area and bathroom. Feeling the pressure of time, Anna opted to try that door first.

Empty. The bed covers were thrown back on either side, and a robe tossed onto the end of the bed. There was a bra on the floor, along with what looked to be a negligee. Anna averted her eyes and pulled Bonnie after her. What had Alejandro planned?

SHE SPUN at the noise of a doorknob turning, shoving Bonnie behind her. Anna held her breath and the hallway door opened, then closed.

Juana stopped in the doorway, startled to see them. The two women stared at each other. Deciding, Juana continued. She approached the bookcase near the couch in the sitting room. Pressing her palm to one side panel, the entire structure swung to the side, revealing a doorway, a Murphy door. Beyond the opening was a landing, then stairs heading down into the darkness. The dawn's light didn't extend this far into the room.

"Where does it go?" To Anna, it represented hope, but it could also lead them to something worse.

"Out. Alejandro had this built two years ago."

"How do you know about it?"

Juana's expression was sad. "Have you not guessed? He is my son." Her sardonic smile spoke volumes. "A son any mother would be proud of, no?"

No!

"Where are the others?" Anna asked.

"Others?"

"The girls?"

Juana shrugged. Perhaps she was not so very different from her son. As Juana's foot touched the first step, a motion-detector activated tiny LED lights on the riser of each stair tread.

Anna listened to the descending footsteps, torn between what to do. Her responsibility was to Bonnie, and rescuing the child was the whole reason she was here. But what about the other women being held?

If the noises outside meant that the law was here, they'd all be rescued. But what if it wasn't the cavalry? As lucrative as this business obviously was for Alejandro, there must be other forces who wanted in on it. These women might receive even worse treatment at their hands.

Should she go back and try to lead them to these stairs? But Anna didn't know for sure where they led. Juana could lure them into a worse fate.

A sound behind her decided for her. Evaline cautiously appeared in the doorway. "I didn't know this was here," she said. "I've been searching for months and never found it. Is this the way out?"

"I don't know. Juana went that way." Anna pointed to the stairs.

"Then I'm going too. Alejandro would have told her about it."

The shouts from outside sounded closer now, maybe near the gates. They spurred Evaline on and she took off down the stairs.

Bonnie regarded Anna, trust in her eyes.

More shouts. That decided Anna. Running to the massive office desk, she grabbed sheets of paper from the printer. Thrusting a pen at Bonnie, she gestured for her to copy. In large letters, Anna printed "aqui" and drew an arrow pointing to the side of the page. They each made several copies of the sign. Racing into the hallway, Anna yelled for the girls to come this way. They laid one paper at the top of the stairs, then spaced several more at intervals along the highway, with one pointing into Alejandro's suite. The last paper she pointed toward the now open Murphy door. She hoped the women would understand and follow the signs.

She also hoped that she was not leading them to a fate worse than they endured here.

CHAPTER 46

*A*lthough there was no sign of either Juana or Evaline, the stairs were well lit as they moved, and the way easy to follow. That is, until it came to an abrupt end with a closed metal door.

Searching showed only two options. Go back up the stairs the way they had come, or push the bar to open the door and take their chances with what lay beyond. Since Evaline and Juana had not returned, it seemed likely that they'd gone through the door. But what would meet them there?

Praying to a god that had never seemed to do an exemplary job of looking after her, Anna pressed on the bar that ran horizontally across the door. Despite its apparent weight, the door opened easily and silently. Trust Alejandro.

They were in the arid jungle. Anna stood, trying to get her bearings. A metal sound had her spinning around. Bonnie had let go of the door. There was no handle on this side, only a keyhole. Well, that pushed the decision to retreat or go forward.

There was no cover for about ten feet between the door and the jungle. Now the daylight Anna had wished for no longer seemed so welcome. They needed to move so they would not be so easily seen.

As quietly as they could and watching where they stepped, Anna and Bonnie made their way through the bush. In some places the going was easier than in others, but there were footprints. They were not the first to traverse this route.

After about forty-five minutes, they spied a clearing ahead. Anna moved them behind a clump of low trees and watched. Shortly, they heard the sounds of a vehicle approaching. Remaining hidden, they waited. Soon another followed that first, then half a dozen more. They were too far away to make out who might be in the jeeps. Was it Alejandro's men coming to collect him? Some rival? The police?

ANNA WHISPERED TO BONNIE. "Stay here and hide. Don't come out until I tell you. I'll check out what's happening, then be right back for you." She waited for the child's nod, but none came. "Bonnie," she warned, "do as I say."

Bonnie crouched behind a bush.

ANNA CREPT CLOSER to the road remaining within the covering of the trees. Then she turned to the right and

made her way parallel to the road, staying hidden. In
the distance were flashing lights, voices, and parked
trucks and jeeps. She was still too far away to tell what
was going on and guess if these people were friend
or foe.

She edged closer and closer, trying to make out the
rapid-fire Spanish. The vehicles blocked the road.
Ahead were the gates to Alejandro's compound, still
closed. Two men were face-down on the ground, their
hands cuffed behind their backs. Other men with
weapons stood guard over them. Anna crept through
the bush toward the last trucks. She'd better get back to
Bonnie. As she neared the last trucks in the line, three
men emerged from it, none of them holding weapons.
They stood together watching what was happening near
the gates.

From the ditch on Anna's side of the road, a small
body hurled itself up and onto the road, racing toward
the men. One man turned just in time to have that body
launch at him with a screaming, "Murph!"

He spun and caught the child as she leaped into his
arms. He squeezed tightly, swinging her from side to
side.

"Can't breathe, can't breathe," Bonnie protested.

He loosened his grip, just a bit.

"Hey, my turn," Jake told him, and reached for
Bonnie.

"Where's Anna?" Murph scanned the road ahead and
behind.

"Here." Anna emerged from the ditch. Soon, very
soon she'd know how she'd be received.

Within seconds, she knew. Murph's arms were around her, his face in her hair. When she pulled back, his face was wet, as was hers.

Jake had moved to one side of them, holding Bonnie's hand. Brendan was on the other side, watching for any movement. His hand went reflexively for his weapon, but it wasn't there. Right. This was not their turf.

A Mexican official joined them, and Brendan made the introductions."Anyone else with you?" he asked Anna.

"There were two women ahead of us."

"Are these the women?" He led Anna to the back seat of a car. There, behind the grill, was Juana and Evaline. "Do you know them?"

"The one on the right called herself Evaline. I think she's one of the girls Alejandro kept. The other woman is Juana. She said she's Alejandro's mother."

"Jackpot!" The officer grinned.

Noises came from the bush. Brendan led them behind the vehicles, closer to the other police officers. "Any idea who that might be?"

"I left signs for the women in case they decided to follow. I didn't see Alejandro, but I think he might have left before we found the stairs."

Looking uncertain, a cluster of young women peered from behind some trees. They were in varying stages of attire; all looked scared.

"It's okay," called Anna. "It's the police. You're rescued." She assumed that that would be good news for them.

The officer waved over some of his men. They surrounded the women, their backs to them, weapons pointed back toward the bush.

The young women came closer to Anna. One officer circulated among them, offering bottled water. Another called for more transportation.

"What will happen to them now?" Anna remembered what it had felt like to be left at a bus station, frightened and alone. She didn't know if these women even had any money.

"They'll be taken to El Refugio in Tijuana. It's an official center, that helps women like this. If they want to return to their families, El Refugio will assist. If they want to start over on their own, they'll work with them."

"And their babies, the ones taken from them?"

The officer's face fell. "We're working on that. Hopefully we'll find records in the house that will give us leads."

Anna doubted they'd find any paperwork there. "And Alejandro? Do you have him?"

"No, senorita. We have not found him."

JAKE WAITED with Bonnie at an In-N-Out Burger near the police station, while Brendan and Murph accompanied Anna for her official interview.

When the officials arrived at Alejandro's estate, two young guards at the gate quickly surrendered. Anna identified them as her brothers, Danny and Manuel, although that was about all she could offer about them. Although she'd had a hasty introduction to the young women, she remembered few of their names, except for Evaline.

As for Juana, Anna was uncertain if had attempted to help them or not.

She told the heartbreaking tale of Sally leading her little boys to the helicopter, then watching the bird fly off with Bonnie's little brothers. The men listening to her tale exchanged grim looks. Anna supplied them with the call letters from the side of the helicopter. At least that was something to go on.

When the officials arrived, the only employees of Alejandro they found were Anna's brothers guarding the front gate. The doors to the back gate were empty, the estate deserted. The women had followed Anna's signs and vacated the building through the hidden stairway. Now, investigators swarmed the place, hoping to find where Alejandro had disappeared to and ways to stop his trafficking operation. They feared that this was just one of his setups, and that he'd continue to operate from another location.

~

"ANNA, we have some news for you." Drawing this out, Jake continued. "It's good and bad."

"Oh, just tell her," Brendan ordered. "She's been through enough."

"Okay. Anna, your annulment is invalid. There is no

record of it being registered anywhere, not with the Church or with any government agency."

Devastation poured into Anna' soul. She was still tied to that viper?

When Jake didn't continue, Brendan shot him a disgusted look and took over.

"But there is also no record of your marriage. It was likely a sham ceremony. You were never officially married."

THE DRIVE HOME WAS QUIET. They'd waited, but Bonnie had not yet asked about her mother and brothers. They'd deal with that later, when she was ready.

The child slept most of the time, her head on Anna's shoulder as they shared the back seat with Murph. He held Anna the entire way home, unwilling to let got of her for an instant. There would be time for recriminations, what ifs, and next times later. For now, they were safe.

Anna had done what she could. She was sure they had seen the last of Alejandro.

*E*lizabeth and Timothy shared a table at a bakery, waiting for Anna, Murph and Bonnie to join them. Timothy played with his iPad, while Elizabeth opened and closed a file folder, flipping pages, reading just a bit, then putting it away. She'd received the report on Timothy's autism assessment. While she understood most of it, Murph was going to go over the whole thing with her this afternoon.

Maybe her nervousness rubbed off on Timothy, because he became increasingly upset as the tablet did not respond as he thought it should. Elizabeth was usually more attentive to the signs of an impending meltdown, but this time she missed it until his little feet pummelled the underside of the glass tabletop, as he rocked back and forth, making that keening sound that made her grit her teeth.

"Shh, son, quiet. It's all right." Why did she say that? Of course, it wasn't all right or he wouldn't be doing that. She took a breath and tried again. "What's wrong with the iPad, Timothy?"

A man wearing a chef's apron appeared at their side. He grinned at her, placing his hands firmly on Timothy's shoulders and pressing down.

"Hey," said Elizabeth. "What are you doing to my son?" She rose, then realized that the kicking had stopped, along with Timothy's moans. She sat back down.

The man released his hands and squatted beside Timothy. "What's going on with your iPad, little man? I hate it when mine doesn't work." He reached for the tablet and, miracle of miracles, Timothy let him have it. The man tilted it toward Timothy, and Timothy pointed to what wasn't working. "Ah, I get it." His index finger moved around the screen. The game refreshed and must have looked proper again.

Timothy smiled. He gave a quick look at the man, then returned his eyes to the iPad.

The guy gave it back to Timothy and stood.

"How did you do that?" Elizabeth really wanted to know.

"The program got stuck; it just needed a reset."

"No, I mean, how did you calm my son so quickly?"

The guy grinned again. "Takes one to know one."

"Elizabeth!"

Expecting to see Anna, it surprised Elizabeth to see Lori, an EA from her son's school. "Hello, Lori. Nice to see you." She indicated the man who still stood there. "This guy just averted a crisis for us."

Lori hooked her arm in that of the fellow. "I see that you've met my boyfriend, Jeff."

"Not officially, but I guess I have now." Elizabeth shook his hand.

Timothy patted Jeff's hand to get his attention, then showed him something on the iPad.

Seldom did Timothy want to share something with others, especially strangers. "You seem to have an affinity with my son, Jeff."

"I can relate to…". Beeping from his watch interrupted whatever else he was going to say…. "Gotta go. My brisket needs to come out of the oven now." With a kiss to Lori's cheek, he was off.

If you enjoyed this book, the author would be very appreciative if you would leave a review on Amazon (https://amzn.to/3mhM589) or Goodreads (https://www.goodreads.com/book/show/57237207-selfish).

Young Anna **(free story)**

You met Anna in *TRUST* then lived her journey with her in *SELFISH*. Want to more about the events that brought her to this stage in her life? Read *Young Anna*, a **free** short story.

https://BookHip.com/PWVTZQH

WOULD you like another free story?

Anything For Her Son is a tale about a mother's love for her autistic child. You'll learn how Keira met Jake before their lives intertwined with that of Elizabeth and Timothy. Grab your free copy at https://dl. bookfunnel.com/a27d9uzou0

～

The psychological thriller series
When Bad Things Happen:

GONE - Book One
TRUST - Book Two
SELFISH - Book Three
INSTICT- Book Four

GONE

Did you read the first book in the series? *GONE: A Psychological Thriller. Book One of When Bad Things Happen.*

A sheltered mother. A medically fragile child. They can't just disappear. Or can they?

A typical day of medical appointments and errands. Elizabeth can handle it, she tells herself. She'll do it all until her husband returns on the weekend.

But someone else has a plan – several someones, throwing Elizabeth's orderly life into chaos and danger. Now, she's on her own. Neither her parents nor her husband is there to protect her. No one knows where they are. If her son is to get out of this alive, it's up to Elizabeth.

Ordinary people, thrown into extraordinary circumstances. Read Gone, Book One of the psychological thriller series When Bad Things Happen.

∽

TRUST

After surviving a kidnapping and betrayal at her husband's hands, Elizabeth wants only to cocoon with her son now that they're safely home.

But the judge decrees that she must get outside help for her son or the State will take over his custody and care.

Trusting no one, she has three choices:
- Comply with the ruling, as scary as that may be
- Ignore the judge's order and hope that all will be well (how likely is that, considering how her life has gone?)
- take her medically fragile son and flee.

Elizabeth thought that after all they'd been through, the bad parts were over. Guess not.

～

INSTINCT
When should you trust your instincts?

Her husband's life came to an end. Cynthia's coming to terms with that loss.
Now the money in her bank account is also coming to an end.
This was not the life she planned, but their little girl depends on her.
After years away, dipping her toe back into her former career is tricky. But it should be doable, right?
Sure, if not for kidnapping, abduction, trafficking, and....

Read INSTINCT, book 4 in the psychological thriller series When Bad Things Happen.

ABOUT THE AUTHOR

Dr. Sharon A. Mitchell lives on a farm, with her nearest neighbor several miles away. Does that seem like a setting to spark the imagination? It does for her.

She's working on her fourth psychological thriller novel for the *When Bad Things Happen* series.

In addition to two (almost three) short stories tied to that series, she's written six novels, each featuring an autistic child or young adult. Two nonfiction books accompany that autism series.

Sharon's been a teacher, counselor, psychologist and consultant for decades and continues to teach university classes on kids who learn differently to soon —to-be teachers and administrators .

Follow her on Amazon to be notified of her next books, and on any of these social media links:

- amazon.com/Dr-Sharon-A-Mitchell/e/B008MPJCYA
- bookbub.com/authors/sharon-a-mitchell
- facebook.com/DrSharonAMitchell
- twitter.com/AutismSite
- instagram.com/autismsite
- pinterest.com/mitchellsha3047

ALSO BY SHARON A. MITCHELL

Made in the USA
Coppell, TX
29 December 2021

70396088R00215